Midsummer's Eve

by

Kitty Margo

This story is a work of fiction. Names, characters, places and incidents are either products of the author's imagination or used fictiously. No part of this publication can be reproduced or transmitted in any form or by any means electronic or mechanical, without written permission of Kitty Margo.

Published November 9, 2012
Second Edition April 25, 2023

Dedicated

TO MY READERS,

PAST

PRESENT

and

FUTURE,

FOR TAKING THIS INCREDIBLE
JOURNEY WITH ME.

I COULD *NOT* HAVE DONE
IT WITHOUT YOU.

Chapter One

Let me start by telling you a few things about my three best friends. Believe me, they are *not* three peas in a pod. One is an incessant whiner, who only dates black men. One is a good sized gal with a heart of gold, who only dates Latino flavored men. One, until a few short years ago, *was* a man. The last one, at times, can also be a royal bitch.

We take turns going to each other's homes monthly for our Monday night gab fests, and tonight is my night to host. I have prepared a chicken potpie, tossed a garden salad, and created a divine concoction of chocolate pudding with whipped cream, nuts, and cherries.

Let's start with the incessant whiner, Mallory. Picture Drew Barrymore with Fran Dresher's grating snivel. She is short, with more curves than Jessica Rabbit minus the boobs, and I must confess that the girl is your classic nympho. She craves sex like I craved chocolate when I still had a period, which I haven't had since cervical cancer marched into my life causing my doctor to insist on a complete hysterectomy at age 41, which was thirteen years ago. Yep, that makes me 54.

As I said, Mallory only dates black men. All her intimate friends have heard her say at least once that just the thought of a white man's penis makes her sick to her stomach. "They are so… pink."

She began dating black men as nothing more than a way to piss her extremely overbearing mother off and in the process got hooked for life. It's amazing what dramatic changes the love of a child can bring about. Mallory has a biracial daughter who is now the very center of her once intolerant mother's universe.

When I am lamenting my pain and angst she tells me what *she* believes I need to hear in order to feel better about life in general. "It will be alright, Eve. He'll call. Just give him time to think about it. Even though I can't stand him, Adam loves you. I know he does. He is just… well… beyond stupid."

Tamara is tall with a fuller figure and has a fondness for Mexican men. She works as a translator at large factory with a mostly Hispanic workforce. Picture Rosie O'Donnell with a lisp.

Her advice depends largely on her mood. If she's in a rotten mood, she will be quick to inform me that I should find someone else. "Adam couldn't possibly love you and cheat on you with Chia like he did."

Now on to my favorite transgendered friend, Teri. Picture Pamela Anderson with brown highlighted hair and much fuller lips. Teri is *decidedly* female now and has one of those bodies to die for. Large implanted breasts with nipples in the epicenter. *I would kill to have my nipples back in their epicenter!* Curvaceous hips, a tiny lipo sculpted waist, cheek implants, chin implant, buttock implants, laser resurfaced skin and all over laser hair removal, tattooed eyebrows, and everything waxed, manicured and pedicured.

She had the final appendage removal a few years ago and was at last able to find the peace, as a woman, that she had craved her entire life. Teri is absolutely gorgeous. The word that comes to mind most when describing her would be diva. You could easily imagine her walking a runway in Paris rather than being the gated community housewife that she is.

Her advice to me is always brutally honest. She tells it just like she sees it. No sparing anyone's feelings with that girl. Hell, no. Not a chance. She has chewed my butt out on more than one occasion until it was left raw and bleeding over who she refers to as *that spineless piece of human offal,* Adam, my ex-boyfriend of three years.

The night I discovered that the love of my life was cheating with a floozy named Chia, after pain pills had finally eased the ferocious pain and nausea of a migraine, Teri stayed on the phone with me for the better part of the night talking me through the heartbreak of betrayal. I received flowers and a fruit basket the following morning, because Teri has the biggest heart of anyone I know. We've been best friends for fifteen years since we met in Cosmetology School.

Teri is a very much in demand hairdresser in Charlotte doing things with a head of hair that most hairstylists can only dream of. While I, on the other hand, knew after only two months of working in a hair salon that I wasn't cut out for a career of catering to the demanding whims of the public, and moved on.

The old queen who employed me in his salon had an elderly clientele and charged $8.00 a pop for a roller set and style. $8.00 mind you, and he had the nerve to take half of that for booth rent and supplies.

This meant that if I listened to the demands of ten persnickety little old ladies, arranged every last spit curl to their satisfaction, and applied an entire can of Aqua Net to each of their heads, at the end of the day I would walk away with the whopping sum of $40.00. Needless to say, after Uncle Sam took his cut, gas to and from work, and the occasional What-A-Burger, I was far removed from living in the lap of luxury.

Teri moved to Charlotte and immediately got a job in one of the swankier salons while I enrolled at the community college for my phlebotomy license. So I have my cosmetology license, and phlebotomy license, and end up scrubbing toilets for a living. Go figure.

"So, Eve, Eve, Eve..." Teri began.

Watch out.

Here it comes.

Stabbing a slice of onion and for once failing to complain about it being mixed in with her greens, she daintily laid it to the side of her plate. "Please tell me you are going to move on and not wait until Chia gets bored with that idiot you seem so fond of and he comes slithering back to you?"

Told you the girl was brutal. I chose to ignore the question since she appeared to be baiting me. Apparently, she had missed a few hormone injections.

Tamara was busily trying to avoid any confrontation and picking what she referred to as chunks of red mush, tomatoes to you and me, out of her salad. The group had a palate that was impossible to please and I had ceased trying years ago, leaving them to pick out the offending vegetables at will.

Teri couldn't tolerate onions because they gave her heartburn and made her breath smell vile. Tamara cringed and swore that tomatoes made her sugar go up. Mallory commenced to gagging if you placed anything that resembled a cucumber in front of her. The salad contained a combination of all three. It was either that or put a head of lettuce on the table.

"You saw Adam and Chia at Bojangles the other day, didn't you Mallory?" Finished with her salad, Tamara set the bowl aside, scooped out a healthy portion of potpie, and asked the words she had been dying to ask, "How does she look?"

Mallory stopped with her fork in midair, positively loving the fact that she was privy to something the other two were still mercilessly in the dark about and bestowed upon me a most pitiful gaze. She shook her head and hesitated, trying to convince us that for the first time in her life she had no comment, when I knew her lips were positively twitching to inform Tamara and Teri of Chia's exquisite beauty.

"Don't be silly." I insisted, even though my heart sank to the floor at the thought of hearing *she looks like a frigging supermodel,* yet again. "Be honest."

I couldn't believe I was giving her permission to utter the godawful truth.

"She looks like a frigging supermodel." With that said, Mallory cocked an eye at Tamara and urged her to consider leaving some potpie for the rest of us.

"Bite me," was Tamara's reply.

Teri seemed wholly confused by Mallory's description. "Don't take this the wrong way, Eve, but how in the hell did Adam get someone who even remotely resembles a supermodel?"

"Same thing I asked." Mallory burst out laughing, then glanced at me. "Sorry, Eve."

"I mean, I know you loved him, but he probably has multiple STD's with the amount of screwing around he does. By the way, did you ever get tested?"

"Not yet." I intended to though. I just hadn't gotten around to actually doing it.

"I'm going to call in the morning and make an appointment for you."

"I'll call," I promised. "I'm due for a physical anyway."

Now that I knew about Adam's rampant sexcapades I had been lying awake at night dreading what the doctor might find. I shuddered, remembering our many nights of unprotected sex.

Suddenly the mixture of cream of chicken soup, Veg-All, and chunks of chicken topped with Bisquick, lost its appeal. My appetite completely deserted me as visions of revenge danced in my head. "Surely I deserve some recompense for being cheated on the entire three years we were together. Can you imagine my humiliation, knowing that everyone at the plant knew he was screwing anything with a pulse, except me? I know this sounds extremely junior high, but I wish there was some way to get back at Adam. A way to make him hurt the way he hurt me. You know, make him feel a little pain, then perhaps I could move on."

"That shouldn't be too difficult." Teri grinned a devilish grin that we were all too well acquainted with. "This potpie is delicious, by the way. It's so nice to enjoy a simple meal for a change." She cut her eyes at Mallory, who had a proclivity to serve soul food such as hog jowls and chittlins on her nights, albeit delicious soul food. "I'm sure if we put our heads together we could devise a plan to serve the imbecile a small helping of pain." It was obvious the excitement of getting even appealed to her. "You could always hire a hit man."

I hoped she was joking, but Lord knows the girl still has a goodly amount of residual testosterone flowing through her veins. "Could we perhaps devise a plan that's a little less criminal?" I set desert dishes and my chocolate concoction on the table. "One that doesn't include the likelihood of me rubbing elbows with a mass murderer in the near future?"

"Well, that certainly takes all the fun out of it," Teri quipped, draining her glass of tea and getting up for a refill. "Anybody want more tea?"

"You know how he loves his little sports car." Mallory brainstormed, holding out her glass. "It could always get accidentally damaged."

"He would know you did it and have the cops on your ass in a hot minute," Tamara warned.

"I don't think he would have the cops on her ass." Mallory scooped out dessert and passed the bowl to Tamara. "He would be extremely pissed and expect her to pay for the damages though."

"How good does this sound? What if Chia fell for someone else?" Tamara nearly swooned as the desert touched her lips. She popped a cherry and giggled before continuing with her idea of a joke. "And dumped him?"

What a beautiful plan.

Why hadn't I thought of it? That would cause Adam volumes of untold misery if the woman he was madly in love with left him for another man.

"That's it! Tamara you are a freaking genius, and why didn't you think of it sooner?" It was a truly brilliant ploy. *Revenge at its best.* "I know just the person to do it." I glanced at Mallory with a sly grin.

"Eric," we both said in unison as Mallory's eyes took on a faraway gleam.

"He could do it," she murmured, licking her lips. She had made an exception and gone a few rounds with his pink dicked self and, judging from the leering grin on her face, was at that very minute contemplating the offer of a repeat performance.

Eric was an employee of mine. Tall, tan, drop dead gorgeous, and he had probably never once heard the word no fall from the lips of a simpering female.

"Okay, we have a plan." Teri was deep in thought. "Now for the details. Where does the trollop live?"

"I have no idea." If I did, odds were great that my Jeep would be parked in the general vicinity of her apartment right then.

"Let's think about this, Eve. Surely someone can tell us where the hussy lives. I mean this is Hanover Falls, not Charlotte. It wouldn't be beneath you to follow her home one night, would it?" the reigning queen of scheme suggested.

"Brilliant." I giggled knowing full well, as did everyone else at the table, that when it came to Adam nothing was beneath me.

"He would recognize your car in a heartbeat," Tamara reminded me. "I'll borrow my dad's truck. Adam doesn't know what he drives."

"But since Adam is always at their little love nest, Eric can't just show up on the doorstep and proceed to seduce Chia."

"It needs to be an accidental meeting of some sort." Teri absentmindedly spooned a tiny portion of whipped cream from the calorie laden dish into her mouth. The second spoon contained what could only be referred to as a dollop of whipped cream and included a cherry. The third scoop of her spoon dug to the bottom of the Pyrex dish like she was digging for oil.

She closed her eyes for a second, moaning seductively and savoring the sweetness that until that very moment had been an all but nonexistent flavor in her diet.

No, no, no!

Not a good sign.

Tamara, Mallory and I exchanged troubled glances. Sugar was Teri's sworn enemy and if her mind hadn't been racing a mile a minute toward Adam's much anticipated downfall it would have never reached her luscious, silicone-injected lips.

"We don't know anything about where she shops or spends her time when the Neanderthal isn't with her." Teri closed her eyes blissfully as she licked a dab of stray whipped cream from her full lips.

"We need her phone number, so Eric can call her," Mallory was attempting to pull her distressed gaze from Teri, who had already scooped out half of the 9 x 13 forbidden delicacy.

Mallory knew, as did Tamara and I, that we would all be on the receiving end of harsh phone calls riddled with obscenities when Teri either remembered this lapse in judgment or stepped on the scales, whichever came first. She would berate us repeatedly for not having the common sense of a warthog to chop off her fingers in an effort to cease the dreaded sweets from contributing to the ruination of her perfect figure.

"Is it in the phone book?" Teri mumbled around a cherry.

"No, I've already checked." Mallory, Tamara, and I shoved Teri's spoon aside and ladled out desert while there was still some left.

Think, Eve, think. How could we get her phone number?

"I've got it!" Teri shrieked, her glazed eyes evidence of a sugar high. "It would be on Adam's home phone."

"Of course it would be." According to Justin, one of my son's friends that worked with Adam and Chia on second shift at the shirt factory, the frisky couple wiled away many lazy afternoons on the phone. On the rare occasion they weren't in each other's arms. "You're absolutely right." I gave Teri a high five. "It would be, wouldn't it? How did you get so damn smart?"

"It's a gift," she answered in her typical matter of fact fashion, all the while scraping the dish for the last smidgeon of desert and seeming overwrought that it was gone. Tamara noticed Teri eyeing her dessert dish and ate faster.

"Can you get in the house and get the number?" Tamara peeked at Teri from under her lashes.

If I know Tamara, and I do, when she got home she would take her phone off the hook until Teri had been given sufficient time to rake Mallory and myself over the coals, hopefully forgetting about her in the process. Somehow, I always got stuck with the dirty work.

Getting into Adam's house could prove to be somewhat of a challenge. I was certain he locked the doors to his house of ill repute before leaving. Then it hit me like a lightning bolt streaking through the bay window behind the sink. "He told me once that he leaves one of his kitchen windows unlocked in case he loses his keys."

"The absentminded lunatic does have cause for concern." Teri rubbed her temples as though the mere thought of Adam caused her head to ache. "There you go. Crawl in the window and get it off his caller ID."

Well, didn't Teri make it sound like the easiest and most perfectly legal act of breaking and entering in the world? Of course, I would do it. It would be worth shivering on a cot in a jail cell for one night to bring Adam a little pain and suffering. Yep, I would do it, but not without an able accomplice. "Will you come with me, Mallory?"

"You know I will." She grinned, rubbing her hands together excitedly. She was always game for any adventure. "When?"

"Let me work out a few details and I'll let you know. I'm so ready to show Adam *firsthand* just how painful love can be."

Chapter Two

Just after lunch a few days later the skies turned a dull grey and light flurries peppered down. I'd been so caught up in my own misery lately that I hadn't heard the weather forecast and, totally shocking, my parents hadn't called with their usual Weather Channel update and urgings to rush to the grocery store for bread and milk.

Food hadn't been first and foremost on my mind in recent weeks. Nothing had really, except the lying, cheating scumbag who had so recently shredded my heart, and dignity. Still, I had to eat. I whipped the Jeep into the Food Lion parking lot to stock up on supplies since I knew I would be having an overnight visitor.

Sure enough, when I arrived back home Mallory was sitting on my porch swing with duffel bag in hand. She has developed a habit of camping at my house during snow and ice storms. The girl is petrified of being stuck in her house alone when the power goes out, and since I have gas logs we can at least stay warm even if it does. I was thrilled to see her, having no desire to be snowbound alone.

We were debating on whether to cook spaghetti or lasagna when my parents called and invited us to supper next door. By the time we walked the path between my house and my parent's the light flurries had changed to big fat flakes and the snow was coming down in earnest.

We were greeted at the door by the enticing aroma of my dad's down home Southern cooking. He had made a mouth watering chicken stew consisting of chicken, potatoes, carrots, celery, onions, one of his red hot peppers, V-Eight Juice, and enough butter to clog at least 90% of your arteries. For desert, he whipped up his famous snow cream.

Mallory ate like a small elephant. She is blessed with one of those amazing metabolisms that allows her to pig out and never gain one stinking ounce. It also helps that her favorite activity is bedroom related and a calorie burning workout in itself. Trust me; she burns an outrageous amount of calories at said activity.

After a supper that had us swearing we wouldn't eat again for three days, we moved to the living room. It was a cozy room with afghans thrown across the backs of a floral patterned couch and chairs that were beginning to show signs of wear and tear. If you mentioned this to my dad, he would insist the furniture still had several good years of quality usage.

Dad grew up during the Great Depression, and even to this day he refuses to waste anything. I kid you not, the man would rather do without than take money out of his bank account. Don't even get him started on buying on credit. It has never been an option for him, and it will bring you a heated lecture on the perils of debt. He firmly believes that if you don't have the money to buy it, you don't have any business with it.

With my belly full, I cozied up by the fire and was reminded of the many autumn evenings our family sat around a campfire and roasted marshmallows when my son was little. What was my favorite campfire activity? Ghost stories, of course. "Do you believe in ghosts, Mallory?" The wind howled through the eaves of my parent's old house causing the living room lights to flicker eerily.

"You know I do. Don't start that shit, Eve." We moved away from the intense heat radiating from the crackling fire. I never understood why Dad didn't just spring for central heat rather than deal with all the trouble and mess associated with heating with wood.

I stifled a smile as we settled back against colorful throw pillows and Mallory turned quite pale. Bless her heart. I really should be ashamed of myself for tormenting someone who fully believes that spirits hover in the very air around us.

"This area is haunted you know?" I leaned toward her, all the while studying her eyes for her reaction. As if on cue one of Dad's guinea hens came running around the house screeching that godawful racket they make and the poor girl almost found herself in the attic.

"Shut up, Eve! Now dammit, I mean it."

"It's true," my mother agreed. The woman could hear a pin drop.

My mom is short and plump, with a head full of white hair that she has shampooed, set, and sprayed, or I prefer to use the term lacquered, into submission every Friday morning.

"There's an old plantation house about a mile from here with a graveyard across the road." Mom arched a brow at Mallory. "There have been strange happenings in those woods. We've lived here for sixty years and I had an eerie feeling about this place the minute me and Joseph moved in."

"What happened?" Mallory leaned forward, eager to hear her answer.

Now you rarely catch my mom without a dip of snuff in her jaw, Tuberose, and tonight was no exception. She picked up her spit cup, an empty Maxwell House coffee can stuffed with tissues, and spit a healthy stream of tobacco juice. "Tell her what you seen, Joseph."

Dad is seventy four and no matter how much my sister and I complain or worry about his health, he continues his daily trips to the garden during the hottest months of the summer growing vegetables to sell at the local Farmer's Market. Age is slowly creeping up on him, but when we were teenagers and watched the *Tarzan* movies every Sunday, without fail, my sister and I were convinced he was the spittin' image of Johnny Weissmuller.

"You might not believe what I'm about to tell you, but it's the God's honest truth, Mallory." Dad settled back in his recliner to get comfortable. "When I was fifteen, a bunch of us went coon hunting back yonder behind the house. It was my daddy, his two brothers, and me and my brother. I won't never forget that night as long as I live. I was walking along carrying a coon in a sack when we heard something running through the leaves and making a terrible racket. We thought it was just another coon." He shook his head. "My daddy shined his light toward the noise, and it weren't no coon."

"What was it?" Mallory was totally engrossed in the story.

"It was a little black boy running as fast as his chubby little legs would carry him. He would stumble and fall, git right back up, and strike out running again. He looked to be about two years old. It was cold that night and all he was wearing was a cloth diaper that looked more like an old strip of cloth. The dogs were getting closer to him, so he stopped at the bottom of a hickor' nut tree and looked up, then looked back at the dogs and started climbing that tree just as perty as you please."

Dad took an orange out of the fruit basket beside him and began peeling it. "The child had a real hard time climbing the tree but he made it to the first set of limbs. He held on to the limb above him while the dogs barked like crazy and tried to jump up the trunk of the tree.

When we got to the tree, we shined our flashlights and watched him for a few minutes. Didn't none of us say a word. It was hard to believe a small child had shinnied up a tree that any of us would have had a hard time climbing, but he did."

Dad chewed on a slice of orange for several seconds, remembering. "The child was crying. I guess them dogs had scared him pretty bad. My daddy finally said to me, 'Climb up that tree and bring that youngun down.' I handed him my flashlight and started up the tree. I kept my eyes on the little boy to see what he would do. He had big ole fat tears rolling down his cheeks and he was trembling. I guess from being cold, and terrified of the dogs."

I watched Mallory's face, as I had heard the ending to this story hundreds of times from my grandpa.

"When I got within arms reach of him, close enough to touch him, the child disappeared in a puff of smoke. Right in front of my eyes. In front of all of us."

"He disappeared?" Mallory glanced sideways at me. She was painfully aware that my parents were telling the truth, since my mom holds regular conversations with God and neither of my parents have ever been known to tell a lie. "What did you do?"

"I reckon I broke some kind of speed record for climbing back down a tree. I was fifteen, but it scared the livin' daylights out of me and my brother so bad we hung on daddy's coattails till we got back out of them woods."

Daddy gazed out the window into the dark night. "To this day I ain't never been as scared as I was that night. I remember walking back home with my eyes glued to the ground. None of us would risk looking into the trees and seeing that little boy. In fact, it was several year before any of us went back to those woods again."

Poor Mallory was about to chew her bottom lip off. "Even now, do you still believe the little boy disappeared?"

"I don't just believe it, Mallory. I know it as well as I know I'm sitting here. I seen that little boy just as plain as I see you sitting there now. Three grown men and two teenaged boys seen him. One person might can imagine something, but when five sets of eyes see the same thing that ain't no imagination."

"Have you seen him since that night?"

"I ain't never seen him again but several other men have been in the woods hunting at night and seen him. He's still out there."

Glancing at the clock, Dad grabbed the remote and switched on the TV to boxing. There wouldn't be any more stories tonight. The man was addicted to the sport.

"We need to get going." I grinned at Mallory and pointed to Dad as he punched the air each time one of the boxers made a jab at his opponent. "Thanks for supper and the snow cream." I hugged both my parents and my mom hugged Mallory.

"Come back to see us anytime, Mallory," Dad said, his eyes never once wavering from the television screen.

We arrived home just in time to see that fine silver fox Anderson Cooper, on *AC360*. I watched for a while, until I heard Mallory snoring. I covered her with a blanket and went to bed. The snow had stopped and it was warming up so most of it would be turned to slush by morning.

Chapter Three

I attended the monthly meeting of the Chamber Of Commerce. I had joined four years earlier hoping to attract business and get to know fellow small business owners. We had a catered lunch consisting of chicken salad with grapes on croissants, chips, pickles, and sweet tea.

I saw that we had acquired a new member during my absence. She was tall, short brown hair, no makeup and she sat next to me.

"Hi," I greeted her, extending my hand. "I'm Eve Bryson. I don't think we've met."

"Marilyn Little." She introduced herself and shook my hand. "No we haven't. It's nice to meet you."

The pudgy owner of a men's clothing store uptown coughed to gain everyone's attention before calling the meeting to order. "Good day, everyone. Thank you all for coming. As our first order of business today, I would like to introduce our newest member." With a flourish, he waved to Marilyn. "Marilyn, would you care to tell us about yourself?"

Marilyn stood. You could tell immediately that she was a take charge kind of gal.

"Hello everyone. My name is Marilyn Little. My husband and I moved here recently from

Pennsylvania and my business is called Inner Awakenings. I am a psychic and a hypnotist."

Oh, she should go far in this town.

I chuckled to myself, as did some others, while a few sat up and took notice.

"Can you make someone stop smoking?" Tom the owner of a Heating and Air business and a chain smoker for 30 years asked.

"I will allow you to answer that question for yourself." Marilyn moved around the table passing out cards. "To drum up some business, I'm giving everyone a free one hour session."

"Free?"

"Great."

"Thanks!"

Tom was immediately interested. He should be with that florid face and rasping wheeze. "Do you have your appointment book with you?"

"As a matter of fact I do."

"Do you have anything available for tomorrow?"

Of the twelve members in attendance four made appointments, then she turned to me. "How about you, Eve? Do you have any questions I could help you try to answer?"

"No, thank you." I laughed somewhat nervously. I wasn't about to spill my guts to a psychic or let someone hypnotize me. Lord only knows what might come out of this mouth.

I should have known she wouldn't let it rest, she had a clientele to build. "Come on, I need someone to spread the word about my amazing talent." *Her smile was very warm and welcoming. She was one of those people you couldn't help but like instantly.* "Help a fellow small business owner out here," she cajoled. "It's free and you have nothing to lose."

I remembered several years earlier when I had first started my business how kind and helpful members of the Chamber had been to me. Evidently, it was payback time. "Okay, pencil me in."

"How does Wednesday at 2:00 sound?"

"Sounds good." I embellished that part. Nothing sounded good about it at all.

Of all the stupid things. How did I allow myself to get talked into a visit with a psychic? Me? Someone who could make a telemarketer wish he had never rolled out of bed that morning. I could just hear my Dad's guffaws if he ever found out.

Chapter Four

All too soon Wednesday afternoon rolled around and I arrived at the destination on Marilyn's card with ten minutes to spare. A long driveway with pecan trees on each side led to a beautiful old country farm house with a wraparound porch, a billowing American flag, and dozens of hanging ferns. Cow pastures surrounded the house, and as I parked under the shade of a huge oak tree cows lowed from all directions. Several large dogs came running to greet me as soon as I opened the car door.

Marilyn came to the porch, calling the dogs by name and ordering them to hush. "Come in the house. Would you like a glass of tea, a cup of coffee, or a bottle of water?"

"Whatever you're having." I was already regretting the decision to come here. This was beyond stupid.

"I'm having sweet tea. I've become quite fond of it since I've been in the South." She stopped long enough to take my hand and squeeze it. "Don't be nervous, Eve. You seem nervous."

"Well, this is a first. I can honestly say that I've never been to a physic before." Taking a glass of tea I followed her up a curving, wooden staircase. "You have a beautiful home, Marilyn."

"Thank you. My husband's parents passed away last year and left it to us. I had a thriving business in Pennsylvania and would have been content to spend my remaining years there, but my husband had a desire to come back home to North Carolina after he retired. So, here we are."

"There's no place like home."

"True, but it's so quiet here. I'm accustomed to the hustle and bustle of a large city. I had the receptionist, the waiting room, an adequate clientele, the whole nine yards." She motioned toward the window. "As you can see, my only companions are dogs and cows."

We went to a bedroom with floor to ceiling windows and a spectacular view of... cows. The room was country chic at its best, with knotty pine walls and wood floors that had been shined and buffed to a high gloss. The breeze coming through the open window ruffled frilly lace curtains and a patchwork quilt covered the four poster bed. Hand stitched embroidery samples adorned the walls.

The focal point of the room was a wooden rocking chair with a thick patchwork cushion positioned in front of the floor to ceiling window. She instructed me to sit in the chair. Marilyn sat on a stool in front of me.

I had already decided that I would pretend to believe whatever she said. You know how accommodating us Southerners are. We love to give folks the warm fuzzies and make them feel welcome.

Here's a thought. How does one know if a psychic has a real gift, or if she's just another scam artist looking for a quick buck? Was it possible for someone to predict the future? *For real?* Perhaps tell me how to plan for the next catastrophe in my life before it swallowed me whole?

Let me just say this from the get go. I am a huge believer in fate. In my opinion, nothing happens purely by chance. There is a reason for everything, even for my life being the pronounced travesty that it is. Anyway, I've never visited a soothsayer, so what could it hurt?

Marilyn looked nothing at all like I expected a psychic to look. You know? Pointed chin. Hairy wart. Not even a crystal ball. She began by shuffling a deck of regular playing cards. She turned over the card on top of the deck, the ace of hearts, and glanced up.

"Let me see your hands," she said, without preamble. Obediently, I showed her my hands palms up. "You have an odd number of children."

"I have one son."

"He works out of town and you don't get to see him as often as you would like." Her eyes fluttered and almost rolled back in her head as she appeared to go into a trance like state.

Wow. How did she know that? The hair on the back of my neck perked up as I felt goose bumps popping up on my arms and thighs. This woman knew intimate details about my life. "My son owns a welding company and travels up and down the east coast." I glanced toward the exit when her upper body commenced to jerking uncontrollably. *Lord have mercy!* I hoped this was her normal behavior and she wasn't going into a seizure brought on by my tragic life.

"You have been treated poorly by a man, haven't you Eve?"

"While I was perusing bridal magazines, my boyfriend of three years dumped me for a little oriental trollop. I guess one could say I was treated poorly."

"You always go for the bad boy, don't you, Eve?"

I guess so.

She had effectively put my life in a nutshell. Bad boys. Men who treated me poorly? Hah! They treated me like something to be scraped from the bottom of their shoe. They then use me, abuse me, and stomp on me on their way out the door. This was the first time anyone had ever actually... verbalized it.

I nervously fiddled with a loose thread on the hem of her lace curtain and blushed to the roots of my hair when it unraveled in my hand.

"Oh, Marilyn! I'm so sorry! Do you have a needle and thread? I will be happy sew it back up." To be so stupid. How could I just sit there and unravel the woman's curtain?

"Don't worry about it, Eve." She pulled my fidgety hands to rest in my lap. "Just talk to me."

"Are you sure?" I asked, glancing toward the ragged hem.

"Absolutely positive. You wouldn't believe how many times that curtain has needed to be re-hemmed."

Why was I suddenly nervous enough to crawl out of my own skin? Why was my heart pounding against my chest hard enough to crack a rib? I leaned back in the rocker, took a deep, calming breath and blurted, "For starters, as you said, I always choose the wrong man. Always. Always. It's a lifelong pattern. The less they have to offer, the more I am inexplicably drawn to them. What else? Oh, I often get accused of being a controlling bitch. Imagine that."

I caught myself reaching for a thread hanging below the curtain, but fortunately stopped myself in time. "I left my husband, who treated me like a queen, for a raging alcoholic. In every relationship since, I end up getting hurt and moving on to another man identical to the previous one. It's a vicious cycle that I would love to break."

"We can certainly work on that."

I nodded, thinking the poor thing had her work cut out for her. It would take years to fix me.

"For now, let's talk about you." She closed her eyes for a second and concentrated. "You are self-employed and very successful in business."

"I own a commercial cleaning company."

Still holding my hands, she whispered, "What are you running from, Eve?"

How did she know?

Who told her?

Deciding to give her a chance to redeem herself, I told her the entire story of how I had recently gone to my boyfriend's house and found him in bed with the petite, stunningly beautiful Asian adulteress named Chia.

She listened patiently. "Do you have a picture of Adam?"

It was nothing more than an astoundingly lucky coincidence that I just so happened to carry a 4x5 glossy in my bag. "I believe I do."

Studying the photo of Adam and me smiling into the camera at Dolly Pardon's Pirate's Voyage, she settled back in her chair. Closing her eyes, she took a deep breath and began her detailed prognostication. "Chia has begun to miss her children, but not enough to actually go home to them."

"Chia has six kids. I would probably prolong my homecoming too. "

"At first she was so in love with Adam that she didn't give her kids a second thought. She was too caught up in the secrecy of their illicit affair. The sneaking around and ever present fear of getting caught was thrilling to her. Now that the excitement of them living together is wearing off, the guilt and regret are beginning to tug at her heartstrings."

"What heart?"

Ignoring my sarcasm, she continued, "It has even crossed her mind to try to convince her husband to allow her to come home, but he has lived with her infidelity for years and has washed his hands of her." She peered at me curiously. "Adam has considered calling you several times lately."

My heart began a clamorous clanging in my chest at her words. Taking a quick peek at my phone to make sure it hadn't accidentally powered off, I sat straight up and fiddled with a basket of potpourri on the end table beside my chair. "What stopped him?"

She breathed a heavy sigh. "He didn't think you would talk to him."

Oh, sweet Jesus. Just to hear his heavily

accented Yankee voice. "He was right," I lied in a feverish attempt to hide the desperation I was feeling. "I wouldn't have talked to him then and I hope I never hear his voice again."

I prayed fervently that I wouldn't get struck by lightning on the way out for allowing that bald faced lie to fall from my lips.

She covered her mouth with her hand in a failing attempt to hide a smile. Her brilliant green eyes sparkled as she glanced at something in the area over my shoulder. Evidently, her clever spirit guide was bouncing with glee and mouthing the words, *she's lying*, and giving Marilyn a clear vision of me bolting to the phone, stubbing my toe on a table leg, and sending whatnots flying in every direction as I snatched it up on the first ring.

I should have remembered she was a freaking psychic.

She recovered, brought her gaze back to me and said with all seriousness, "He will be calling you within three weeks."

Stop the presses!

"Be warned. This man will never stop cheating. It's in his blood. If you allow yourself to get involved with him again it will lead to a life of heartache. When he calls, don't answer. Ignore him. This is your year."

My year?

"Aside from the fact that you won't have Adam, everything else in your life will improve. By midsummer there will be so much happening in your life, you will rarely give Adam a second thought."

Seriously?

If she honestly believed there was even the most remote possibility of my life improving without Adam in it then she, along with her inept spirit guide, might consider registering at the local community college for a semester of Remedial Fortune Telling. Adam might be able to switch his feelings on and off like the bubbling mechanism on a hot tub, but it wasn't that easy for me. We were meant to be together!

I have the frigging wedding dress!

I mean, come on. *Adam and Eve?* It's biblical. If that isn't a sign that we were meant to be together please, tell me what is.

I noticed an abrupt change in her demeanor as she gathered my hands in hers. Hers were so warm and comforting I felt like I had known her for years. Closing her eyes for several seconds, she opened them and gazed at me with such a depth of sadness that I wanted to cry. This couldn't be good.

She took a deep breath and exhaled slowly. "I must tell you some bad news."

No shit!

Imagine that!

Certainly no beating around the bush with this woman. How bad could it be? I had no desire to find out. Nope. Time to go. I wasn't going to wait around to hear bad news. I don't need to hear it from a stranger when I live it daily.

Jerking my hands from hers, I braced them on the arms of the chair in preparation for a hasty departure. I shouldn't have come here. She didn't know anything about me, or my life. She was a quack. She was guessing. Plus, I wasn't at all sure my fragile mental state could withstand more bad news.

My traitorous legs refused to cooperate and lift me. It was almost like my body was forcing me to listen to what she had to say. I tried to speak, but couldn't. Either she had placed a spell on me, or I really didn't want to leave without hearing her prophetic words. I saw her getting ready to speak.

Don't!

Hush!

I wanted to cry out but the words refused to leave my numb lips. Please. Whatever it is. Don't say it. Just let me go home unscathed.

Her lips parted and the words that had the ability to destroy my life tumbled out. "Chia is pregnant."

That couldn't be true. She was lying. I felt sick. Chia's seventh child would belong to Adam? Surely her devious spirit guide was playing a horrible joke on me.

"Chia doesn't want the baby. She wants to have an abortion. She has no desire to be tied down with an infant now that her children are in school." She leaned back in her chair seemingly oblivious to the pain her words were causing. "The thought of an abortion devastates Adam."

"He's a big boy. He'll get over it."

"I know you don't want to hear this, Eve, but I must be honest with you."

"Trust me, I don't mind if you lie."

"Adam loves this woman more than he has ever loved anyone. He knows what kind of woman she is and accepts it. He believes that her having his baby will be a way to tie her to him forever, convincing her to settle her down and accept his proposal of marriage."

Did she say proposal?

"What makes him think one kid will tie her to him when her husband couldn't keep her with six?" I sobbed, imagining Adam in labor and delivery with Chia as the irritating *Peter Peter Pumpkin Eater* nursery rhyme played over and over in my head.

"He doesn't care about any of that." She shook her head sadly. "He's head over heels in love with her, and love is blind."

"Will she marry him?" Tears of hurt, pain, and betrayal coursed down my cheek.

"Probably, but it won't be the happily ever after Adam dreams of. By summer, Chia will have met yet another man she can't live without. Adam will be devastated."

Happy! Happy! Joy! Joy!

"He will feel like his life is over, exactly as you do now, only worse. Always remember my dear, we reap what we sow."

"That's what my mom always says." I hiccupped, but the flow of tears had slowed just a bit. "Is she going to have an abortion?"

"Yes, that's when Adam's world will begin to slowly crumble." Her face took on an irritated expression. "Do you know who he will turn to for comfort when this happens?"

"Me?" If only her words could be true.

"Like I told you before, Adam will never change. He will always be a skirt chaser. A doctor might even diagnose him with a condition known as sexual addiction."

I had often heard the term but never had the

common sense to apply it to Adam. As with most obsessive disorders there were probably medications to keep the powerful cravings of this addiction under control. I would go online the minute I got home and learn everything there was to know on the subject, and call a Help Line.

It was crystal clear now. His cheating was an addiction. He couldn't help it. Bless him. The poor man just needed someone to understand his sickness, and some counseling.

The dreamy smile on my face must have been a dead giveaway that I was having a rare jubilant moment because she swiftly wiped it from my face with her hateful words. "Adam's ideal woman is Asian. He likes the different little things they do in the bedroom. He rarely finds an American woman sexually appealing."

Her *I must be honest* mantra was about to piss me off. Why couldn't she let me savor even the tiniest bit of hope before she stomped on it and crushed it into the carpet like a two year old with a bag of chips? "Does Adam think about me?"

"Occasionally, when he needs something."

Did she take pleasure in telling me that, or had I only imagined it? Why did this woman take an immediate dislike to me? Had she never heard of little white lies to protect the innocent? Couldn't she see I was close to slipping over the edge here? Maybe she needed to twist the knife a little deeper next time she plunged it through my liver.

"He thought often of you during the first couple of weeks after the breakup. Now you rarely cross his mind." She stood, signaling that our time was up.

I might be getting the last laugh after all. No matter how in love Adam was, just knowing his little Chia pet was going to break his cheating heart thrilled me to the very core. Spring was just around the corner. A few more weeks and he would be feeling the pain I was feeling now. Marilyn had said so herself. Pay back is a bitch.

Passing her a twenty dollar tip, I shook her hand as she said, "Come back whenever you need me."

That shouldn't take long.

Chapter Five

The following night Mallory and I put on our spy gear. The only thing missing from this *Mission Impossible* scene was Tom Cruise.

Adam's shift ended at 11:00 and he would be home by 12:00, on the off chance that he wasn't sleeping over with his paramour. It was 10:15, so time was of the essence.

Don't you know two grown women have never looked quite as ridiculous as we did skulking around in our black coats, gloves, and toboggans? The gloves were so we wouldn't leave fingerprints, of course. You know I read every word Patricia Cornwell writes.

What about my Jeep? Was I supposed to park it in his driveway during our daring venture into espionage? No, there was a wooded lot across from his house. I could park on the back side and cut through the woods. Then we would cross the dirt road, hopefully without being seen or heard.

Parking the Jeep as close to the edge of the woods as possible, I switched off the engine as adrenaline gushed through my veins. Thankfully, clouds were covering the full moon so we felt semi-safe. "Let's do this."

Stepping out, we were greeted by a chorus

of croaking bullfrogs, buzzing mosquitoes, chirping crickets and a hooting owl. Now that was unusual. Whoever heard of mosquitoes being a nuisance in the dead of winter? I might have given that thought further contemplation if Mallory hadn't rushed up beside me and began her nonstop, nervous chatter. We stealthily scooted from tree to tree like amateur cat burglars, trying to stay in the shadows.

"Hush, Mallory!" The girl squealed like a pig when a whippoorwill in the tree directly overhead issued an alarm. He was fulfilling his duty as night watchman by signaling to the forest creatures that a stranger was in their midst. "It was just a whippoorwill."

"Well, he needs to be quiet!"

"Don't count on it. Once those birds start singing they never hush."

"What if the cops ride by?"

"They won't."

"What if Adam has an alarm system?"

"He doesn't."

"What if a neighbor has dogs and they start barking?"

"They don't."

"I just know someone is standing at the window watching us."

"Well then, stop talking so much and start moving your big ass."

"Men never complain about my big... Oh! Oh! Oh! I just felt something scurry over my foot!"

"It was your imagination, Mallory. Please, lower your voice. When you feel something *slither* across your foot you will have cause for concern."

"Why did you say slither? There could be a

copperhead pilot or a rattlesnake at our feet and we wouldn't even know until it was too late."

After a short while the girl's eternal whining could grate on your last piece of nerve and her sniveling would no doubt wake even the neighbors with hearing aids.

"What if the window is locked?" she whispered.

"I brought a credit card, just in case. Have you opened a door with a credit card?"

"Lots of times." She chuckled as we cautiously raced across the street. "It's easy."

Somehow I knew she had, but we had reached Adam's house so I didn't question her motive for having acquired that particular life skill. With our backs pressed against the house we slid around the brick wall checking windows until we finally hit pay dirt. The one in the dining room was unlocked.

"Crawl in, Mallory."

"Me?" She actually had the nerve to appear shocked by my request. "Why don't you crawl in?"

"Because I am ten years older than you. Now stop your caterwauling and crawl in before someone sees us."

"Eve, sometimes you worry the piss outta me." She complained loudly, but raised the window and hauled her oversized derriere over the windowsill. Although she let it be known by loud huffing and puffing that she was *far* from happy about it.

I heard her stumbling around inside until she finally found the back door and opened it. "How are we going to see? Surely the neighbors will notice and call Adam at work if we turn on a light."

I slapped my palm against my forehead in frustration. "Of all the idiotic things. Can you believe I forgot to bring a flashlight?"

"Well, it was kinda spur of the moment. We didn't case the joint for days like most master criminals would. Where's the phone?"

"To your right on the wall." I anxiously felt around the pitch black room and prayed Adam didn't have the forethought to set booby traps for a situation just such as this. Never mind, as a general rule Adam doesn't have forethought.

"Ouch! Shit!" Mallory yelped, banging her thigh against the kitchen table. "Here." She handed me the cordless phone, followed by the sound of her vigorously rubbing her thigh. "That's gonna leave a bruise and you know I hate bruises."

"Just turn out the lights and the man of the hour won't even notice it."

My eyes aren't what they used to be and I hadn't thought to grab my reading glasses, so I grabbed the phone and opened the refrigerator door for light. I hit scroll on his caller ID and there was Chia. About a hundred times. The talkative trollop.

Grabbing the pen and paper from my pocket, the only things I had remembered to bring in my haste, I jotted down her number and suppressed the urge to send the phone sailing through the nearest window. As I was writing, my eyes were drawn to a blinking red light in the corner. His answering machine. Well now, I wonder who was leaving messages. It certainly hadn't been me. Should I or shouldn't I? I pressed play.

"Hey, baby." A sultry, Asian voice purred

from the machine. "Are you wake? How you sleep without me in you arm?"

Well gag me with a fucking fork.

The pain in my chest felt like someone had my heart in a vise grip. "Let's get out of here." As I turned to leave, I noticed one of those disposable cameras on the kitchen table. *Who still uses those?* Let's see. Should I or shouldn't I? I was already breaking and entering. I might as well add theft to the charge. I slipped the camera in my pocket without the worrywart even noticing.

"Whip-poor-will." The woods were even creepier and more ominous walking back to the Jeep with the song of a whippoorwill echoing through the still forest. "Whip-poor-will. whip-poor-will."

I had a serious case of jitters and prayed the sounds I heard were only the workings of an over stimulated imagination. The sounds such as limbs breaking too close to us with loud snaps that echoed through the woods like a rifle shot penetrating the darkness.

Maybe it was a deer.

Dead leaves being crunched on the damp, moss covered ground as if someone were skipping through the woods a short distance from us.

Maybe it was a deer.

The sound of leaves rustling and stirring in the trees, when the leaves had long since fallen from the trees.

Okay. Even Bambi can't make leaves appear on barren trees.

At that moment, the moon shone through the clouds and illuminated the skeletal limbs that towered above us. We stopped dead in our tracks as the woods suddenly filled with the haunting melody of a child's playful laugh.

"What's so funny?" Mallory demanded.

"It wasn't me," I whispered, peering into the trees with building apprehension.

"What do you mean, it wasn't you!" she screeched, taking off in a sprint.

Glancing up, I saw a small shadowy form or something considerably larger than a whippoorwill or an owl perched on a limb in the tree directly overhead. I stood still, too terrified to move a muscle.

"Mallory," I whispered hoping not to draw undue attention to myself. "Look at that limb right above your head."

Mallory was long gone. The girl left me in a trail of dust and didn't slow down until she stood trembling and gasping for breath beside the Jeep. When I realized I was alone in the woods with... something... you can believe I wasn't far behind her.

"Why did you lock the door?" Mallory whimpered, her breath catching in her throat as I caught up to her. "Did you see him, Eve?"

"I..."

"It was the little boy, wasn't it? It was the same little boy your Dad saw, wasn't it? I saw him in the tree. He was laughing. Did you hear him laughing? Oh Lord, we have a ghost after us for real. You know I can't take this shit, Eve. Why did I let you talk me into doing something so stupid? Did you hear his sinister laughter, Eve? The kid was laughing at us!"

"Yes, I heard laughing and no, I don't know who or what it was. I thought I saw something, but it was probably just my imagination." Leaning back in the seat I took a deep breath and tried to calm my frazzled nerves. "It gets kinda spooky around here at night."

"Spooky? Are you kidding me? These woods remind me of the woods in the *Blair Witch Project*."

It had to be my imagination, didn't it? Of course it did. When I could finally get my trembling fingers to fit the key into the ignition, I put the Jeep in reverse and backed into the road slinging gravel hither and yon. I drove home terrified that the little boy would skip across the road in front of us, or swing down from an overhanging tree limb as I drove under it, or leap on the hood and press his hideous face against the windshield. Here I was selfishly worrying about myself. Poor Mallory would have a seizure on the spot.

When we arrived at my house Mallory adamantly refused to drive home alone. I heard her rummaging through my dresser drawer until she found pajamas that fit over her supersized backside and crawled into my bed. I double checked the locks on all the doors and windows and joined her. The delayed thought struck me that if the child could appear and disappear at will, a locked door probably wouldn't present much of a challenge for him. Screw the electric bill. I left every light in the house on.

I had just pulled the covers over me and was reaching to set the alarm when the phone rang. Picking up the receiver I heard, "I cannot believe how truly ignorant the lot of you are. *The Three Stooges* in female form. You know how taxing it is for me to maintain this figure, yet you sit idly by and allow me to stuff my mouth with enough pure cane sugar to send me into a diabetic coma and…."

I handed the phone to Mallory. "It's for you." I put a pillow over my head to drown out Teri's ceaseless tirade and went to sleep.

I was awakened sometime during the night when a whippoorwill perched on the ledge outside my window and called, "whip-poor-will, whip-poor-will, whip-poor-will" in his mournful echo through the otherwise quiet night.

I felt like one of the walking dead when I rolled out of bed the following morning, grateful for the light of day. Visions of the little boy had danced through my head for the better part of the night. When the child had finally taken a break from disturbing my sleep, the whippoorwill filled the silence with his haunting lament.

I stumbled down the hall to make coffee and heard Mallory rapping in the shower to a song about the joys of sex, smoking pot, and drinking something purple.

Only after I had my first cup of the steaming aromatic brew in my hands did I remember I was anxious to drop off the pilfered disposable camera and get to work so I could talk to Eric. Hopefully he would agree to the plan the girls and I had cooked up and *Operation Pay Back is A Royal Bitch* could commence.

Chapter Six

Eric agreed totally and enthusiastically to the plan. Especially after Mallory's gushing rendition, she told it to anyone who would listen, of the Fair Chia's resemblance to a frigging supermodel. Quite frankly I had long since tired of the comparison. When was the last time she had witnessed a 4 foot 9 model sashaying down a runway?

There were still a few kinks to be worked out of our plan. Eric couldn't call Chia from work because we couldn't block calls, and I couldn't have my work number showing up on her caller ID. He didn't want to call from his cell because he didn't trust the block feature on cells. His number at home was private, so I gave him an extra long lunch break to call from home.

I ordered barbecue chicken with creamed potatoes and green beans for lunch in the cafeteria. The first bite settled sourly on my stomach. I slid the plate toward Mallory who mumbled, "Thanks," around her cheeseburger. The girl was a bottomless pit and I had never once known her to lose her appetite. You can talk about snot 'til the cows came home and she won't even flinch.

How could I possibly concentrate on toilets

and scuffed floors at a time like this? I was a bundle of nerves waiting on Eric's return. This was torture. I had to do something to occupy my mind, so why was I sitting here when I could be at CVS picking up the purloined photos?

Twenty minutes later, I sat in the parking lot staring at the unopened pack of photos. Did I really want to see what was inside? *Yep.* My hands shook violently as I settled back in the seat and found the courage to open the pack. Believe me, the second I saw the photos I wished fervently that I had left the damn roll of film on his table. I should have known nothing good would come from stealing.

The first photo was of Adam and Chia in front of the Biltmore House with their cheeks pressed against each other, standing arm in arm and behaving like a much in love and blissfully happy couple.

At Thanksgiving Adam had told me his parents were flying in from Massachusetts to meet him in Asheville and spend the holiday in the mountains. I remembered his exuberance over what I had thought was a family gathering as I *helped him pack*. Instead, he had taken Chia to the scenic destination. This reality and the depth of Adam's lies was another crushing blow as I sat alone in the parking lot and had a good cry.

I shook off the building despair and continued through the photos. There were snapshots of each of them plopped down on boulders with Grandfather Mountain in the background. Chia's photo was of her blowing a disgusting kiss to the photographer. There were shots of them holding hands, evidently taken by an innocent bystander, while crossing the Mile High Swinging Bridge. Shots at snow covered Blowing Rock, and even a few shots at Tweetsie Railroad with Chia giggling and clearly flirting with a wild west gunslinger.

There were still more photos of her in provocative poses on the bed in a hotel room with a come hither look in her seductive gaze. Then I came to the shots of her in a bikini at the indoor pool and hot tub.

Oh Joy! Oh Joy! Oh Joy! There is a God!

Her stomach looked like someone had pulled the plug on a hand grenade just under the skin. I grinned wickedly at the sight of her wrinkled globs of lumpy, over stretched folds of mottled flesh spilling over her bikini bottom. Ugly red stretch marks at least an inch wide riddled her abdomen causing it to resemble a road map, and the girl had the nerve to wear a bikini.

Had she no pride?

It was a profound relief to know that she may be extraordinarily attractive from the neck up, but her stomach resembled that of a 600-pound woman a year after gastric bypass surgery.

Obviously Adam hadn't found the overlapping folds of flesh repulsive. Judging from the number of photos he had taken I could only assume that he wanted to remember this trip with her through infinity. The slimy bastard. The most I had ever gotten out of him was dinner, a movie, and the occasional fishing trip.

I searched for signs in the photos to give me a clue as to which hotel they had checked in to. Please, don't let me discover that Adam had rented a room at the luxurious Grove Park Inn, as many times as I had suggested that *we* go there. *Whew.* He didn't. It was more like one of those motels where they leave the light on for you.

After lunch, Eric came swaggering up the sidewalk beaming from ear to ear.

"Spill." I said, scooting over and motioned for him to join Mallory and me at the picnic table. I was so nervous I had chewed three fingernails to the quick.

"She seemed a little uncertain and suspicious at first," he drawled in his charming Southern boy way. "She wanted to know how I had gotten her number. It took about 5 minutes to convince her that one of her friends at work had given it to me. When I told her it was because she was so stunning and I had to meet her, she was putty in my hands. The girl loves to hear that she's beautiful."

"Wait until you see how beautiful her stomach is," I quipped.

"What's wrong with her stomach?" "Eric glanced at me with a disconcerted frown. Mallory and I had both assured him that Chia was exquisite and he wasn't at all pleased with the suggestion that the object of his intended seduction might possess an unsightly flaw. After all, he had a reputation to maintain.

"You'll see, and it's not that bad really," I fibbed. "Finish telling us about the call."

"Okay, for starters, she has a real problem with English. You know that, right? I had to keep asking her to repeat what she was saying." He was lost in thought for a minute, trying to remember the pertinent details of their conversation. "Oh, I asked if she was seeing anyone and she said, 'Not really'."

"Did you ask to meet her?" Mallory simpered, leaning over the table to provide him a better glimpse of her less than generous cleavage. The girl's ample behind was her best calling card to the opposite sex. Even Sir Mix-a-Lot would agree that Mallory had a supercharged motor in the back of her Honda.

"Nope. I'm gonna talk to her a few days on the phone and let her get to know me before I rush in." He was taking full advantage of the view so blatantly offered and even went so far as to lick his lips.

Practically drooling now, Mallory purred, "Smart move."

"I just kept telling her how beautiful she was, since she soaks that up like a sponge. I'm supposed to call her tomorrow at noon. I asked about calling her tonight when she got off work and she said, 'No. Sorry. I busy tonight'."

Shocking. At least one female was capable of telling him no, but for how long? "Adam will be with her tonight." My heart sank with the knowledge as I stood. "Oh well, it's time to earn our paychecks."

Eric offered me an incredibly sexy wink. "I thought I had already earned mine, and you would give me the rest of the afternoon off."

"You don't know Eve very well, do you?" Mallory was fanning herself as we headed back inside. "Eve would pop a blood vessel if you tried to leave after lunch before the cafeteria was spotless."

Feeling much better, and confident that lover boy Eric would have Chia eating out of his skilled hands in no time, I informed Mallory that I was leaving to go home and take a nap. Actually, I was going home to pray for forgiveness for my sinful ways.

The next day, after a two-hour lunch, Eric sauntered up the sidewalk with even more impressive news. "I didn't even have to ask to meet her. She asked me. Seems one of her friends at work has seen me and... I guess told her I was kinda cute."

No the boy was not trying to be modest when we both knew any modesty he possessed would fit in his smallest toe bone.

"We have a lunch date Friday at Applebees."

That was certainly a news flash. Chia was willing to go to a public restaurant with Eric? She didn't seem overly concerned about her afternoon tryst reaching Adam's jealous ears, now did she? I asked what was first and foremost on my mind. "Can you hook her, Eric?"

"She's already hooked." His lips curved into a conceited grin as he brushed invisible lint from his shoulder. "I can't believe you ever doubted me. Oh, by the way, you're paying for the motel room."

"No problem. Just let me know how much." Hell, I would give him my credit card, the gold American Express without a spending limit, if it would rush the proceedings. This was moving faster than I hoped.

"Will do."

"That is one self assured man." We both watched as Eric strutted toward the plant, pausing long enough to wink at one of the female employees puffing away in the smoking section of the patio.

"He has every reason to be." Mallory's eyes never once wavered from the seat of his jeans.

"I have to go," I announced, trying to draw her attention from Eric's backside. "I need to drop by the Employment Security Commission and ask them to send over applicants to interview for the new contract at the county offices."

"Hire some good looking black men," she purred.

"I will hire the most qualified person for the job."

"I wish you would let me do the interviews."

"I just bet you do. The employees you hired wouldn't begin to know what to do with a mop or broom but they would certainly be well qualified in other areas, wouldn't they?"

"You know it, girlfriend. If they weren't qualified I could teach them the basics in one afternoon in the broom closet."

"I know you could, Mallory." I couldn't help but laugh. "I know you could."

On Friday, Eric returned from a *four hour* lunch with a satisfied grin splitting his handsome features. "Well, I gotta say. I know why Adam is so crazy about her now."

Oh, good Lord.

Why did he feel the need to say all that? Did I really want to hear what he was fixing to bust a gut to tell me?

"I can't speak for other Asian women," he purred, "but Chia is one hot little tamale."

I was almost positive that a hot tamale made reference to a female of Hispanic origin, but I chose to keep that contemplation to myself. Just because Eric's looks are well above average doesn't necessarily mean his IQ followed suit. Nor his pay scale, because I was quite certain that his complimentary commentary concerning said tamale was on the verge of eradicating any future pay raises. Still I had to know. "How is she different from an American woman?"

Eric's eyes glazed over with… passion? "For starters, she brings a whole new meaning to the term bucking and thrashing."

"Really?" How much bucking and thrashing could one woman do? Not that I was prone to either buck or thrash, but it sounded extremely tiresome.

"You can't keep her still. That girl is all over the place." He had a nauseatingly dreamy smile on his face. "From top, to bottom, to sideways. She really gets into it."

"What else?" A feeling similar to that of impending doom seeped through my entire body. Eric's face was flushed and he absently nudged his groin just thinking about her.

"Well, she's very… vocal." A leering smile played across his lips, evidently remembering Chia's choice of obscenities. He moved behind the picnic table and sat down, obviously in an attempt to hide the erection that no one at the tables, especially Mallory, had missed.

"Like talking dirty?" Okay. That wasn't something I was prone to do either. I mean, how embarrassing. I had to be beside myself with anger to even utter the F word.

"That and moaning and groaning and screaming. She *really* enjoys sex."

"And?" So she was a screamer. I wasn't. Big whoop dee do. I couldn't remember one time when I had even come close to feeling the urge to raise my voice during a sexual encounter.

"Anything goes." Eric was on a roll. "In fact, the kinkier the better."

"Such as?" What was I missing here? Very rarely had the word *kinky* entered my boudoir vocabulary. She bucks, she thrashes, she talks dirty, and screams. What else was there?

He hesitated and a bright blush lit his face and neck. "Like I said anything goes with her. Anything. Anywhere."

"Anywhere? Like on top of the washing machine or in the back of the car at the drive-in or, heaven forbid, in a public restroom?" *Just think of the germs.*

Eric's eyes sparkled as he shook his head. "Um… no."

"Well, where?"
Oh.
Oh!
You…don't… mean…"
Oh!
Ouch!
Say it isn't so!

"Yep." He must have been having a particularly naughty memory the way drool was forming at the corners of his mouth. "I swear, you will have to buy me some vitamins, and perhaps a prescription for Cialis to keep up with the girl."

Always the glutton for punishment, I had to ask. "Okay. Be honest. On a scale of 1 to 10 how would you rate her in bed?"

"Are you sure you want the honest truth, Eve?"

Nope, I didn't, but tell me anyway. "Yes."

"15."

Such a dreamy look settled over his handsome face that I was tempted to fire him on the spot. Still, I was sure that was a slightly exaggerated figure. It had to be. Eric had worked for me for almost a year and I had never known him to give one of his numerous conquests a score higher than 10.

Oh man, if looks could kill Eric would be a dead man at the hands of Mallory, whom he had ranked at a measly 10. I never should have told the girl her ranking but at the time it was the ultimate compliment. "Then you shouldn't have a problem going back for seconds, should you?" I snapped, close to tears.

"Hey, don't get mad at me." He came around the table to hug me. "You asked for the truth."

"I know. Of course, you're right." I couldn't be angry with him for being honest. Although he certainly could have lied just a little given the enormity of the subject matter. "I'm sorry, Eric," I mumbled, as the number 15 sliced through my heart like a Ginsu knife.

"It's okay," he said with what he surmised were comforting words. "I've known people who've been dumped and they say it hurts like hell."

Dumped. Such a vicious little word.

He snapped his finger. "I almost forgot to tell you something else. Her cell phone was ringing like crazy the entire time. I guess it was Adam. She finally turned it off."

"So, other than the spectacular sex, is she falling for you?" I had heard enough of Chia's porn star theatrics for one day. "Enough that she will end it with Adam?"

"I'm meeting her tomorrow night at 8:00." With that, he proceeded to grin one of those cocky grins that only good looking men can carry off. "Does that answer your questions?"

Yep, sure did. That one sentence spoke volumes. Chia was giving up a fun filled Saturday night of erotica with Adam to spend time with her new boy toy Eric. What woman of mediocre intelligence wouldn't? Alas, that could only mean Adam had been knocked from his vantage point of the highest perch on Chia's totem pole and would be alone on Saturday night.

Poor baby. He should have known.

Once a ho, always a ho.

I didn't have time to gloat, I had planning to do. "Do you think you can get invited to her house, so Adam will see your car there? I don't want her sneaking around behind his back in her accustomed manner. I want it thrown in his face and smacked right between the eyes with it."

"I take that to mean you want me to spend the night at her house tomorrow night." Eric thought about this for a minute, a bit hesitantly it seemed. "He won't do one of those crimes of passion things and come after me with a machete will he?"

"Heavens no." I couldn't help but laugh, just the thought was humorous. Anyone who knew Adam would know Eric had nothing to fear. "Adam will park down the street and wait. When he realizes you're spending the night with the precious one he will leave, beside himself with grief, and call tomorrow assuring her of his undying love and begging for another chance. You have to convince her, beyond the slightest shadow of a doubt, that you are the man of her dreams. Can you do it?"

"In my sleep."

"I don't believe you'll be doing much of that." To be so young and arrogant. "Call me and let me know if you get invited to her sleepover."

"If?" He seemed to find the word insulting. "I will pretend I'm calling my mom to tell her I won't be home. Chia doesn't know I don't live at home and probably wouldn't understand me if I tried to tell her. She only wants my body." *Duh!* "When I call it will be my signal that I'm staying over."

"Perfect." If he spent the night at her house our plan would be a resounding success.

I was a nervous wreck the following day. To keep my mind from rambling and imagining plan gone wrong scenarios, I took my mom for her first ever pedicure. She complained incessantly, like I was taking her to have her toenails removed instead of polished, during the entire drive to Perfect Nails.

"Ain't nobody got no business touching my feet," she insisted.

"Okay, Mom."

"You know them folks don't wanna be handling somebody's feet that they don't even know."

"They don't mind, Mom."

"I could go to the Dollar Store and get three bottles of polish for a dollar and paint my own toenails."

"I'm sure you could, Mom."

"Why would I pay good money to have a stranger rub my feet?"

"You're not, Mom. It's my treat."

"I don't know if I want another woman rubbing my feet."

"They do it all the time, Mom."

"Why would a woman my age care if her toes looked good or not, when her legs look like somebody took a blue magic marker and scribbled on them?"

"Women should try to look their best at any age."

When we arrived I led her to the polish section and instructed her to choose a color. Instead of the reds, which I assumed she would choose, her hands fluttered over the neon section.

Go ahead, girl!

She chose a bright fluorescent orange, then sank back in her chair sullied up like a bull, although I could tell she was secretly excited.

Excited was putting it mildly. She nearly swooned with pleasure as the petite Asian lady vigorously massaged her feet and scraped a neat pile of dead, calloused skin from her heels. She chatted with the lady in the next chair with a vibrating voice and relaxed contentedly in her massaging chair, which had been adjusted to the highest speed.

I had recently gotten a pedicure, so while receiving my manicure I glanced back at her and could tell she was positively loving every minute of her pampering, but she would never admit it to a living soul.

Finished, Mom ever so carefully padded over to where I was sitting. She was a colorful sight with her bright blue cushiony toe separators still in place between fluorescent orange toenails that I was sure would glow in the dark. Grinning broadly, she complimented the artistry of the lady who had painted dainty white flowers in the center of each of her big toenails and said, "Do you think I need a manicure too?" all the while eyeing my French manicured nails.

"I believe you do." Well now, a manicure *and* a pedicure? Mom was stepping out of the country for real. "Go up to the front desk and add your name to the manicure list."

She wrote her name, while I steadfastly prayed she wouldn't choose the same fluorescent orange for her fingernails. She didn't. She extended her hands for inspection to the lady at the desk and received her own French manicure while I chatted with Kim, the owner of the shop. We had been good friends for over twenty years.

Okay!
Okay!
I know what you're thinking.
Chia is Asian.

Admittedly, I detest and loathe her with a passion that alarms even me, but I would feel the same deep abiding repugnance if she were American, Hispanic, French, Spanish, Italian, Icelandic or Native American. My feelings for the slut are directed toward her as an individual.

I have zero problems with the remaining Asian populace. They are a wonderful people, judging from the ones I have met.

It's my fervent belief that those who choose to snub their noses at an entire race of God's creation, (be it the color of their skin, the slant of their eyes, or a language barrier) are playing with fire in its hottest form. So, please believe that I am in no way prejudiced, with the exception of home wrecking adulteresses.

"How often do we need to get this done?" She admired her fingers and toes during the ride home, commenting on how cute they were.

Don't you know, sometimes I could just pinch her?

Later that night, I was a bundle of raw nerves waiting for the phone to ring and almost jumped clear out of my skin when it finally did at 12:02.

"Hi, Mom. I won't be coming home tonight," Eric mumbled around what sounded like someone trying to swallow his tongue.

"My God!" I cried. "Is she on you?"

"Yes."

"You likey?" she purred very close to the phone. This was followed by some enthusiastic smacking and slurping.

The horny twit. She changed men like I changed underwear. "Have a nice time, Eric."

Just before he hung up I heard her say, "Oh… Ewick!"

At 12:10 the phone rang again.

There it was.

Oh, my God.

It was him.

Adam's name flashed in slow motion across the caller ID and almost succeeded in stopping my pounding heart.

Chapter Seven

Could it be?

Was it really him?

"Hey, Eve," Adam's sweet Yankee accent sizzled across the air waves.

His sexy purr sent a flood of wild emotions ranging from elation to seething rage racing through me. It was the sound I had lain awake night after night on a tear soaked pillow waiting to hear, while consuming multiple bottles of anti-depressants because I wasn't hearing it. Was it really the man who had gleefully purchased me a one way ticket to hell? The man who had caused me to question my very existence on this earth?

"What are you doing home on a Saturday night, Eve?" He may have asked the question, but it didn't sound like he cared one way or the other what my answer might be. Couldn't he at least sound just a little excited to be talking to me after all this time? "I thought you would be on a date tonight."

Miracle of miracles.

Could he be jealous?

If so, it was a pathetic attempt at emoting. Inhaling a deep breath, I tried to sound as casual as possible under the circumstances and took the liberty of embellishing the truth just a little. "I have been on a few dates, but nothing serious." There was total silence on his end, so I took the opportunity to question him. "Why aren't you with Chia? I was of the opinion that you two were joined at the hip." *Shit!* Now I was the one sounding jealous and, unlike his, my voice carried the appropriate depth of emotion.

"I ended that." *He was falsifying information again.* "She wasn't what I wanted, Eve. The girl was trying to get too serious and you, better than anyone else, should know I'm not ready for a commitment."

He was lying through his teeth. He wanted to get serious and commit to Chia more than he wanted the winning numbers for the next Mega Million Jackpot. I about chewed my tongue off to keep from blurting this out.

Not ready for commitment my dimpled ass.

He continued with his outrageous lie. "Being with her made me realize what I really wanted."

The way he spewed this verbal diarrhea might lead one to believe he was referring to me, when we were both painfully aware that wasn't the case at all.

"It's Saturday night and we're both alone. Can I come over, Eve?"

At that moment, I would have given all my worldly possessions to be in his arms. Still, I wasn't blind to the fact that if Adam could be anyplace of his choosing right now, it certainly wouldn't be with me. He would be happily ensconced in Chia's arms if she weren't already draped across lover boy

Eric like a rebel flag. Somehow the victory wasn't as sweet anymore.

"Sure, come on over." My short lived joy was being rapidly replaced by miserable defeat.

He was there before I could comb my hair and apply lip gloss or even consider changing into something sexy. Not that it mattered. I swear the man resembled someone who could just as easily have marched in a funeral procession. Nonetheless, when I opened the door I almost collapsed at the sight of him standing on my threshold, just like old times. Somehow, against all odds, I held myself aloof.

"Can I at least have a hug?" He didn't appear to be overly enthused by the prospect, more like pitiful and disheartened.

And it was all my fault.
Ha!

"Sure." He drew me into his arms and I immediately felt safely home again after a long and dangerous journey into the abyss. It felt so right to be back in his embrace, where I belonged. I didn't want to let go. Ever. Why couldn't he just love me?

With another one of his heartfelt sighs, he whispered, "I've missed you, Eve. You don't know what I've been going through, wondering if I had lost you forever."

Not a whole hell of a lot, I would imagine. "When did you find time to miss me, Adam, when you were spending every waking moment with Chia?" Suddenly, thinking back over the months of agonizing pain he had caused, made me angry enough to spit in his adorable face.

"I was confused, Eve." Taking my hand, he

led me to the sofa, pulling me down beside him. "I was chasing the wrong dream."

I'll say. How many nights had we sat side by side on this very sofa, when I had erroneously believed the love we felt for each other was equal and would last through eternity?

"What's wrong, Adam? You look like you've lost your best friend." I was thrilled to the core that he was feeling exactly as I had months ago. Exactly as Marilyn had foretold he would feel, in fact.

"It's been a rough couple of days, Eve." His eyes were red and puffy as if he had actually shed a tear over the floozy, and his poor fingernails had been chewed down to the nub.

Well, I just bet it had. What with the ever randy Chia undulating with Eric on her waterbed and ignoring both him and his phone calls. That wasn't a good feeling. I should know. He was finally getting a taste of his own medicine and *Mary Poppins* couldn't make it go down without choking him.

"I've been thinking about all the bad choices I made." Putting his arm around my shoulder, he drew me close until our faces were only inches apart. His breath carried the ever present fragrance of Budweiser. "I made a terrible mistake, Eve. I was wrong to cheat on you with Chia."

I pulled away from the suffocating nearness of lips that were begging to be kissed, but not far enough. Scooting forward, I perched on the edge of the sofa and absently twiddled my thumbs as he continued.

"Would you believe me if I told you that

when I was with Chia, I was thinking of you?"

Not no, but hell no!

Great balls of fire!

I didn't think it was possible for him to top some of the unbelievable nonsense he had told me in the past, but he just had. I could almost hear Teri's outraged reaction when I repeated that one to her.

"You will never know how much it pleases me to learn that I crossed your mind during your frequent romps with Chia, Adam, but I'm curious."

Now it was my time to twist the knife a little.

"What happened? Did you just decide you didn't want to see her anymore and break it off? Why, it must have broken her confused little heart."

"Oh, she cried and screamed and threw a serious tantrum, but I had to end it. I couldn't take her jealousy anymore, or her need to be with me every single minute." He threw his head back on the sofa for emphasis as he tried to persuade me of what a trying ordeal her alleged dumping had been. "To tell you the truth, I was getting tired of her."

Truth?

Here we go again.

"Don't worry, Adam. There are plenty more Asian women at the factory. She shouldn't be too difficult to replace."

"I don't want another Asian woman." Adam turned to me with a maniacal glint shining in his eyes. Good grief, was he on drugs? If so, it was the hard stuff. Talk about a mood swing. He seemed as close to slipping over the edge as I had been a few weeks earlier. "I want you, Eve."

While I realized that I should probably

humor him and not agitate him further until he calmed down, I've never been a shining example of when to hold ones tongue. "How can you sit there and lie with a straight face, Adam?" His vast array of untruths were about to cause me to throw a tantrum as well. "You're only attracted to Asian women. Neither of us can deny that. You can't make yourself be attracted to someone you're not. Is sex with them that much better than with an American woman?"

The idiot felt the need to eclipse every lie he had ever told me. "Actually, Chia was pretty boring. She has a tendency to just lie there and make me do all the work. She's not nearly as exciting in bed as you are."

The pathetic, lying bastard. Never had there been born a more compulsive liar. I didn't scream, talk dirty, or *perish the thought* take it up the rear. For a split second I wondered if Chia had found him as boring in bed as I had. Maybe it had taken lover boy Eric to bring out the hidden tigress in her. No, that wasn't the case at all. Even Marilyn had mentioned that's why Adam was so crazy over Chia. The fireworks in the bedroom.

"I love you, Eve." He had a forlorn look in his eyes that was almost believable. "I didn't think you would date while we were apart."

"I picked at a nonexistent hangnail on a perfectly manicured nail. "Did you expect me to sit around waiting patiently for you to tire of Chia and come crawling back."

He grabbed my nervous hands, clutching them between his. "Yeah, something like that." He had the nerve to confess it? He was either drunk or had been slipped a vial of truth serum. "I was wrong, Eve."

"I'll say."

"Would you give me another chance?" With an urgency bordering on desperation he pulled me into his arms. "I promise, you won't regret it."

I will admit that being in his arms almost caused me to forgive his past discrepancies. Never had anything felt more wonderful, but I was far from convinced as to the authenticity of his murmured declarations of love.

"I could never trust you again, Adam. You know that. Every day when you left for work I would suspect that you were on the prowl again. From what I hear you hit on every Asian female who walks through the factory doors."

"That's a lie." Dropping my hands, he stood and sauntered into the kitchen. A cork popped and he returned with a bottle of Chardonnay and two wineglasses. Filling the glasses with shaking hands he handed one to me.

"Thank you."

"I've told you people are jealous of me and love to start rumors. Haven't I told you that all along? If I so much as speak to a girl at work rumors spread like wildfire throughout the plant that I'm sleeping with her."

I moved to stand in front of the fireplace. Mistake. The rug brought unwanted memories scrambling through my brain. Memories of the nights during the first couple months of our courtship when we had made love on the rug, leaving me with severe carpet burns on my knees.

"Give me one more chance, Eve." He

moved to stand in front of me, slowly, so as not to spill his precious wine. Taking my glass, he placed it on the mantle and drew me into his arms.

Why did he insist on having me in his arms when he knew the position made it impossible for me to think straight?

"I can earn your trust back, Eve."

"I doubt it."

"I could find another job."

Those words instantly succeeding in grabbing my full and undivided attention. "You have been employed at the factory for fifteen years. You aren't going to find another job that pays as well, not when factories are closing in North Carolina at an alarming rate."

His voice held a note of sincerity when he said, "I would quit my job tomorrow if it was the only way to get you back."

He held me by my shoulders as unshed tears glistened in his brilliant blue eyes. *I so loved a sensitive man who wasn't afraid to let his emotions show.* "You would?" My steady resolve melted as quickly as the pumpkin spice scented candle burning on the mantle. "Really?"

Adam was warehouse supervisor, a status that required years of ladder climbing to achieve. I found it difficult to believe he would leave his job, or the large supply of female Asian employees, for me. That had to mean something. But what? Could it mean that Adam had been doing some deep soul searching? Had he perhaps finally realized there was more to life than great sex with Asian women?

"If I have to, I will put in my notice Monday." He held my face to gaze deeply into my tear filled eyes. "I love you, Eve."

"Oh, Adam, I love you too." Every last defense shattered as I fell into his waiting arms, praying that this time his words could somehow be true. "I never stopped loving you for a second."

"Will you give me another chance?"

"Yes," I whispered. "Of course I will."

He kissed me and I swallowed bile as I forced myself not to think where his lips had recently been. Shoving Chia to the darkest recesses of my mind, I was dripping with desire when he grabbed the wine bottle and took my hand, leading me to the bedroom.

Let's just say the encounter skidded downhill from there. No butterflies in the stomach. No tightening of the nether region. No waves of raging passion racing through my veins. Actually, there wasn't a whole lot of feeling at all. All that would return in time, I was sure. He had a lot on his mind, plus, he had downed the remaining wine from the bottle before crawling into bed with me.

Afterward, Adam kissed me on the cheek, rolled over, and asked me to rub his back until he fell into a restless sleep, leaving me alone with my thoughts.

Marilyn had it going on. As I lay with my hand on Adam's shoulder, constantly touching him to assure myself that he was really there, I realized she hadn't missed a beat. She had foretold that Adam would call within three weeks, after his beloved Chia had fallen head over heels for another man. Eric. "Don't answer the phone," she had strenuously cautioned me. "Ignore him." Thank God, I had ignored her instead.

It was impossible to ever love another man with the intensity I felt for Adam, so why bother trying? Sliding my hand around to cradle his steadily increasing beer gut, I snuggled contentedly against the warmth of his back and breathed a contented sigh.

Having a great sex life wasn't crucial for a successful relationship, was it? Naturally we weren't going to be burning up the sheets every few hours like someone in there 20's. Laughter was the glue that held our relationship together, although I couldn't really remember the last time I had heard a robust belly laugh from him.

Bottom line, I couldn't live without him, nor did I want to. At long last I had him lying next to me and felt the pain and hurt of the last couple months slowly fading into oblivion, hopefully never to return. With a contented smile I closed my eyes and slept blissfully, even though that aggravating whippoorwill returned to his new roosting spot on my windowsill.

The next morning, I awakened feeling all was right with this wonderful world of ours. I wanted to stay cuddled up to Adam and just kiss, well *maybe one or two more things,* for the better part of the morning. Judging from the look of things, there wouldn't be sweet kisses or anything else with Adam. He was snoring so loudly that I giggled, expecting the ruffled curtains to lift and flutter like they did in the *Tom and Jerry* cartoons.

I made coffee and spent the morning watching a movie in my pajamas. Adam rolled out of bed around noon, resembling a zombie from one of the *Night of the Living Dead* movies, with a hangover. He made the motions of going to the kitchen to pour a cup of black coffee without the evidence of a clear focus.

It was painfully obvious that the haggard man had some heavy stuff on his mind and wasn't in the mood to convey these thoughts, or any others, to me. Leaning back on the sofa he closed his eyes with a woeful expression that suggested he might be feeling exactly as I had after catching him with another woman. I couldn't recall ever seeing a more pathetic sight, except in my own mirror.

How could he still be thinking about Chia when he had irrefutable proof that she was with another man?

Duh?

Who was I to ask such a foolish question? The answer was, evidently the same way I had yearned for him during his Chia phase. Could he still be in love with her? Was I just someone to pass the time with until she tired of Eric? I couldn't think about that right now. I might plunge into the ranks of the stark raving mad. "Are you really going to work a notice next week?"

"Yes, Eve. I told you I would, didn't I?" He sounded much less sure of his plan than he had the night before. Was he already having troublesome second thoughts about his hasty, alcohol induced decision to quit his job. "I just don't know how I will keep my house."

Did he have to lay every ounce of guilt for his decision to quit at my feet? It was his idea, not mine. Maybe that was the cause of his hard to conceal distress this morning. Odds were that he wasn't even thinking about Chia. Surely he was more concerned with the nagging question of how to pay the bills that arrived like clockwork, than with a piece of ass.

If he truly loved me, as he so adamantly professed to do, wouldn't he be able to withstand the slanted eyes of temptation at work? I couldn't risk Adam losing everything he owned on account of my jealousy. That wouldn't bode well for either of our futures. I took the opportunity to ease his mind. "You don't need to quit your job, Adam."

"Do you really mean it, Eve?" This caused a beaming smile to light his boyishly handsome face as his blue eyes fairly danced. "I have to admit I'm shocked?"

"I know. Just hearing you say you would quit was enough for me." I hoped this would elevate his mood and we could have a good day. "I would be tearing my hair out if I didn't have a job and a no way to pay my mortgage next month. How could I ask you to put yourself in such a stressful situation?"

He glanced over his coffee cup for a long, appraising look and reached to caress my cheek. "You are one of a kind, Eve. Do you know that?"

Was that an actual tear twinkling in his baby blues? Had he finally seen the light and realized the error of his ways?

He winked. "You won't regret this, baby."

Please, don't make me regret it.

"Just promise to keep those roving eyes to yourself at work." I laughed with a sound that lacked even the smallest trace of humor.

"That is one promise that will be easy to

keep."

At times he could sound so sincere.

"I only have eyes for you now, Eve."

That was surely a first. "Okay, that's settled. What's on the agenda for today?" I reached under the counter for the frying pan. Bacon and eggs over easy with buttered toast was his favorite breakfast.

Draining the last of his coffee, he stood. "Get dressed and let's go to Charlotte to the mall."

Huh? I had feared earlier that I might need to fetch a walker to support his weary body as he struggled down the hall, now he was feeling spry enough to go gallivanting around a mall? What was the reason for this sudden burst of enthusiasm? I wouldn't allow myself to dwell on the possible causes of his unexpected jubilation. It couldn't be attributed to the fact that he would continue to see the enchanting Chia every day at work. Could it?

"Don't cook breakfast." He stretched and grabbed me for a bear hug and a quick kiss before heading to the shower. "I'm taking you to lunch at your favorite restaurant."

On the ride to Charlotte I couldn't help but wonder how many times Chia had plopped her skinny behind in my passenger seat. I caught myself glancing around for any lingering long black stray hairs. *Stop that.* Don't ruin the day obsessing over that foreign adulteress.

After an hour drive, Adam pulled his fancy little sports car into Olive Garden. I was happy to see he was his old self again, laughing and making his usual corny jokes. He chatted with the couple in front of us in line as if he had known them all his life and especially enjoyed when Southerners commented on his heavy Yankee accent.

After we were seated, I sipped a delicious bloody mary while we discussed the cabin he wanted to build in the woods, in the spring. I ordered Fettuccini Alfredo and he ordered Ziti and held my hand while rambling on and on about the bait and tackle he needed to purchase at Outdoor World. He didn't release my hand until the best salad on the planet arrived.

At Carolina Place Mall he purchased jeans at Macy's and shoes at Finish Line. I picked up a couple of cute shirts at The Gap. We were standing in line for Aunt Annie's homemade pretzels when he said something that left me puzzled and slightly uneasy. "Let's shop separately for a while."

"Why?" I cried, drawing the rapt attention of several fellow pretzel lovers. My suspicious mind immediately leapt to the worrisome conclusion that he was trying to slip away and make a clandestine phone call.

Aware that he was the center of attention, Adam grinned. "Would it be too much to ask to do a little shopping in private? Look around you, Eve."

Humoring him, I gazed around the mall and saw red hearts hanging from the ceiling and taped to every window. How had I missed it? "Valentine's Day."

"Valentine's Day is Tuesday." An attractive sixtyish gentleman in front of me chuckled. "Now can the man have some privacy to shop?"

"If I was you, I'd give him all the time he needs *and* point the way to the jewelry store," a charming elderly lady behind us joked.

"You take all the time you need," I assured Adam as my mind raced with possibilities. Wasn't it nothing more than a thrilling coincidence that we happened to be standing a few doors from a jewelry store when the sudden need for privacy occurred to him?

His Christmas present, a Lucky Brand blue jean jacket, was hidden in the back of my closet. I was glad I hadn't relented to the relentless urge to watch the jacket go up in flames. I would change the Christmas wrapping paper, making it the perfect Valentine's gift. Before I turned the corner toward J C Penney's, I glanced back to see Adam walking into a jewelry store.

What if he was getting an engagement ring at this very moment? He was. I just knew it. Why else would he insist on privacy to enter a jewelry store? I was too excited to shop. I couldn't think of anything except the likelihood that I would be receiving an engagement ring in as little as two days.

In a determined effort to calm down I took deep breaths, bypassed J C Penney's, and headed to Starbucks for a Grande Mocha Frappachino, my second greatest weakness in life. Even my mailman probably knew that Adam currently held the tarnished trophy.

When we met later, Adam carried a little white bag with gold lettering from Jared's Jewelry Store. Yep, *JARED'S JEWELRY STORE.* To say my excitement was hard to contain would be a gross understatement. I could have easily joined the nearest gaggle of scantily clad teenaged girls and giggled and squealed over my possible engagement for the next several hours. I so wanted to snatch the bag from Adam's death grip and take a quick peek inside. Curiosity could definitely kill this kitty.

"What's in the bag, Adam?" As hard as I tried, I couldn't suppress the urge to ask.

"Just something to show someone how very much I love her." His tender words caused my eyes to sting. "I hope the contents of this bag will finally prove that my heart belongs to her forever and ever."

Oh, I wanted to break into Oprah's ugly cry right there between Abercrombie and Hollister. I would surely blubber like a blithering idiot when he placed a sparkling diamond on my finger. I decided to watch my salt intake over the next two days. Good Lord, what if I swelled up like a toad and the ring refused to fit my finger? Why, oh, why did I eat that salty pretzel?

I also warned myself not to get overly excited about a supposed engagement ring and go jumping to all manner of conclusions, as I was very prone to do. It may be entirely too soon after what's her name. I couldn't allow myself to sound too disappointed if it was a bracelet or necklace or even *God forbid* earrings. With Adam, who knew? I was sure he didn't have a few thousand bucks lying around for frivolous expenditures. Life was so unpredictable with the man.

Having more bags than we could carry comfortably we returned to his snazzy sports car, which I secretly hated. Give me a comfortable sedan any day. He made a point of locking the little bag securely in the trunk. Surely, at my advanced age, I was too old to even consider sneaking into the bag while he was asleep, wasn't I?

"What's so funny?" he asked, as I struggled to keep from chuckling at the absurdity of the thought. So I told him.

I could see the worry in his eyes. *Bless his heart.* "In other words, I need to sleep with my keys under the pillow tonight?"

"It probably wouldn't hurt," I admitted as he reached over to kiss me. Good Lord, the man could kiss.

"We could visit Teri while we're in Charlotte, if you want?" he suggested. "Doesn't she live close to the mall?"

I had to think fast. "No." Adam didn't want to be the victim of one of Teri's tongue lashings any more than I wanted him to be. As strong as her absolute disgust was for him, who knew what version of misery her conniving brain would conjure up with him actually in her domain, instead of having to plot his demise from afar? "I'm exhausted. Let's go home. Her husband can barely tolerate company at his age."

"Would you marry a man for money, Eve?"

"I might consider it if he had a bank account similar to Lawrence's."

"It would just be a consideration and we both know it." He reached for my hand and brought it to his lips for a soft kiss that sent shivers curling down my spine. A stoplight caught us and he leaned over to kiss me, leaving me breathless. "You are a hopeless romantic and would never marry for anything short of true love."

I found it to be more than just a mind-boggling coincidence that he was discussing the concept of marriage shortly after placing a package, *from a jewelry store*, in the trunk of his car.

Believe me. It was a beautiful, sunny day in the hinterland.

At home we made a batch of fudge and popcorn and plopped down in front of the fire to watch one of those boring action flicks with an aging celebrity that failed to hold my interest long enough to keep me awake. Sometime during the night he woke me and we went to bed.

And to sleep.

I just bet if he was crawling in bed with Chia he wouldn't roll over and snore like a lumberjack. *Nope.* Not going to think about that right now. I snuggled up to his back, breathed a contented sigh, and was asleep in seconds.

Adam came stumbling down the hall the next morning around 11:00. After his requisite two cups of coffee, he pulled on his shoes. "I'll see you tonight after work, Eve. That damn whippoorwill kept me awake half the night. Next time I come I'm bringing my shotgun." Then he kissed me on the cheek and left. The poor thing would never be accused of being a morning person.

I called him at 12:00, then 1:00, and then 2:00 to ask if he wanted me to buy steak or chicken to grill later tonight, but he didn't answer. What could that mean? Was he on the phone and not accepting my call? No, he had most likely crawled in bed to take a nap before work.

Chapter Eight

It was the second Monday of the month and that meant girl's night. We were going to Teri's house for dinner, not supper as Tamara, Mallory, and I referred to our evening dining experience.

Teri lives in the exclusive Piper Glen section of upscale South Charlotte, where you tend to feel like you're walking into the Smithsonian the minute you enter her three story manse. She happens to be one of those domestic goddesses who, if you drop a crumb, is at your feet with a dustpan, broom, and a look that begs the question, "Must you be eternally clumsy?"

Hey, we didn't tell her to order the installation of pristine white carpeting throughout the house, and talk about cold. The girl is extremely hot natured and the house could easily substitute as a meat locker for Perdue Farms. I couldn't understand why her frail husband hadn't perished from a fatal bout of bronchial pneumonia years ago.

Immediately upon entering her house I stop at the entry closet and grab an afghan, which she keeps there just for me. It remains draped around my shoulders for the entire visit. It never fails to annoy the hell out of me that she can traipse around her glacial dwelling wearing daisy dukes and a tank top as if the thermostat might register a sweltering 99 degrees.

Once she notices my lips beginning to turn an unsightly shade of blue she breathes an irritated sigh and, as a great sacrifice to me, ignites the gas logs in the fireplace. Within the short span of five minutes she commences to perspire heavily, turn a bright vivid red in the cheeks, and appear to have difficulty breathing. Since I can gather warmth from my afghan, while she seems on the verge of an impending attack of apoplexy, I clutch my life supporting cover tighter and shut off the logs.

Get this. She listens to show tunes. Angela Lansbury was bellowing from the stereo, singing something about a lady called *Mame*. "Don't you just love this song?" Teri trilled in between singing to the high heavens with her arms thrown in the air and spinning gaily around the room.

"Yes," Tamara cried with a stricken look.

"Liar," I whispered in her ear as Teri waltzed us through her imposing manor. Her husband is a wealthy, geriatric stockbroker and doesn't mind flaunting it.

"Surely she won't force us to listen to that music throughout the entire meal will she?" Mallory asked with a put upon look similar to Tamara's. Her shoes clicked on the black and white marble floor of the foyer as she trailed behind. She knew the deeper you ventured into Teri's abode the louder the music would become.

"You know she will," Tamara moaned. "Doesn't she always? Do you think Lawrence ever complains?"

"Hell no," Mallory moaned. "He only has to

remove his hearing aids."

"It sounds like the poor woman could be in pain." I glanced at Teri and sighed heavily. "Why do you feel the need to torture us whenever we come to visit?"

"How can you call *Mame* torture? Why, I never heard such a ludicrous notion." She actually pretended to be shocked. "It's a classic."

Then she fell into dance and twirled around the room for the entire song as I huddled in my life supporting afghan while praying for the song to end. The other two glared at her as if scientist had just discovered a new form of life on planet Earth.

Years earlier, prior to her sex change, Teri had been a popular stage performer/drag queen with lurid tales of her onstage antics that could cause your ears to sizzle. I had been to several of her shows and remembered her doing an excellent Cher. Teri was then, and still is, an exhibitionist at heart. She had paid good money for her triple D's and had no intention of shielding them from the casual observer.

At Teri's domicile, if show tunes weren't blasting from the Bose speakers hidden in the walls, she was playing songs from the 80's. Laura Branigan, Joan Jett and the Blackhearts, and Blondie were a few of her favorites.

Where was the extra strength Tylenol?

To top it off, she has an obnoxious affinity for anything with a coat of fur or feathers. There is either a dog running, a bird flapping, a rodent (*in others words a freaking rat, which I keep about a hundred glue pads in my basement in an effort to annihilate the horrid creatures*), spinning on a wheel, or a rabbit hopping through the house at any given moment. She treats them like her children. You never know what will greet you when you arrive on Teri's doorstep.

"Oh, would you just look." I cried, glancing around her Victorian inspired living room. Four stunning vases of gorgeous roses sat at various locations around the room, one each of red, yellow, pink and orange. "They are exquisite."

"Lawrence had four dozen roses delivered for Valentine's Day. One for each year we've been married." She frowned as we all moved to a different vase to touch and smell the delicate floral arrangements. "After four years of wedded bliss the man still hasn't figured out that roses are my least favorite flower and I haven't the heart to tell him."

"Today isn't Valentine's Day, tomorrow is," I informed her, sniffing the orange bouquet.

"We know. He said my real Valentine's gift will be delivered tomorrow."

"What do you think it is?" Mallory was savoring the fragrance of a delicate, sunshine yellow rose.

"I'm guessing a convertible Porsche Carrera since I made the mistake of commenting on one last week." She grinned mischievously.

It hadn't been a mistake. We all knew Teri well enough to realize that her comment had been timed with painstaking precision.

She led us up the curving mahogany staircase to her computer room to show us her latest online acquisitions. The girl is an Ebay junkie, purchasing an amount equivalent to my mortgage payment on a weekly basis. She has enough shoes, clothes, and handbags to supply a small country.

The Fed Ex man has become such a regular at her house that she has taken to inviting him inside for tea and crumpets and… whatever, while Lawrence enjoys his daily round of golf. More aptly put, his round of being chauffeured around in his tricked out golf cart.

We followed her into her bedroom to admire her latest Louis Vuitton collection. What a diva. Who actually changes their purse daily? I consider it no small feat if I find time to change mine every six months. I shouldn't complain, since after a couple of weeks she often tires of a new bag and passes it along to me. I have a stash of handbags in my closet, while Mallory and Tamara are quite content with their Walmart bags, thank you.

We made the appropriate oohs and aahs at the latest additions to her cleavage revealing and curve hugging designer wardrobe, then meandered to her husband's weight room in a mannerly effort to speak to him. He was having his twice weekly session of physical therapy due to last year's massive heart attack and gave us a cursory wave.

Lawrence begrudgingly tolerates us on Teri's night to entertain, when it's obvious that he would much rather spend the evening alone with his voluptuous wife. He is a very peculiar person who guards his privacy zealously and wishes Teri would as well. *Like that will ever happen.*

"When was the last time you two had sex?" Mallory whispered, moving into Teri's bedroom and taking a seat at her vanity to spritz perfume on various locations of her body.

"Oh, we don't have actual sex per se. Every

night I sit on the edge of his bed naked and he fondles my breasts until he drifts off to sleep with a satisfied smile." Teri swiftly took the perfume bottle from Mallory. "Why must you insist on smelling like a French whore?"

Mallory ignored her and began sampling different shades from the vast array of lipsticks before continuing, undaunted. "When was the last time you had actual bumping and grinding sex?" She settled on a rich peach color and added a topcoat of gloss.

"With Lawrence, you mean?"

"Yes, Teri," she huffed. "Your husband."

Well, while there was no bumping, or grinding, involved, we had sex just before I called 911." A pained expression crossed Teri's face. "That was the night of his heart attack."

The night of Lawrence's heart attack had been a terrifying ordeal for Teri, for all of us, in fact. She might not be *in* love with him, but she loved him dearly. I knew this beyond a shadow of a doubt that awful night.

She called from the hospital sobbing hysterically that Lawrence was going to die. It was only a few months after her sex change surgery and she had insisted, rather loudly, "It's all my fault! I know it is! I killed the poor man with my brand new, silky smooth, extremely tight, state of the art twat." She said this from Lawrence's somber room in ICU. God only knows how many nurses, doctors and patients needed resuscitation after that heartfelt confession.

The three of us had rushed to her side and were witness to her genuine relief when Lawrence was taken off life support and smiled at her for the first time.

"Is anyone hungry?" Teri asked as we headed back downstairs, where blessedly the soundtrack had ended. "Now that you have snooped into my personal life, when was the last time you fornicated, Mallory?"

"Today. Twice, and it was damn good." Her lips curved into a dreamy smile. "

"I'm starving," Tamara announced, clearly grateful for the silence. "What is that wonderful smell?" Her gratitude was short lived however, as the next CD that fell into place contained the coma inducing rendition of one of the most annoying songs on the planet

Supercalifragilisticexpialidocious.

"How does Beef Wellington sound?" Teri removed a dish that smelled scrumptious from the oven. The girl is a culinary marvel.

"Great," we all said in unison as we plopped down on bar stools at her kitchen counter. None of us, given a choice, would have chosen to suffer through a meal in her elegant dining room with its exquisite French lace tablecloth and window treatments.

I personally would have been more inclined to choke from thirst rather than risk picking up a crystal wine goblet in the elaborately appointed room. It was difficult to enjoy libations with the ever present fear of tipping the glass and having to watch in absolute horror as red wine soaked into her plush snowy carpet.

"So Eve, when was your last romp in the hay?" Teri queried, returning to her favorite topic of discussion.

Did she seem suspicious or was it all in my mind? I had asked Tamara and Mallory not to tell her that Adam and I were back together until after girl's night. I didn't feel like being the victim of her catty comments or insults tonight.

"To be honest, I don't even remember." I laughed, unable to look her in the eyes.

"What about you, Tamara?" Mallory scooped out a healthy portion of beef, a side of asparagus, and about a pint of potato salad.

"Saturday night, but it wasn't that good." Tamara plucked a roll from the napkin covered breadbasket. "He didn't do the bestest thing."

The bestest thing, in Tamara lingo, being the predominant use of lips and tongue on ones nether region.

"Why ever not?" Mallory seemed both shocked and appalled by the notion that a man would actually refuse a woman oral sex. She appeared downright distraught.

"He said he didn't believe in doing it. That he had never done it, in fact." Tamara took a bite from a yeast roll and slathered more honey butter on it. "He said it was nasty, can you believe that shit? I bet he wouldn't think Shakira's was nasty."

"Hell, even I wouldn't have a problem nibbling on her twat," Teri was quick to say. "I don't know what his problem is, Tamara. I only hope you didn't suck his lollipop before you found out about his aversion to juicy fruit. At any rate, I suggest you move on. He hardly sounds worthy of your time."

Teri poured us each a glass of sweet tea,

since none of us liked wine with our meals. "In my opinion, it's one of the necessary life skills.

"You know, I had always heard that black men wouldn't go down on a woman either. Well, I can assure you that's a lie." Mallory grinned and wiggled her bottom on the stool. "Antwan slurps mine like it's a vanilla ice cream cone."

"You girls won't know the true meaning of slurping until you get with a man who can remove his teeth and use his gums," Teri simpered, shivering at the thought. "Devine."

That was *not* the mental picture I needed during dinner.

One of the perks of having Teri as a friend is that she cuts and colors our hair for free. After the meal, Mallory commented that her ends needed a trim. Teri led us upstairs to her bathroom and eagerly shoved Mallory down on a stool, draping a cape around her. This was a highly unusual event, as I felt reasonably certain that some of the hair would have to land on Teri's immaculate floor. I couldn't imagine her allowing this to happen but, as shocking as it was, that seemed to be her plan.

Mallory had been attempting to allow her inch long, spiked hair to grow, which annoyed Teri to no end. "You have a round face, Mallory, and all that hair fluffed out around your face only makes it appear rounder, fuller, and for lack of a better word... fatter." Teri's tone implied that she had informed Mallory of this on more than one occasion. Admittedly, Mallory's hair was naturally curly and very, very full. "Before I cut it, why don't you let me straighten it and take out some of the fullness?"

Teri was a huge fan of straight hair and given the fact that she could be very persuasive, few of her clients even owned curling irons.

"Will I look good with straight hair?" Mallory's words came out in her typical annoying whine.

Teri cast a sideways glance at me with eyes that questioned if the girl could make it through one entire day without talking through her nasal passages? Yet, for once, she almost held her tongue. "It couldn't look any worse than it does now." While that would have seriously pissed some people off, we were accustomed to Teri's biting sarcasm and it rolled right off her.

We suffered through an entire CD of *Barry Manilow's Greatest Hits*. In between belting out songs, and the occasional random twirl around the room, Teri applied chemicals and combed Mallory's hair straight.

After drying and styling, Mallory's appearance changed dramatically. She was transformed from country to city chic in less than two hours. The switch from curly to bone straight was sensational. It added an air of sophistication and erased several years from her appearance. Given the amount of parading she was doing in front of the mirror, Mallory loved it too. "Teri, you are a miracle worker."

"So they say."

"Next month, it'll be my turn for a makeover," Tamara stated.

"Let's not make this a habit." Teri was quick to point out. "You girls know you need to book appointments at the salon. I made an exception tonight because I simply could not tolerate the broom-straw on Mallory's head for another second." She cast a doleful gaze at Mallory and continued, "How you could appear in public with that unsightly bush sprouting from your head simply behooves me."

Ignoring her rhetoric, Mallory hugged Teri and thanked her profusely.

Glancing at the clock, I saw that it was almost 9:00. Adam's shift would end in two hours. I needed to hurry home and be waiting with open arms.

As we were getting our coats, Teri turned off the music and came to stand directly in front of me.

Oh, boy.

Here it comes.

When she turned off her music watch out.

Leaning over to help me with my coat, she whispered, "Please tell me that what I heard isn't true, Eve. Ease my mind and reassure me that you did *not* take the imbecile back? Surely you have more pride than to allow that lying weasel back into your heart."

I cast a wicked glare at the traitors who suddenly couldn't seem to pull their rapt attention from one of Lawrence's horrible abstract paintings. A lot of good it had done to ask them not to broadcast the fact that Adam and I were on speaking terms again. It was Mallory. I knew asking her to keep a secret was like asking Adam not to tell a lie, impossible.

"I don't know if you would exactly call us being back together." I was hedging and she knew it.

"Oh, you don't call him spending the last two nights with you being back together? Then please forgive me for jumping to ridiculous assumptions."

Here we go.

"What's the plan, Eve? To pay Eric to keep Chia's bed hot, so you can keep Adam?"

Three sets of eyes looked at her in shocked disbelief. That was cold even for Teri. It rarely happened with her, but I felt my blood begin to simmer. How could she be so spiteful and vindictive? To me? "I'm not paying Eric a dime."

"You're not? Oh, then forgive me once again if I spoke out of turn. I was under the impression that he remained on the clock during his mid afternoon romps with Chia."

She had me there.

Then, totally confusing the three of us as we stood on the stoop of her front steps, she stepped back in and slammed the door. Immediately she opened the door and informed Tamara and Mallory that she desired a private word with them. I didn't care to hear what she had to say anyway, since it obviously concerned me. I started toward the car mumbling unkind things under my breath.

Tamara had driven, and her car had an oil leak, so she had parked on the paved road in front of the manse. I took the shortcut across the lawn and had only taken a few steps when the Pamela Anderson wannabe actually had the nerve to turn on the sprinkler system, soaking me from head to toe.

I screamed as the ice cold water soaked me through and through in seconds. I bolted across her lawn, which was the size of the Panther's football field at Bank of America Stadium. In my confusion, I ran away from the driveway and into a field of Lawrence's beloved sod where I was inundated with huge blasts of frigid water at every turn.

Get a grip, Eve!

I stopped, took a deep calming breath, swiped at the rivulets of water pouring into my eyes and finally spotted the driveway, seemingly about a mile away. I charged back through the sprinkler system and ended up on her doorstep looking like a drowned rat. *Just let me get my hands on the spiteful bitch.* I would kill her! I pounded on the door with frozen fists.

Teri opened it, appearing quite astonished by the fact that my hair and clothes were soaked and I was dripping large amounts of water on her stoop. "What on earth happened to you?"

"You did, you conniving bitch!" Failing to think clearly in my icy rage, I slapped her soundly across her implanted cheeks.

She slapped me back. With a quickness. Since she still had the inner workings and strength of a man, her slap sent me staggering backwards on the steps. "Excuuuuuse me!" she ground out.

Fortunately, she thought enough of me to catch me before I hit the ground.

Few people could call Teri a bitch, let alone lay hands on her, and get away with it.

"Don't even try to pretend you didn't turn the sprinklers on. I was already frozen clear to the bone from being inside your igloo," I cried through chattering teeth. "I'll probably have pneumonia by morning."

Snatching my hand, she rushed me inside and forced me into a hot shower fully clothed, while at the same time cooing, "Eve, those sprinklers are on a timer, honey. They come on at this time every night. You know how Lawrence obsesses over his sod." She stuck her head in the shower and glowered at me. "Do you honestly think I would do that to you?"

"Yes."

She screamed with laughter. "Me too. Damn! I wish I had thought of it."

While I sat huddled in one of her thickest terry robes and an electric blanket, she applied a palm filled with styling gel and vigorously massaged it into my hair. Tamara and Mallory looked on with apparent amusement at the flaming handprints on both our cheeks as Teri dried and styled my hair.

"You know I tend to blurt things out when I should just keep my mouth shut," she shouted above the noise of the hairdryer. After applying hairspray to force each strand to stay exactly where she wanted it, and with what I supposed was her idea of an apology, she admitted, "I should probably work on that."

"Amen, sister." My anger evaporated as we fell into each other's arms. The girl's words could cut to the bone, but it was impossible to stay mad at her.

"I'm just so tired of watching that low life piece of dog excrement hurt you. Is he coming over tonight?"

"Yes." I couldn't help but smile at the thought of seeing Adam and she read me perfectly.

It was also impossible to hide my emotions from her.

"Then go home and get ready for him, at least you won't have to do anything to your hair. There is nothing I can say that hasn't already been said. You know I love you."

"I know." I smiled as she closed the door behind us. "I love you, too."

An hour later, I arrived at home about the same time as Adam and was quick to discover that he was in one of his foul moods.

Going straight to the fridge, he cracked open a beer. "Where have you been in your bath robe, Eve?"

I explained the events at Teri's with him failing to see the slightest bit of humor in the situation. At times the man could be so trifling.

We planned a vacation to the mountains in a few weeks, with him failing to mention his recent visit to the tourist attraction with Chia. I wondered if he had missed the disposable camera yet?

We grilled barbecued chicken, baked potatoes wrapped in aluminum foil, and corn on the cob with the shucks intact, but the laughter we normally shared was glaringly absent. Since he didn't seem inclined to conversation we snuggled on the couch and watched a movie. While I was deliriously happy to have him back home, his mind was a zillion miles away from my living room.

When he left the next morning, without so much as a Happy Valentines Day, I filled the tub with bubble bath and hot water and sank down into it as nagging doubt assaulted me.

Adam would see Chia at work every day. That was a given. What would happen? Would a sexy smile from her cause him to fall mindlessly back into the same pattern of lust? Was the dashing Eric succeeding in his attempt to eradicate all thought of Adam from Chia's mind? Could she settle for the admiring attention of just one man? Did Adam really love me, or was he filling my head with his customary lies? So many questions with so few answers.

Eric was at work, which meant Chia was alone and could quite easily pick up the phone. Would Adam answer if she called? Good Lord, I would go insane if I didn't stop the multitude of doubts from swirling around in my head. Adam had continually asked me to trust him, insisting that he could earn my trust. Could he? Who knew? I could call and try to find out though.

"Happy Valentine's Day, Adam," I chirped, when he finally answered his phone.

"Happy Valentine's Day, Eve."

I couldn't contain my excitement another second. "Tonight's the night I get to open the sequestered box."

"What box?"

He was so scatterbrained. I heard the pause on his line as he received a beep.

"Hold on a minute, Eve." I waited several minutes for him to click back over. He did and hurriedly said, "Hey, Eve, it's my mom. I'll call you later, okay?"

"Okay, give her my love." His mom was calling to wish him Happy Valentine's Day. How sweet. I should send her flowers from him. Lord knows he wouldn't remember to.

My skin was beginning to prune so I forced myself out of the tub . I was feeling the need of a liberal dose of caffeine. The smell of fresh coffee in the morning *is* the best part of waking up.

In an effort to convince myself that I'd made the right decision by taking Adam back, I drove to the lingerie shop in town and bought a sexy lace teddy. After considerable debate, I chose a slinky red number with garter belt, hose, and 6 inch heels.

With my sexy attire laid across the foot of my bed and me counting the minutes until midnight, I called all three of the girls hoping to wile away the hours. Teri was in the process of applying chemicals to a client's hair, Mallory was riding the floor scrubber around the plant, and Tamara was busy translating. None of them had time to talk to me on what was sure to be one of the most momentous days of my entire life.

Some friends.

Why was this day going by so slow? I couldn't sit still long enough to watch my favorite cooking show, *Barefoot Contessa*. I was a bundle of nervous energy so I went next door to my parent's house.

We feasted on a delicious supper of barbecued chicken, creamed potatoes and gravy, pinto beans, homemade biscuits, and a plate of sliced tomatoes and cucumbers while I answered countless questions about my confusing social life. My dad said things like, "Be careful, Eve. A skunk ain't gonna lose his stripe," and "Some men just ain't the settling down type." Mom had to add,

"Sometimes it's best to cut your losses and move on."

As usual, I ignored their words of wisdom.

Finally at 9:00, I soaked in a steaming tub of water and rubbed Japanese Cherry Blossom Body Lotion from Bath and Body Works over every inch of skin. I placed candles throughout the bedroom, popped Adele into the CD player, and slipped into the new teddy I bought for my Valentine. Everything was perfect. Now came the interminable waiting.

Finally, at long last, I would be allowed to open the jewelry box and see which setting he had chosen for my brilliant diamond. I did so hope he had asked for a few suggestions from the sales lady.

The phone rang and I knew the girls had finally found time in their busy schedules to talk to me. Mallory and Tamara were positive it was an engagement ring and they were already discussing color schemes for their bridesmaid dresses. Teri insisted that if it was a ring, it would be a toe ring.

In my heart, I was convinced that it was an engagement ring and after tonight I would be Adam's betrothed. I practiced the word several times and just hearing fiancé roll off my tongue sent a shiver of excitement racing through me. I would without a doubt tie up Ma Bell for days as I called family and friends to inform them of our engagement.

Who knew, we might even set the wedding date tonight and I could spend every waking second planning the big event. I would suggest June. I love June weddings.

I pulled my old robe over the teddy, anxious

to see Adam's surprise when I let it drop during the little strip tease I had rehearsed after watching *Striptease* three times. This was going to be a night neither of us would ever forget, and the night that relocated the illustrious Chia to the back of his mind forever.

I was sitting on the couch, watching the clock and tapping my high heels impatiently on my polished wood floor when the phone rang at 10:58. It was Justin who unexpectedly burst forth with, "Chia got a dozen red roses delivered to her at the plant today."

"Who were they from?" I asked, elated that she had received flowers and was hopefully moving on with her life. "Eric?" Maybe she and Eric were fast becoming an item. "I imagine she was quite giddy."

His next words held an ominous tone. "She was giddy all right."

Chapter Nine

I'll just bet she was.

"Was she rambling on and on about Eric's finer attributes?" I giggled.

"The roses weren't from Eric, Eve."

Why did he sound so solemn?

"Well, since the girl seems to have any number of admirers," I mumbled around the rising hysteria that threatened to choke me, "I really couldn't begin to guess who they were from."

"Eve, you know exactly who they were from," he insisted harshly, seeming unwilling to go along with my *what you don't know can keep you sane* philosophy.

I most certainly did not know who the flowers were from. Although I did know they weren't from Adam, as Justin seemed to be so callously insinuating. I should just hang up on him.

The nerve!

Adam wouldn't send Chia roses!

He couldn't have!

Not when he was about to propose to me.

"What makes you think they were from Adam?" I strangled on the words, furious with him for even alluding to such an insane notion. He was way off base on this one. The roses were probably from Eric. After all, a 15 should be deserving of a dozen roses at the very least. Then again, who knew how many other men Chia was currently carrying on illicit affairs with? The floral arrangement could be from any number of devoted admirers.

"They were from Adam." The way he said this left no doubt. "Chia told my girlfriend Alicia."

I crumbled where I sat as Justin continued with his torturous tale of treason.

"Alicia said Chia had ended it with Adam and had been seeing this other guy for awhile. Some young stud she was absolutely crazy about."

Eric.

"Then yesterday at lunch this guy just up and dumps her. She told Alicia she wasn't about to spend Valentine's Day alone, so she called Adam. Can you believe she told him that she loved him just so he would get her a gift for Valentine's Day? Is he really that gullible?"

"Yes," I whispered around rising panic.

"She was also bragging to Alicia about how she had him wrapped around her little finger, and get this. During break, he took Chia out to his car and showed her a package from a jewelry store. Alicia said she was jumping up and down and hugging and kissing Adam and trying to persuade him to let her see what was inside the box. He told her she could open the package tonight. When they went back to her place."

When they went back to her place? He wasn't going to her place. He was coming here. This couldn't be happening.

Again.

On Valentine's Day?

Something from a jewelry store?

For Chia?

"Thanks for calling, Justin," I mumbled, hoping to avoid the head on collision with hell that I knew was fast approaching.

"No problem." His soft words dripped with sympathy. "I just thought you should know."

I would wait to see what Adam had to say when he arrived at my house after work, before I jumped to irrational conclusions. This could all be nothing more than a colossal misunderstanding. He had already promised that he was coming over tonight and I would be allowed to open the little box that was safely tucked away in the trunk of his car. It was Valentine's Day for crying out loud. Adam wouldn't lie to me about something so important, on this of all days.

Justin was wrong. Alicia was wrong. Chia was lying. Adam loved me and would be here shortly to ask me to be his wife and slip a sparkling token of his undying love on my finger.

Striving to make since of Chia's sickening lies and utter nonsense, I called Eric. "What happened with you and Chia?"

"I couldn't take it anymore, Eve." He sounded as if he had decided to wash his hands of the entire situation. "That girl is crazy. All she wants is sex."

"And that was a problem?" I attempted to laugh while swiping at a torrent of scalding tears.

"That and the fact that she called every five minutes to tell me how much she loved me and wanted to spend the rest of her life with me. Did you know she has six kids?"

"I thought I told you that." I was becoming quite adept at fabrications myself. I should have heeded the Bible, especially the part where God says, "Vengeance is mine."

"You left that part out. Get this. She wanted me to take her and her six kids to Carowinds this weekend. Aside from the fact that I have no desire to develop a relationship with her children, there's no way I could afford tickets for six kids and two adults. Is she nuts?"

"Evidently."

"She came to my job yesterday and brought me a plate of rice."

"When exactly did you end it with her, Eric?" I whispered as my body began to shake with uncontrollable spasms.

"Yesterday, when she brought me the plate of food. I lied and told her I had met someone else and wouldn't be seeing her anymore. She shouted and spluttered words I couldn't begin to understand, so I walked back into the plant before she could cause a scene."

"I'll see you tomorrow, Eric." I felt dazed and dizzy as my world once again began the oft-repeated process of collapsing around me.

"Are you okay, Eve?"

"I'm just tired."

Of life.

Alicia had told Justin that Chia had been dumped yesterday at lunchtime. Eric had verified that.

I could confirm there was a package from a

jewelry store in the trunk of his car. My package.

Yesterday, when I called Adam for hours on end, he hadn't answered. Today, he had taken a beep and told me it was his mother.

Lies.

All lies.

"Bye, Eve."

Feeling as though I might be experiencing one of Sylvia Browne's out of body episodes, I removed the high heels, went to the liquor cabinet, and made a bloody mary minus the tomato juice.

Teri was spending Valentine's Day with her husband. Tamara and Mallory were happily spending alone time with their men of the hour. I could only wonder how my Valentine's Day would turn out. At 11:36 I received the much anticipated and dreaded answer when Adam called from work.

"Hey, Eve."

Downing the glass of vodka, I gasped as my throat caught fire. "Why are you still at work, Adam?"

"I have to work over tonight." He was talking fast, as if he only had a few minutes to waste with talking to me. "I really hate to, but we are shorthanded tonight."

"On Valentine's Day, Adam?" I felt a tightening in my chest and the threatening approach of a full blown panic attack. He wasn't working over tonight anymore than he had all those nights he had lied about it in the past. How could I have been so blind?

He was going to propose to Chia.

Tonight.

And place my ring on her finger.

My throat was closing, blocking even the smallest breath from entering my lungs. "You aren't going to see me tonight, on Valentine's Day, Adam?"

"I can't, Eve. Didn't I just tell you I have to work over tonight? Besides, it's just another day."

Just another day? In my estimation it was the most romantic day of the year and meant to be spent with the person you loved most in the world.

That was Adam's intent as well.

Inching ever closer to my breaking point, I headed into the kitchen for a refill. "If it's just another day, then why did you send Chia roses?" I needed to end this charade once and for all, before Adam succeeded in his vicious plot to see me institutionalized, or in the grave.

A long silence ensued. "How did you find out?" He sounded vastly annoyed that someone had gone behind his back and informed me of the floral delivery, while the pain in my voice didn't seem to bother him at all. "What makes you think the roses were from me?"

"I know about the roses, Adam. How could you do this to me? Again?" I hadn't meant for him to hear me cry but the pain gushed from my very soul.

"It wasn't my intention to hurt you, Eve," He snapped. "It just happened."

I had to have some answers or give up my slippery grasp on the pretense of sanity and he was going to give them to me before he hung up the damn phone.

"What's in the box in your car, Adam?" I struggled to breath, deciding not to bother with a glass and drink vodka straight from the bottle. "The one from the jewelry store."

"An engagement ring."

"When you bought it, who did you intend to give it to?" If we never spoke again I had to know the awful truth to this one burning question.

"I actually bought it for you. Then Chia called, begging for my forgiveness and reassuring me of how much she loved me and telling me what a horrible, horrible mistake she had made with some guy named Eric." He didn't think he had hurt me quite enough, so he added, "She was on my mind when I picked out the ring. It would have been too small for you anyway."

"Is she pregnant?"

"She was, but she had a miscarriage."

"Don't you mean abortion, Adam?"

"Whatever. It doesn't really matter now. We have plenty of time to make more babies."

I could hear the anguish in his voice. Not from hurting me, but from the betrayal he felt over Chia having the abortion.

He took a long shaky breath and exhaled slowly. "Okay, I'm just going to be honest with you, Eve. I love her. I can't help it. I know I could settle down with you and be content, but I don't want to settle for mere contentment."

Mere contentment.

"Chia is like a drug that I can't get enough of. The only time I feel alive and deliriously happy is when we're together. When we're apart, I feel... lost. While you might find this hard to believe, I have actually cried myself to sleep over her, especially the last couple of nights, knowing she was with another man. I thought I would lose my mind."

Join the club.

"I bet you never cried over me, did you, Adam?"

He gave a harsh little chuckle designed to let me know exactly where I stood. "I would never cry over an American girl. You're all so ordinary. There's nothing exciting, or exotic, or special about you. Now, you take an Asian girl, or a Mexican girl, or an girl from one of the Islands and you have a real woman."

I hung up the phone, threw the empty vodka bottle into the trash, and staggered down the hall toward my bed and my beloved bottle of Valium.

It didn't take long to discover that life without Adam, the man I had *devoted* the last three years of my life to, hurt worse than the eternal fires of hell. Sinking deeper and deeper into a dark, suffocating depression, within a few weeks I was questioning my reasons for even getting out of bed. Getting dressed? Brushing teeth? What exactly was the point again?

I worked, went home, ate, and slept. Emotion of any kind, other than pain, was something that I rarely felt anymore. In an attempt to convince myself that the pain would pass, my mind took charge and blocked the pain. I erected an invisible concrete barrier between myself and my friends, my family, and anything outside the shelter of my bedroom. Blessed numbness had settled over me like a warm blanket.

I lost about fifteen pounds. It didn't seem

like a big deal to me, but Teri, Tamara, Mallory, and my family harped on my gaunt appearance as though I was a candidate for an intervention. Admittedly, my clothes were beginning to hang loosely and I would benefit from an entire new, two sizes smaller, wardrobe, but I had absolutely *no* desire to go traipsing around a mall. I found it an almost insurmountable challenge to go food shopping.

Without fail one of the girls was calling every hour on the hour with some ridiculous and boring anecdote, when their sole intention was to obtain a progress report on my sanity. I was sorely tempted to have my phone disconnected.

I hadn't been to a girl's night in three months and unless some drastic changes occurred in my life, would probably never attend another one. Why couldn't they just pretend I had moved to Alabama, to my son's current construction site, and stop constantly harassing me? On cue the phone rang and with extreme irritation I wondered which of the Tiresome Trio it could be.

"It's time for you to snap out of it, Eve," Teri droned in a seriously annoying tone.

"Okay. I will." I held my fingers to the phone and snapped. "Done. Gee thanks, I feel much better. You should have demanded I do that months ago, before I had personally tripled the quarterly profits for the Kleenex Tissue Company."

"Thank God you never lost your sarcasm. Anyway, have your bags packed Friday."

"Why? I'm not going anywhere." I was beyond bored with her monotonous and redundant *get out of the house* routine.

As was usually the case, she totally ignored my comment. I was beginning to believe I might have to piss the girl off to get her to leave me the hell alone.

"Yes, you are," she insisted.

Much to my dismay, I could tell by the lilt in her voice that she was in one of those argumentative moods where she resists taking no for an answer. She was convinced that if she yammered enough about a subject she could bend anyone to her way of thinking. Not this time.

"The girls and I are taking you to the beach for your birthday, Eve." This was uttered as if she expected me to flip out of bed and do cartwheels around the room at the mere thought of a fun filled weekend getaway.

"My birthday is May 30." I tried unsuccessfully to stifle a yawn.

"Duh."

Was it May already? Good grief! I guess it was. "I'm not going." I was grateful they had thought to include me in their plans, although I truly wished they hadn't. I wasn't in the mood to join in the fun of an exciting beach excursion. "Y'all go and have a good time. If you happen to stop at one of those souvenir shops along the way bring me back a pecan log for my birthday."

"Please do us both a favor, Eve, and spare me the wearisome litany of why you can't go, because come hail or high water you are going to get out of that damn house for your birthday."

"No, I'm not. I am turning fifty five, Teri. What about that is cause for celebration?" I hoped she missed the slight edge of hysteria that drifted into my voice.

She didn't.

"I'm coming to spend the night with you Thursday night and we're leaving first thing Friday morning for Myrtle Beach, whether you like it or not. So you might as well go ahead and start shaving the furrier parts of your body that probably haven't seen a razor since Valentine's Day. You know how you tend to ignore even the most basic hygiene when you're depressed."

"Screw you, Teri. Bathing is basic hygiene, which I do daily, thank you. Hair removal is not a prerequisite to cleanliness, regardless of what you think."

"Well, if I were you I'd go ahead and call a plumber ahead of time, because you know damn well all that hair is going to stop up the bathtub drain and I will *have* to bathe come Friday morning."

I started to give her a piece of my mind, but instead I burst out laughing. "You are a bitch from the depths of hell, Teri."

"I know. Don't think you are the first to insult me. Kids started doing that in elementary school and by high school I was getting my head slammed in lockers and shoved in toilets daily, just because I dared to be different."

It was true. Teri didn't remember her childhood or teen years fondly. Her homosexuality had made her a prime target for the cruelest bullies in school and caused her to suffer terribly at the hands of fellow classmates.

"While you're more than welcome to come and spend the night Thursday, I can assure you that

I am not going on a beach trip."

"I'll pack your suitcase myself if I have to," she chirped. "Gotta go, love you, bye."

Good luck with that. Like I had anything to pack that would actually fit.

She was pissed. Good. Maybe she would delete my number from her phone. I didn't really give a flying flip. No one was going to make me get out of bed, cover my atrophied body in something other than pajamas, unplug my Kindle Fire, turn off the Lifetime movie network, and close my bag of Reese's Pieces when I didn't want to. So there.

Now, if I could just think of a way to piss off *Thelma and Louise*. The phone was ringing and I could only guess that Teri had called the two remaining musketeers for backup. She had wasted her breath, for Tamara or Mallory weren't going to convince me to go someplace I didn't want to go either.

It wasn't Tamara or Mallory on the phone. I shivered involuntarily when I recognized Justin's deep Southern drawl. This couldn't be good. Thinking back, it occurred to me that Justin had never once called with good news. I held my breath as he casually asked, "Hey Eve, did you see the diamond Adam gave Chia?"

"I saw the box."

"It's some rock. One of those marquise styles."

I had often joked to Adam that when he finally proposed I expected at least a two carat marquise diamond.

"My girlfriend Alicia says Chia sticks it in the face of practically everyone she comes in contact with at work and squeals and giggles."

Well, wasn't I was just tickled pink and positively ecstatic for the dear girl.

"I asked Adam when the big day was and he said Chia wanted to marry him as soon as possible. To hear him describe her wedding plans it will be the social event of the season, with all his relatives flying in."

Like Hanover Falls boasted of a social season.

"Can you believe he had the nerve to ask me to be an usher, Eve?"

Could we please continue this conversation at another time? I just noticed a new mound of fire ants in the back yard and I need to welcome them to the neighborhood.

"I told him, 'Hell no, I wouldn't be an usher'." *I could tell by his voice that the request had actually offended him.* "Anyway, Chia already has another man on the side, you know."

"Oh, really?"

"Yeah, Chris at work. Every night when I go to the smoking booth he and Chia are whispering and getting intimately acquainted in a dark corner."

"Evidently she isn't afraid of being caught by Adam."

"Not at all. She knows Adam believes every word out of her mouth, especially when spoken in the bedroom."

"Adam will never receive accolades for his comprehension skills, will he?"

"Nope, if he's too stupid to see what's right under his nose, he deserves to look like the consummate fool she's making him out to be. If he had one iota of common sense he would still be with you."

"Thank you, Justin." His words brought a slight smile to lips that had all but forgotten how to turn upward. "That was nice to hear."

"It's the truth. The men at work tell him how stupid he is on a daily basis for choosing her over you. His excuse is that he can't help himself. Chia is like a drug."

"It sounds like he might benefit from a 28 day program at Ho Anonymous."

He chuckled. "Anyway, I just thought you might feel better if you knew Chia wasn't being faithful to him.

"Thanks for calling, Justin."

He took a deep breath and exhaled slowly. "There's something else I guess I should tell you."

I couldn't think of a single thing he could say to cause more pain than I was already feeling. "Just tell me."

Taking a deep breath, he blurted, "Adam and Chia's wedding is Sunday at the Catholic Church."

Wedding?

Adam and Chia?

It couldn't be so.

Breathe, Eve.

Just breathe.

I gasped, in an effort to force air into my lungs as a vision of Faith Hill singing the song flashed through my mind and I struggled to obey her. Adam couldn't be marrying someone else. I had convinced myself that Chia was nothing more than a heart wrenching phase that would pass and he would come to his senses and realize that he loved me. "Thanks for calling, Justin. I'll talk to you later."

"Bye, Eve. Don't be a stranger," he urged. "Call me if you ever need to talk."

"I will."

I took a long hard look at what my life had become and fell back on the bed, covering my flaming face with a pillow.

A travesty.

That's what it was. My life was one humongous travesty. I wasn't living each and every day to the fullest. Hell, I wasn't living at all. I was merely existing, struggling through one monotonous day to the next, and in serious danger of sinking.

No more.

For crying out loud, Adam was a flesh and blood man. Not some deity with the power to dictate my moods on a daily basis. I was so much better than this mewling, sniveling creature I had evolved into over the last few months. Adam didn't have the power to control my emotions. He wasn't doing anything to me. I was doing it. To myself. Forget the bastard. For God's sake.

Get a fucking life.

I hung up with Justin and dialed Teri's number. "I'll have my suitcase packed and ready to go." I tried to sound cheery, though the catch in my throat was a good indicator that my wound was gaping open and spilling blood. Even to me my voice sounded an octave above normal.

"What brought on the sudden change?" I caught the sudden note of alarm in her voice.

"Nothing, I just decided to go. After all, it's

my birthday."

"You're lying, Eve." *The girl knew me too well.* "Cut the bullshit and tell me what happened."

"Sunday is Adam and Chia's wedding day."

The dam finally burst and I sobbed uncontrollably as those seven words lodged in my throat like a sideways fish bone.

Teri immediately went into damage control mode. "It will be okay, honey. We'll have a blast at the beach and you know how men hang on you the minute you walk through the door at Studebakers. Remember that one man…"

"Hush, Teri. Don't prattle on like you need to talk me out of puncturing an artery or something. Granted, I lost it for a few minutes, but, I'm okay now. I just needed a good cry. I decided to go to the beach because I don't care to be in town for the celebration. I wouldn't want to accidentally ride by the church and see Chia in her wedding dress." I had a heartrending vision of her in her bridal finery, posing on the steps of the church for her official bridal portrait. "She will be a stunning bride."

"Stunned is more like it. How long do you think it will be before Adam has his first affair?"

"Not long." I swiped at a tear as the thought almost caused me to smile for the second time in a day. I would be doing stand up comedy if the merriment continued.

Friday morning we piled into the Jeep, the only one of our vehicles with enough trunk space to hold Teri's outrageous amount of luggage. She had one each for her designer wardrobe, designer shoes, cosmetics, and hair care products. "Must you pack like you're leaving for an extended cruise around the world?" I snapped, trying to squeeze my one suitcase in.

"I never know which outfit I'll wear, so of course I bring several to choose from," she informed me.

"Of course."

"Just imagine my distress if I arrived at the hotel and realized that I didn't bring a matching pair of Jimmy Choo's for each outfit."

"No!" I cried. "It's simply too unfathomable to imagine!"

Slamming the trunk, she gave me a serious go to hell look. "Drop the attitude, will you? This is supposed to be a fun weekend remember?"

"Oh, boy," My tone dripped with sarcasm as I slid beneath the wheel. "Let's get this party started."

She frowned at Tamara and Mallory in the backseat. "Can't you just feel the love?"

"She'll feel better when she's on the floor tonight doing the *Electric Slide*," Mallory quipped.

"And when some gorgeous hunk buys her a drink," Tamara added.

"No man is going to buy her a drink with that sour puss expression on her face," Teri insisted. "Let alone ask her sully old ass to dance."

"Bite me, Teri." I had to giggle. "Who are you calling old?"

"That's better." She was digging in her latest Dooney and Burke bag. "I brought the *Phantom of the Opera* soundtrack to sing along to."

"Not hardly. Sorry, my dear, but you have been out ranked. My car. My music." I pushed power on the stereo and Adele's *I Set Fire To The Rain* filled the car. I must admit Teri's look of abject misery thrilled me to the core.

"I knew I should have driven my own car," she huffed. "It's only fair that we each play our own music in thirty minute increments."

"Okay, Mallory," I mouthed to Teri.

"Hey!" Mallory complained loudly from the backseat, as neither of them particularly cared for the comparison. "I heard that and I do not whine."

"Let's vote on it then," I stated diplomatically. "Raise your hand to cast your vote to listen to opera during our two and one half hour trek to the beach."

Not even a finger twitched.

"Okay, fine," Teri complained loudly, tossing the cd back in her purse. "There is no accounting for taste."

I was feeling rather smug over my small victory until she started singing, "Happy birthday to you! How old are you?"

"Remember, Teri. I don't get mad, I get even." Then, the strangest thing happened. I actually laughed out loud for the first time in months. It felt so good. I opened the window and sunroof and Mallory, Tamara, and I joined Adele and sang *I set fiiiiiiiiiire to the rain and watched it burn!*

After we had driven for about an hour, Teri, of the weak bladder, insisted we stop for what she referred to as a twinkle break. "I need a Diet Pepsi and a bag of Fritos Corn Chips to snack on, anyone else want anything?"

"Yoo Hoo and Skittles," Tamara said.

"Diet Pepsi and a Snicker bar," I said.

"Mountain Dew and a Zero bar," Mallory added.

"For crying out loud, this isn't a restaurant where you all place separate orders from the menu. Just come in and pick out what you want." As she slammed the door and was walking off in a snit, she called over her shoulder, "I should have known you cretins wouldn't have the decency to all ask for the same thing."

By the time we reached the beach even Teri was singing along to *Rumor Has It*.

We checked into the Patricia Grand Hotel, choosing a suite with an ocean view. Leaning over the balcony rail I filled my lungs with salty sea air and knew this, at long last, was where I would begin the healing process. Water, sand, the sea, and plenty of nightlife surrounded me.

Adam who?

"Stop ogling all the studs from afar and get your suits on so we can gaze upon their lean, mean, hard bodies up close and personal," Teri called from the bathroom.

I turned just in time to see her stuffing, and by stuffing I mean the same way you would a turkey, her jugs into what looked to be a bathing suit top that a woman with 32B breasts would fit comfortably in. Surely she wouldn't go out in public wearing that thing.

Even the most casual observer would have to notice the top was several cup sizes too small for her. I'm sure there were indecent exposure laws here. Good grief, would she be arrested? Would parents race to shield their innocent children's eyes when she waltzed across the sand?

Now I knew why Teri always slowly glided when she moved. I had always assumed it was just for effect, so no one could miss her abundance of beauty. Now, I realized that wasn't the case at all. She had to move slowly. If she ever moved too fast and those things got to swinging, especially unfettered as they were now, there would be hell to pay for all concerned.

Searching for any good in the situation, I was happy to notice that at least her nipples were fully covered. I was extremely grateful for that small concession on her part. Glancing over at Mallory and Tamara, I found them to be watching the X-rated fashion extravaganza with eyes bugged out and jaws dropped as well.

"What?" Teri giggled. "For the love of God, you all act like you haven't ever seen a set of tits before."

"We haven't. Not like those anyway," I cried. "I think you have scarred us for life."

"Well, get used to them. I didn't come to the beach to cover these bad girls up."

And she didn't cover them, not once.

Tamara, Mallory and I put on our suits and followed her to the beach. We wouldn't have gotten any more attention if Angelina had been hotfooting it across the sand with Brad and the kids in tow. Every eye was on Teri, who looked spectacular in her bikini, even though her entire suit could have fit in a thimble.

I was in a constant state of unrest wondering

when one of her boobs was going to spill out of her top, resulting in chaos on the Grand Strand. Mallory looked just as curvaceous with her ghetto booty spilling out of her bottom. Tamara and I had sensibly chosen tankinis. I had given up showing my stomach years ago.

The trio took their chairs and laid them directly under the scorching sun, while I sensibly placed mine under the shade of a wide, rented umbrella. I fought dreaded wrinkles on a daily basis and wasn't about to lie in the sun and invite them to march in formation across my face. Not as long as Neutrogena continued to make their wonderful tanning mouse anyway. Taking a deep breath of salty air, I let it out slowly. This felt so good.

"Would you look at that?" Mallory almost purred as an extremely well built black man jogged down the beach with another fellow whose very next call should be to Jenny Craig. "Look at those dreads."

"Dreadful aren't they?" Teri shuddered.

"Hell, no!" Mallory laughed, rising to jog toward them and immediately strike up an animated conversation with the contrasting duo. The girl certainly didn't lack for confidence. With an ass like that, who would? She waved to us, and left walking between them.

We watched her laughing and flirting outrageously with the men until they were out of sight.

"I guess we won't be seeing her again until check out time Sunday." Tamara's voice carried a slight tinge of jealously. "Lucky her, I don't see a single Mexican."

"Just keep watching," Teri said. "There isn't a town in North Carolina that hasn't taken in dozens of Mexicans. Surely, a gaggle of fine Latinos will happen along soon." She turned her evil eye toward me. "What about you, Eve? Any prospects?"

"Not that I can see. Just a bunch of family men," I said to pacify her for the moment.

"I'm glad that I'm happily married and don't have to do the whole man hunt thing." Teri claimed, all the while peering over her Ray Ban's at a handsome man splashing in the nearby surf. "Now that is a physique."

"Too bad you are happily married," Tamara reminded her, while looking forlornly up and down the beach for anyone with a hint of Latino blood.

"Tell me about it," Teri groaned while slathering her voluptuous body with oil. "Always remember, Tamara. What happens in Myrtle Beach stays in Myrtle Beach. Anyway, it's 2:00 now. We can lie in the sun for two more hours and then we must go to the mall."

"Whatever for?" I asked, wondering at the girl's mental stability. It would require an act of Congress for me to leave this idyllic setting and enter a crowded mall.

"To get you an outfit to wear to the club tonight, of course." She rolled her eyes as if it should be the foremost thought on all our minds. "Did you bring a single ensemble that doesn't hang on you and resemble a muumuu?"

She had a good point. "Well no, but it doesn't matter since I'm not man hunting."

"Yes you are, and trust me, you are going to look the part if it kills both of us. Then we are going back to the room to color your new growth." She lowered her sunglasses and peered over the top of them with squinted eyes. "You have at least three inches of gray going on up there, granny. How did you miss *that* when you passed a mirror?

"I didn't miss it." Stevie Wonder couldn't miss it. "I just really could care less about my roots."

She removed her shades and pointedly glanced at my bikini area. "Thank God, you took my advice and bush hogged the briar patch before you left home."

Tamara found this extremely funny and almost fell out of her chair laughing. When she had calmed down enough to speak, she told Teri, "There's a gift shop on the first floor of the hotel. I saw some cute sundresses earlier when I went to buy a Pepsi."

"Great. I'll be right back." Then she was gone, with her triple D's bouncing.

Tamara and I people watched until Teri returned about an hour later. The bathing suits that some people choose to parade around in never fails to amaze me. I mean, do these people not own mirrors?

"I found the perfect dress and shoes for you, along with a few things for me. You will absolutely love them." Teri paused to lick her lips as a handsome father build a sandcastle with his daughter a few feet away. "Come on, let's go color your hair. It's a good thing I brought supplies. I was afraid you would try to prance around Myrtle Beach looking like Betty White, and I was right."

Thankfully, she had thought to bring hair

coloring supplies, which I desperately needed, But, oh boy, would I ever be a candidate for *What Not to Wear* with the clothes she chose for me? I had no doubt the neck would be slit to my navel and the hem would fall slightly short of covering my butt cheeks. At least my hair would be gorgeous.

We remained on the beach until 6:00, making frequent trips to the poolside bar for my all time favorite drink, bloody mary. By the time Mallory came sashaying back, looking flushed and satisfied, my head was spinning, I was sunburned, and my vision was slightly blurred. Tamara wasn't feeling any pains either, so Teri drove the Jeep to a Calabash restaurant for a fabulous seafood supper.

"So spill." Teri said to Mallory once we had filled our plates with flounder, oysters and shrimp, deviled crab, and lobster from the buffet and were seated in our booth. "Did you do one or both of your recent acquaintances?"

"How can you ask me something like that?" Mallory actually had the grace to blush while cracking a lobster. She dipped the succulent meat in butter and moaned in pure bliss as it touched her lips.

Anxious for the juicy details, Teri totally ignored her lobster. "I'm guessing you had plenty of practice at perfecting that moan today. Just answer the question and don't bother trying to play some coy debutant, when we both know you will fail miserably. Meryl Streep would have to dig deep to pull off that performance."

Mallory threw back her head and laughed. "Both," she confessed with a satisfied smile. "How could I do one and not the other? You know his feelings would be hurt."

"Together or separately?" Tamara inquired, sucking a raw oyster, that reminded me of nasal secretions, out of the shell with apparent relish.

"Tamara, I can't believe you would ask such a thing." Mallory was deep in thought as she dug through her salad, always alert for an offending cucumber. "Do you honestly believe I would be a willing participant in a threesome?"

Teri almost choked on her unsweetened tea. "Three would just be an appetizer for you, Mallory. Just answer the damn question."

"Fine then, if you all must live vicariously through me, we had a most entertaining threesome," the nymphet finally admitted.

"You should have called me," Teri deadpanned. "I could have shown you the true meaning of entertainment. Although I'm sure the heavier of the two shed copious amounts of sweat and grunted like a farm animal during his entire performance. That couldn't have been pleasant."

"Did either of them have any outstanding features?" I asked, knowing Mallory was diligently searching for a man who did. For quite some time "humongous" had been her word of the day.

"Hell no, just average. At least Tyrick, the cute one, was average. I couldn't really bring myself to look at the heavier one, naked, but he felt about average."

Tamara and I were left speechless.

After the meal, it was back to the room to shower for the club. Teri had chosen a pink, floral, cleavage revealing sundress and pink flip flops.

While the dress looked surprisingly cute on my rail thin body, it also announced the fact that my chest was flatter than a pancake, which Teri was quick to point out.

"Honey, you either need to gain some weight or call Charlotte Plastic and schedule breast implants. Talk about fried eggs."

"Screw you, Teri. and your milk jugs." Though it was a thought I *had* seriously considered.

Chapter Ten

We hadn't been at Studebakers ten minutes when I made eye contact with a fairly handsome middle aged man leaning casually against the bar. He smiled and made his way toward our table.

"Didn't take you long, did it?" Teri whispered.

As he approached, I noticed he was a few inches taller than me with black hair and a dark tan. He was one of those rugged, outdoorsy kind of men that just made you feel all warm and cozy.

"What are you drinking?" He grinned, showing perfect white teeth.

He had passed my first requirement. Good teeth. I can kiss for hours on end if my partner is even reasonably proficient at it. For this to happen, good teeth, oral hygiene, and pleasant breath are an absolute must.

"Bloody mary."

He lifted my hand to kiss my palm before heading toward the bar. "I'll be right back."

As it turned out he was from Winston Salem, single, 57 and divorced. Requirement number two was checked off my list. He was single. I introduced him to the others, "This is Stephen."

"Hi Stephen." Teri beamed, extending her

bejeweled hand.

"Hello there," Mallory simpered, grinning from ear to ear as she did when introduced to any member of the opposite sex regardless of age, physical appearance or nationality.

"Hi, Steven." Tamara sounded so depressed that even I was praying for a bevy of Mexicans to bum rush the door.

Steven turned to me, his green eyes twinkling. "Would you like to dance?"

"Sure."

He led me to the dance floor where we swayed and talked for the next several songs. I learned that he had two grown children and three grandchildren. He had been divorced for five years. The divorce was supposedly due to philandering on his ex wife's part. I discovered that he was self-employed also, owning a successful printing business. He had passed requirement number 3 with flying colors. He was gainfully employed.

On his next trip to the bar, he returned with another round of bloody marys and a red rose with a cute little bear attached. How long had it been since a man had presented me with a gift? "Thank you, Stephen." I inhaled the heady fragrance of the gorgeous red rose. "How very sweet. I love it."

"You're welcome." He squeezed my hand as he leaned toward me. "Be right back. Going to the men's room."

"Look at you, already receiving gifts!" Teri shouted to be heard above the music. "The man is divinely handsome."

"He smells good enough to take a bite out of."

"Down girl." Teri snickered as she sipped from a dirty martini. "Wait until he tells you his name before you go nibbling on him. What's he wearing by the way?"

"Jean Paul."

"Not Jean Paul! You will be putty in his hands. The poor man never knew when he was getting dressed tonight that his choice of cologne would get him laid."

Jean Paul Gautier cologne for men, to be exact. I knew the fragrance immediately since over the years I have purchased gallons at Christmas for my son and other male family members. A more delicious fragrance for men doesn't exist. Honestly, the scent makes me melt.

"You gonna do him?" Teri inquired.

I didn't have to answer as Mallory and the slimmer of her acquaintances from the beach, Tyreek, came bouncing to the table after a hip thrusting routine to Lady Gaga's *Poker Face*. Tamara sat, looking forlornly toward the door.

"Why don't you give a white boy a chance?" Stephen asked upon returning to our table.

"Or a brother?" Tyreek chimed in. "I could hook you up."

"Nothing against you two," she informed them sadly. "Mexican men really know how to treat a woman, and they are so sweet."

"I'm sweet," Tyreek insisted.

"Me too," Stephen added, grabbing my hand to pull me back on the dance floor and into his arms.

Good Lord the man could dance. He was extremely handsome, smelled positively scrumptious, and had a smile that could knock your socks off. I had already decided I wasn't going to jump in the sack with him. There wouldn't be a notch added to my *one night stand at Studebaker's belt* tonight. My life was slowly inching back toward a semblance of normalcy and I wasn't about to throw a curve ball into the chaotic mix now.

When the club closed, even though Stephen begged me to go for a walk on the beach, Tamara, Teri, and I left him at the hotel entrance. It was too soon, but I did promise to meet him back at the club the following night.

Back in our room I opened the balcony doors before crawling into bed. No matter how hot it is I sleep with the doors open at the beach so I can hear the crashing waves and feel the ocean breeze. "Teri, do you think Mallory is doing both of them again?"

"At the very least the two of them, but I imagine she picked up enough strays in the club to have a full fledged orgy." She sounded slightly envious.

"Weren't you tempted to go with them?" I teased.

"Not really. As twats go, mine is relatively small. This is both good and bad. On one hand men absolutely love it, on the other I still have to insert spacers into my vagina occasionally to keep it open. As much as I would love to, I'm afraid a black man would rip me a new one."

"You better stick with white men then," I advised. "Or have you ever tried a Latino man? I hear they are about average."

"Not true!" Tamara was quick to voice an

objection. "Most Mexican men are definitely above average."

"I'm sure they are, Tamara." Teri pacified her, then turned to me. "To answer your question, yes, I've had Latino men. Not many though since I would rather be able to understand a man when he is talking dirty to me. What if he tells me in Spanish that he wants to choke me until I turn blue, or chain me to the bed for the weekend, or use a whip on my ass, and I unwittingly agree to it?"

I was still giggling when I drifted to sleep.

The next day while Tamara and Mallory basked in the harmful rays of the sun, Teri and I hit the mall. They didn't seem to grasp the concept of going to the beach and wasting time shopping any more than I did, but I couldn't send Teri out alone.

The girl could shop until the soles of her flip flops melted and keep on going, especially the outlet malls where she thought she was getting a bargain. She had 75% of her Christmas shopping completed when we finally left the mall and I had four cute new outfits.

Satisfied that I could look presentable for at least four consecutive days, Teri and I went back to the hotel and met the girls at the poolside grill for hotdogs and hamburgers.

Oh Lord, they were setting up karaoke. Of all things. If Teri stepped up to the microphone we would never get it out of her hands in time to make it to the club before closing time.

"Look girls! Karaoke!" she squealed with unabashed delight upon spying the microphone. "What are we going to sing?"

"*We* aren't singing anything," I said. "What are you singing, and please don't embarrass us by singing something from a Broadway musical?"

"Well, that certainly takes the fun out of it and when did you become such a killjoy?"

Ignoring her question, I made a suggestion, hoping to sidetrack her from the ever popular show tunes. "Do *Black Velvet*. You sing that really well."

"I do, don't I?" She was busily searching through the book for song numbers and jotting them down. "I also do a mean *Betty Davis Eyes*."

She waltzed up to the microphone, cleared her throat a few times, leaned slightly forward for added effect, and belted out the song. She really could sing, and finished to a round of robust applause, along with raucous shouts of encore from a table of men in the corner. She bowed, waved to the men, and headed straight for the song selection book to choose her next number.

In less than a minute she was back on stage singing *Dancing Queen* by Abba, which was equally impressive. She followed these with several more songs from the eighties and showed no sign of slowing down anytime soon. The girl was in her element and loving it.

Around 8:00, I went to the room to bathe and change for the club with disco mania ringing in my ears. Teri refused to give up the stage, informing us that she was having too much fun to leave since she had befriended two couples who shared her passion for music from another era.

Heaven help them all.

Tyreek had shown up looking quite sexy, to the point you could almost see drool forming in the corners of Mallory's mouth. He and Mallory remained at the foot of the karaoke stage sipping drinks appropriately named Sex on the Beach and shouting encouragement to Teri.

When Tamara and I arrived at Studebakers Stephen was waiting patiently at the door, looking every bit as handsome as he had the night before in Bermuda shorts, a Carolina blue Myrtle Beach tee shirt and Hey Dude's. Believe me, the man smelled so delicious it was a physical challenge to keep from locking lips with him right there on the sidewalk. My resolve not to add another notch to my *one night stand at Studebaker's belt* was steadily weakening. We are talking super-sonic speed.

Mallory swears she would never be caught dead in public with a man wearing sandals. Tyreek was wearing Rainbows, but I don't think she even glanced at his feet. I, personally, would prefer that my man not wear Jerusalem cruisers, but flip-flops on a man are rather sexy in my opinion, especially at the beach.

Steven hugged me, presented me with yet another rose, and led us to a reserved table. How thoughtful. I had yet to find a single flaw with the man.

The Studebopper Dancers were performing on the dance floor when Stephen went to the bar for drinks. As soon as the dancers finished their routine, we heard *It's Electric* and that was our cue to hit the floor. You just know I consider myself to be the Electric Slide Queen.

At Studebaker's the *Electric Slide* continues

through at least three songs and Tamara and I never missed a beat. Next came the *Cupid Shuffle* and when the dance ended we made our way through the masses to the table where Stephen waited with another round of bloody marys.

"Next slow song is mine," he whispered against my ear sending a delicious shiver traipsing along my spine. "I've been thinking about holding you in my arms since I left you last night."

I don't know about Stella, but Eve was definitely getting her groove back. My breath caught in my throat as I turned my head so that our lips lightly grazed each other. "I can't wait." The blood was certainly pulsing through the old nether region tonight.

My head was beginning to spin as we danced and drank several more rounds of bloody marys. I wondered if Stephen really liked that particular cocktail or was simply funneling them because it was my drink of choice?

We were on the dance floor, with Stephen holding me sinfully close, when he pressed his moist, soft lips close to my ear. "Would you look at that?"

"What?" My head was on his shoulder and my nose was pressed to his neck breathing in his glorious fragrance. I didn't want to move a single muscle.

"Look, Eve," he insisted.

Humoring him, I glanced over and talk about a total shock to the system. I couldn't believe my eyes. Tamara and an apparently rich and slightly less than attractive white boy, were in a passionate embrace right there on the dance floor.

Stephen and I returned to the table to wait. We couldn't miss this introduction. When the song ended Tamara brought her dance partner to our table.

"This is Melvin. Melvin, this is Eve and Steven."

"Hi, Eve, Steven," he said, shaking Steven's hand.

I leaned toward Tamara and whispered, "A white boy? What's up with that?"

"I felt sorry for him sitting all alone. Plus, look at him, you can tell he's loaded. If I'm going to do a white boy he'll need money coming out his ass."

"From his appearance, I would agree that his family is probably loaded, and you felt sorry for him sitting all alone? Tamara, honey, the world could use more good women like you."

At some point in the evening the DJ announces the names of major cities in neighboring states and you applaud if you live in that city or close to it. When he mentioned Charlotte, Tamara and I stood up and whistled and clapped since it was the closest city to our hometown. He wasn't likely to announce the booming metropolis of Hanover Falls. I glanced at the surprisingly quiet Stephen when Winston Salem was announced.

Then to my complete astonishment and utter regret, he stood and applauded loudly for the city of Myrtle Beach. Admittedly, he'd had several drinks. Evidently, a few too many, because when I asked if Myrtle Beach was his home he forgot to lie. Adam would have done much better at hiding the truth.

"I have a home at the country club, why?"

"You told me your home was in Winston Salem." I took one last whiff of his marvelous cologne, knowing it would be my last. "I can only assume that was a lie."

"Oh." He had the decency to blush, remembering the mention of his fabricated hometown. "Damn, I guess I'm getting to old for this shit."

He had proven to be just another typical, sweet smelling, lying member of the male species. Nothing new there. "You aren't divorced either, are you?"

"No," he slurred, well on the way to being drunk. "But I wish I was."

"Me too." Damn, I wished Teri was here. She was so good at giving people their comeuppance. "Yet, wishing and doing are two entirely different things. Why don't you go home to your wife where you belong? If you aren't happy, tell her. If you can't work it out, leave her. Don't go club hopping, spinning lies, and trying to hook up with innocent women. Be a man for God's sake," I snapped, leaving my seat to move to another table.

Apparently the imbecile had a problem with comprehension as he had the unmitigated gall to follow me and put his hand on mine, causing me to wonder if perhaps his hearing wasn't all it should be. "Can't we just be together tonight? You can't come to the beach on a girl's weekend and not get laid."

"You wanna bet." I snatched my hand from his. "If I do decide to get laid, as you so tactfully put it, it won't be by the likes of you. The way you pick up women I wouldn't go within ten feet of your nasty and probably disease ridden pecker. In other words, my advice to you would be to get the hell out of my face."

I adamantly refused to let another despicable member of the male species ruin my weekend. It was almost closing time at Studebakers, and as Katie Scarlett would say, "Tomorrow is another day."

Tamara left the dance floor with Melvin and came to our new table with her hands held out, apparently wondering why I had switched tables and left poor Stephen sitting all alone.

"What's wrong, Eve?"

"Our Stephen has difficulty deciphering fact from fiction as he is not only very married, but resides here, at Myrtle Beach."

"No shit. The lying bastard." She practically snarled, turning to give him an evil glare. "He spent a fortune on drinks and flowers, serves him right."

"Are you a typical lying man, Melvin?" I asked, pointedly gazing into the eyes of the most homely man, reminiscent of Disney's animated Ichabod Crane, I had ever had the privilege to encounter.

"No, ma'am," he insisted, blushing to the roots of his horribly highlighted hair. "I try real hard not to ever lie, especially to a female."

It would seem the old adage was true. Everyone looks better at closing time. Bless his heart, I hadn't partaken of enough vodka to make poor Melvin attractive. I'd had too much to drink, for even the name Melvin sent me into convulsions of hilarity.

"What's so funny?" Tamara queried.

"Nothing, this is the last song and I am going to borrow your man, Tamara. Come on, Melvin, let's dance."

"He's from Charleston, or at least he said he is," Tamara shouted, turning to give Stephen a withering glare.

After the dance ended and we had returned to the table, Tamara whispered, "It's almost closing time so we're going to walk you home, then go to Melvin's room to watch a movie."

"Sound like a plan." Although, I was sure neither of them would be watching TV tonight. I almost suggested they stop off at the Piggly Wiggly for a paper bag, but fortunately my drunk ass held my tongue.

I entered our room to find Teri sitting with her feet propped on the balcony rail, gazing across the ocean at the moonlight reflecting on the water.

"What are you doing here?" she mumbled sleepily.

I had hoped she would be in dreamland by now. "Why wouldn't I come here?"

"You know exactly what I mean, twit." Placing her drink on the table, she stood and stretched. "Why aren't you with that sweet smelling hunk?"

"I'm not ready for a hunk just yet, no matter how sweet he smells."

"When will you ever learn, girlfriend? I thought I had raised you to know the only way to get over one man is to get under another."

The thought of getting under any man right now actually made me nauseous.

"Obviously, I have more work to do with you. Put on your suit and let's go get pickled in the hot tub."

I gazed with intense longing toward my side of the bed. "Didn't the sign at the pool say the hot tub closes at 10:00pm?"

"Since when have you and I obeyed rules? You weren't worried about rules when you broke into Adam's house confiscating everything from phone numbers to a disposable camera, now were you?"

She was slightly tipsy, I could tell. It was 3:30am and I didn't see much chance of my over imbibed ass getting any sleep tonight. "Give me a minute to change."

"Hurry up," she insisted. "I don't intend to spend my last night at the beach sleeping."

Minutes later I slid into the hot tub as steaming, churning water enveloped my body and lapped around my chin. It felt heavenly. Totally relaxed, I laid my head back and gazed at the beautiful night sky trying to bring my blurred thoughts into focus. I knew there was something important I should remember. *What was it?* "Oh! Guess what?"

"What?"

"Guess?"

"Okay," she said, gazing up at the stars and pretending to ponder. "Stephen only has one nut?"

"I wouldn't know, he might." I grinned. "Tamara is with a white boy."

Her eyes flew open and she sat straight up so suddenly her too skimpy bathing suit top was left hanging beneath her massive mammaries. "Stop lying."

"I'm not lying." For emphasis I crossed my heart. "They were going to his room to watch a movie, I swear."

"Uh huh, the only movie they'll be watching tonight will be on Porn Hub." She laughed, mirroring my thoughts exactly.

"I don't imagine it be any more titillating than the scene old boy is watching." I nodded to the man a few feet away, drooling over his balcony rail at Teri's bare bosom.

Far from being embarrassed and hastily covering herself, as I would have, the exhibitionist sat up straighter, placing her elbows on the edge of the hot tub to make her boobs jut out even further and bounce merrily on the surface of the water. "Let him look. I'm sure the poor man rarely sees a set of girls like these."

I half expected her to squeeze her nipples and moan for him and she probably would if I hadn't shocked her with my tale of *Tamara and the White Boy*.

"How did he look?" She cut her eyes toward the man to assure that he was still partaking of the bountiful feast displayed before his eyes. He was.

"Um... well."

"Seriously? Did the poor thing look that bad?"

"Worse. Tamara *really* wants a rich boy. She's tired of struggling as a single parent. I think she wants to be you."

Teri leaned her head back and closed her eyes. "It wouldn't take her long to realize that wealth isn't everything."

"It helps though."

"True. At least she's getting laid. That's more than I can say for the two of us." She glanced at the mesmerized man on the balcony. "I wonder if he would be interested in nibbling on a set of lips?"

I was almost positive she wasn't referring to the silicone set either. "Surely, you aren't going to ask?"

Laughing raucously, she slid under the water and adjusted her top. "He has seen enough to get his jollies." She nudged my leg with her toe. "How are you doing, Eve? I mean really? None of your contrived bullshit."

I thought about this for a minute before answering. "I guess it's true what they say about time healing all wounds. I have actually been having fun this weekend. Who would have thought? Thank you, for insisting that I come, Teri."

"Anytime, sweetie. Next time don't be such a pain in the ass when I suggest something. Just remember that I know best."

"I'll try to remember. I find that each day it seems to hurt less and less. Since tomorrow is Adam and Chia's wedding day, I hope to finally have closure."

"Who knows? That yummy smelling Stephen just might be the man to help you forget Adam, even if he does only have one nut."

"Afraid not." I really hated to burst her bubble and inform her that the mighty Eve had struck out once again. "I found out tonight that our Stephen not only lives here, but is also very married."

"Good Lord!" she cried. "Must every man

you meet be a chronic liar?"

"Sure seems that way, doesn't it? Anyway, it's hot as Hades in here and I'm getting out."

"Me too. Let's go to bed. I'm totally exhausted from singing." Wrapping a towel around her waist, she handed me one. "It felt like I was performing again and I had a blast. This has been a weekend to remember."

All of us would agree to that.

Ever mindful of the wedding back home, we asked for an extended checkout time and lounged on the beach until late afternoon.

Tamara left the beach considering herself to be on easy street for the rest of her life with Melvin the trust fund baby. It would seem he had the ability to do the *bestest* thing with such proficiency he had succeeded in wiping the entire Mexican population from her feverish mind. He had promised to visit her the following weekend.

Mallory was strongly considering leaving Antwan, her live in boyfriend, for Tyreek. If she asked my opinion, I would urge her to stay with Antwan. Anyone could tell Tyreek was the very definition of a player.

Teri was still hearing the applause from last night's karaoke performances ringing in her ears, humming 80's songs, and planning our next adventure. A fun filled Caribbean cruise.

"Teri gave an encore performance after karaoke last night." I couldn't suppress a snicker as I brought them up to speed on her hot tub debut.

"Mallory," Teri asked, "have you ever had your lips nibbled on while in a hot tub. It is the most divine sensation."

"Hell, no. It almost gives me a spontaneous orgasm just thinking about it, but you know most black men aren't fond of water."

They talked nonstop sex on the ride home while my mind, against my will, drifted to the Catholic Church. Today marked a new chapter in my life.

Today Adam would be a married man.

Chapter Eleven

On a Monday night in June we were at Tamara's house for girl's night. Teri licked her tongue around the salted rim of her margarita glass. "Tamara, have you heard from the limber lipped Melvin yet?"

"Hell, no. The lying bastard! Not a word." Tamara chugged her margarita. "I with I could get my hands around his skinny neck."

"It's a unfortunate fact that the world is full of lying me," I hated to inform her.

"What about you, Mallory?" Teri asked. "Any word from Tyreek?"

"Nope, and his phone has been disconnected." Mallory bit into a taco. The sauce dribbled down her chin as she chewed with a vengeance. Then she drained her margarita. "Can you believe that shit?" She held her taco in one hand and motioned toward her camel toe with the other. "Can you believe a man didn't come back for seconds of this?"

"That's a conundrum that will cause me to lose sleep for months to come," Teri deadpanned, while salting her glass and pouring another drink. "What about you, Eve? Do you have any encouraging news from the dating front?"

I would swell up like a toad and my blood pressure would shoot out the roof of my head if I consumed that much salt. Don't get me wrong, I love salt but my body can only handle it in very limited doses. "Nope, no news."

"Nope," Mallory was quick to agree on my behalf. "She sits at home watching CNN and waiting to see what the next disaster will be. How depressing is that?"

"I like to keep abreast of current events, Mallory. Is that a crime?"

"To answer your question about Eve's love life, or lack thereof, the answer is no. She never goes out. She refuses to even go to clubs with me. I guess we need another beach trip."

"I *choose* not to go out looking for men, Mallory. I'm not ready to dive into another relationship so soon." I spooned huge dollops of sour cream onto my taco. The tacos would be so much better with diced tomatoes, but Tamara had never been known to purchase a tomato. "I'm going to be alone and learn to be happy with myself. I don't need a man to complete me. That is unless Bradley Cooper comes to his senses and decides to give me a call. What has what's her face got that I don't have anyway? Just one hour with him. That's all I would ask for."

Teri grinned. "At least Eve is beginning to think about other men, even if Bradley is slightly out of reach. The part about her being alone for a while and learning to be happy with herself is the smartest thing I have heard her say in, well, forever."

I clasped my hands under my chin and

gushed, "Thank you, Teri. Your approval means so much to me."

"Lying bitch."

"I wonder how Adam and Chia are doing." Tamara had to ruin the evening by pondering this question out loud.

"Justin told me Chia has begun slipping out at night to meet Chris. It seems that Adam has awakened several times and found her gone. He said Adam was also complaining about how much money Chia spends. Apparently he's forced to let his bills pile up in order to finance her Walmart shopping sprees every Friday and keep her happy."

"Serves the imbecile right," Teri said. "He deserves to be treated the same way he treated you. I hope she ruins him financially.

"I bet if Adam lost his job and couldn't buy her everything she wanted, Chia would leave him in a hot minute," Mallory chimed in.

"Of course she would," Teri agreed. "Even Adam is smart enough to realize that."

Tamara brought out what we had all been waiting for, a banana pudding made with Splenda to satisfy the diva, and we were too busy eating to talk for a while.

While we were clearing the table, Tamara said, "I can't wait to start planning our cruise."

"Let's plan it for the fall, after hurricane season has passed." My life was turbulent enough. I had no desire to sail on stormy seas.

"Let's make it a singles cruise," Mallory added. "You know there won't be any single men on one of those fun ships that cater to families."

"I'll go online tomorrow and start checking

websites for a good deal," Teri said. "Any particular destination in mind? I hear the Atlantis Resort in the Bahamas is spectacular."

"I've always wanted to go to Jamaica," I said. "There is so much history there. I could spend days researching pirates and maybe tour a working sugar cane plantation."

Tenderhearted Mallory asked, "Does Haiti have a cruise ship port? I would love to spend my vacation doing whatever I could to help those poor people."

"I don't know for sure, Mallory, but I will check." Teri grabbed her latest Louie and stood up to leave. "So which is it, Jamaica or the Bahamas?"

Tamara leapt to her feet with a fierce look of determination in her eyes, placed her hands on her hips and said with meaning, "Have you lost your freaking minds? You know damn well we are cruising to Mexico."

Evidently, we *had* lost our minds. Tamara very rarely voiced an opinion. She always went along with the crowd. We felt terrible that she hadn't heard a single word from Melvin since returning from the beach, so we were thrilled to witness this new and *hey, I have an opinion too* version.

"Okay." We were all in agreement. "Cozumel it is."

"I'll call you all tomorrow and tell you about the deals I found," Teri quipped. "Start shopping for cruise attire, girls."

Chapter Twelve

On a sweltering July evening my son Levi was working close enough to home that he was able to take the day off and go fishing with his grandpa. Around suppertime, Dad called from the river to say they had a mess of catfish and for Mom and me to come to the river for a fish fry. I helped Mom load up Dad's old river truck and we headed toward the river.

It was such a beautiful day, and since recently deciding that I needed to jump back on the exercise bandwagon, I hopped on my bike and pedaled down the dusty river road.

When we arrived at the river, Levi had cut the catfish into nuggets, rolled them in House Autry seasoning mix, and was dropping them into a frying pan filled with corn oil. He had already cooked French fries and hush puppies and had them in a covered bowl. Mom had brought a bowl of coleslaw and I had made a large jug of tea and grabbed a cheesecake out of the freezer.

I don't know why, but food tastes better when it's cooked outside, especially on the riverbank. I was totally content to sit by the river and have a fish fry with my mom, dad, and son on the riverbank. I hadn't told anyone about my visit with Marilyn but several had noticed a surprising change in me. The simplest way to explain it, I guess, would be to say that I no longer sweated the small stuff.

Just before my session with Marilyn ended, she had asked if she could hypnotize me and plant a suggestion. Willing to do anything to ease my pain and suffering, I had readily agreed.

Over the last few weeks I had lost that nervous, wound up tight and threatening to explode at any given minute, energy that everyone associated with me. For the first time in my adult life, I wasn't singing the *some man done me wrong* song. I still found it hard to believe that after fifty years I had successfully put the past where it belonged. In the past. I don't know what Marilyn said while I was under hypnosis, but I was eternally grateful.

My dad and Levi practically inhaled fish that tasted even more delicious than what you could order at our local Rocky River Springs Fish House. They were anxious to take the boat downriver to one of the deep holes where the flathead catfish lived and get in some night fishing. I had seen several fish reeled in from the river that when held in front of a 6 feet tall man would reach his chin.

Levi waved and faced the front of the boat, steering it through dangerous clusters of underwater rocks that he knew by heart. The rocks had been the cause of many failed fishing trips attributed to busted propellers by boaters less skilled at navigating the hidden dangers of Rocky River.

"It's so peaceful here, isn't it, Eve?"

"If only the rest of the world could be this

peaceful, Mom."

"I worry about what's going to happen to this old world. We have wars and rumors of wars all over the world. The Bible is fulfilling itself. Anybody who has any doubt about it should read Mark 13:8."

She quoted: "For nation shall rise against nation, and kingdom, against kingdom: and there shall be earthquakes in divers places, and there shall be famines and troubles: these are the beginnings of sorrows."

"I agree, Mom. The bible does seem to spell it out and we've certainly had earthquakes in diverse places in the last few years."

"The bible is fulfilling, Eve."

"What really bothers me is the amount of hatred so many Americans feel for their fellow man. Politics has divided us, and it's scary."

"It is scary, Eve. You can't hardly turn on the television without seeing some new disaster that's befalling this old earth, or men and women fighting in the streets." She gave me a big hug and hopped in the truck. "Do you want to put the bike in back of the truck and ride home with me?"

I decided to ride my bike home and get a little more exercise. I waved to Mom as she left in a cloud of dust, still ruminating on her prophetic words.

I sat in a lawn chair gazing at the river that had been such an integral part of my life. Leaves swirled on the surface of the water and floated by on a lazy current. A woodpecker pecked noisily in a tree overhead. A trail of determined ants made their way across the cleared picnic table searching for crumbs. Fish, that always got playful just before dusk, jumped out of the water and fell back into the river with a loud plop.

The sounds provoked new memories to stir inside my head. Pleasant memories. It was like the floodgates in my mind suddenly opened up and for the first time, my childhood came rushing back to greet me. I remembered Christmases, Easters, Halloweens, Birthdays and Thanksgivings. I even remembered my Valentine's Days spent passing out cards at school. I remembered them all.

I recalled that almost every weekend during the summer my family had camped out on this very spot, along with my mom's sister and her family. I remembered sliding down the muddy riverbank and landing in the cool water with my sister and cousins giggling beside me, along with the time Mom had lifted the cover off a platter of grilled hamburgers and found a blowfly inside. She had panicked in a major way.

Not knowing any better, she was certain we would all die from maggot infestation since we had snacked on the burgers most of the day. She and my aunt had thrown every last child in my dad's old river truck and rushed home at breakneck speed. Once there, they made us take a dose of Castoria, undoubtedly the nastiest substance on the planet, to clean out our stomachs.

Just remembering the horrible taste of the laxative was enough to make me gag now. I had to laugh remembering the sleepless night my sister and brother and I had spent trotting back and forth to the bathroom. It was good to have memories again, some of them anyway. At least now I know why I have such an aversion to Castoria.

I could just make out the edge of Dad's boat going around the bend in the river in the growing twilight. I had been so caught up in my onslaught of new memories that I hadn't noticed the sun slipping behind the trees. It would soon be dark.

I hopped on my bicycle, not relishing the thought of riding home alone at night, but Mom was long gone. Since the men had taken a lantern I knew they wouldn't be returning until much later. Better leave now while there was still enough fading light to still see the road.

The narrow dirt road from the river to the main road was surrounded on both sides by cornfields. In fact, the road twisted and turned in such a way that you were surrounded by towering stalks of corn as far as the eye could see.

The corn stalks rustled and crackled, their tasseled tops swaying in the gentle breeze. Wiping the sweat from my brow with the back of my hand, I closed my eyes for a few minutes to savor the feeling of being alone in my cocoon of corn. As I breathed deeply of the cool evening air, I suddenly realized that I had been wrapped up in my own misery for so long I had ignored the peace and tranquility in my own back yard.

That was about to change. I intended to start communing with nature. Life was good again for the first time in a long, long time. I laughed out loud and startled a covey of quail, sending them into a noisy, scattered flight along with a grasshopper that landed on my knee and promptly spit a wad of tobacco juice on me.

Levi would be coming back home for two

weeks at Thanksgiving, I had a new contract at the county offices, and crying myself to sleep at night was a thing of the past. Huh. I suppose time does heal all wounds. Well, time and a good hypnotist. Amazing, since a few short months ago I would have bet my last pecan log that the wound Adam had inflicted on me would fill my body with enough pus and canker to give my shattered heart gangrene.

After twenty minutes of strenuous pedaling I was beginning to feel the burn in my thighs. I had forgotten the return trip was mostly uphill. You can believe I was doing some heavy breathing, and I had just slowed down to catch my breath when I heard a loud thrashing in the corn. It must be a raccoon or fox or other small creature that called the cornfields home, but man was he ever kicking up a fuss.

The furry little critters were notorious for making a mad dash across the road, I would swear they had turbo jets built into their hind legs, causing you to slam on brakes to keep them from an early demise. Although in this case, with me on a bike, if we collided the odds were better that I would be the one picking my bruised bottom up off the ground after I took a harrowing flight over the handlebars.

I stopped the bike, squinting into the dying light and waiting for the animal to cross the road. It must be a fast little critter the way it was charging through the cornfield. It got closer and closer as I waited impatiently for it to emerge in front of me so I could be on my way, but it didn't. "Come on, would you! We're losing daylight here!"

The thrashing noise suddenly stopped and all was quiet. The animal must have spotted me and was too frightened to come out in the open. Good. I had just placed my foot on the pedal when I heard what sounded like a giggle. As a general rule, raccoon's don't giggle. It had been my imagination for crying out loud. I pushed on the petal, when curiosity got the best of me. My nosiness has always been a curse. I leaned slightly into the corn for a better look.

Oh, my sweet Jesus!

Why did I do that? Why didn't I leave when I had the chance? And what in the *hell* was that glaring at me through the corn? Those eyes certainly did not belong to the animal kingdom. A horrified scream froze in my chest and my heart pounded against my ribs like a jackhammer as I saw large emerald green, laughing eyes staring back at me.

They were human eyes.

But not... quite human eyes.

While the urge to leap from my bike and run screaming through the soaring rows of corn was strong, there was no way I was leaving my bike and being stuck, at night, in the middle of a cornfield with whatever that... thing was. I might be scared shitless, but I wasn't stupid. It was time to follow my golden rule and run, or pedal, like hell.

Before I could get the wheels in motion a chubby little black face peeked out from behind the corn stalks. I shut my eyes for a second, praying feverishly that when I opened them he wouldn't be there and we could pretend this never happened.

No such luck. He was still there and he had his full lips pursed as if he were puzzled to find a middle-aged woman on a bicycle in his cornfield. I took a slow steadying breath, trying to calm my rattled nerves and see what the child intended to do. He was such a beautiful child. He could have easily graced the cover of a parenting magazine. I couldn't be afraid of him. Could I? He seemed perfectly normal. Well, bless his heart, he was filthy, but normal.

> *Except for the eyes.*
> *Eyes that just looked different.*
> *Too brilliant.*
> *Too green.*

Like he had colored contact lenses, or had just climbed out from under a rock.

Judging from the green eyes and his coffee with just a touch of cream skin tone, I assumed that one of his parents was white. He didn't speak, but just looked at me with two dirty little fingers tugging on his bottom lip as the sun dipped below the cornfield. I shuddered at the thought of being trapped in the cornfield all night and pushed on the petal once again. The child grabbed a cornstalk and shook it vigorously to gain my attention, then he held out his other chubby, dimpled hand and playfully stuck one finger out, motioning for me to follow him.

> *Bless his sweet little heart.*

The child had bumped his head on a corncob if he thought I could ever, in this life or any other, find the courage to go hiking through the corn with him. Nope, you'll just have to wait for the next hapless cyclist to wander by sweetheart.

> *Me?*
> *Follow him?*
> *Me?*

Who couldn't even work up the nerve to stroll through a haunted house at Halloween?

As the child's green gaze locked with mine, I remembered Dad's story.

The little boy in the tree!

Like the little boy in his story, this child was wearing nothing more than a saggy cloth diaper as well. He wasn't trembling and crying, possibly because dogs weren't chasing him in freezing weather. He seemed to be in a rather playful, albeit a troubled, mood like he had heavy things weighing on his young mind. Nope scratch young, he was probably a few hundred years older than me.

Without speaking, I shook my head from side to side to let him know that I couldn't possibly work up the courage to go traipsing through the corn with him. My weak constitution, which was getting frailer by the second, simply wouldn't allow it.

What to do? *Run.* Could he read minds? Possibly, because before I could lift a foot toward the pedal he again motioned determinedly with his little finger.

He must understand that he had the wrong person for the job here. *I suddenly had a rare light bulb moment.* "You come with me," I croaked, given the fact that my saliva glands had ceased to produce even a drop of spittle. In a determined effort to convince myself that the child was indeed human, I foolishly added, "Let's go find your mommy."

At the mention of his mommy his face hardened to stone, his eyes filled with tears, and he again motioned for me to follow him, but not just with his finger. Now his entire hand was gesturing toward the cornfield behind him with hard, jerky movements.

"I can't." I licked my suddenly parched lips, while shaking my head vigorously from side to side. "I can't follow you. Wait here and I'll go find someone who will, okay?"

When I said this his eyes took on a menacing, reddish glare and the cheerful smile that had brightened his face earlier was replaced by a sinister frown. He began to tap one dirty little bare foot on the ground.

This couldn't be good.

Trust me, red eyes erased all doubt from my mind. This child was not human.

As I live and breathe he was a tanned version of Chucky.

I took a second to look toward the sky as the gentle breeze became a forceful hot gust that felt like it was blowing out of a furnace. I glanced back at the child and his eyes no longer had a reddish glare. They were blood red.

The wind speed was leaping in volumes by the second. The cornstalks swirled and the dry leaves crackled as the wind began to scream around me. I glanced back at the child but quickly averted my gaze from his menacing red glare. Within seconds, the wind was pounding me with a gale force.

Fearing that I would be sucked from my bicycle and into a funnel cloud at any second, I glanced around for the nearest ditch. Dad always said, "Get in a ditch if you get caught outside in a tornado."

There were no ditches, only rows upon rows of corn. As I glanced toward the sky in the growing twilight I was shocked to see there wasn't a cloud in sight, but it had to be a tornado. What else could produce wind this ferocious? My only thought was survival as my hair whipped wildly around my face and the powerful blasts of wind seemed determined to rip the clothes from my trembling body. I tried to scream for help but the powerful gusts blew the words away before they left my lips.

The stalks of corn twisted and jerked, doing a violent dance in the relentless wind. I heard a popping noise and glancing sideways saw corn actually popping off the cob. I kid you not. On both sides of the road the ground was as white as snow, with popcorn.

Oh Lord, please get me out of here.

Then the wind became even fiercer and I covered my face with my hands to keep the sand and dirt that felt like needles jabbing into my skin, out of my eyes. Sand, dirt, and cornstalk debris swirled around me in a stifling cloud of dust making it difficult to breathe. I covered my face with my shirt and gasped for air.

I was absolutely terrified that at any second I would be blown into the cornfield where the child had wanted me to begin with. I could feel the cornstalks brushing against me as they bent almost to the ground and the roar of the vicious wind was deafening. I cried out when the bicycle crashed to the ground.

I knew the corn, even as flimsy at it was, was better than no cover at all so I crawled toward it. I had to find shelter from the funnel I expected to drop from the sky at any minute.

Then, as suddenly as it had started, the wind stopped blowing. The corn stopped rustling and dancing. All was calm. It wasn't a gradual dying down of the wind either, it was a complete dead stillness. Not a single breeze stirred the cornstalks. I heard frogs croaking in the pond, crickets chirping, and bumblebees lazily buzzing.

Strange, I thought, lowering my shirt and pulling deep gulps of sweet air into my deprived lungs. You would think the frogs would be hiding underwater and the crickets and bumblebees would have been blown into the next county. Then, I remembered that Dad, and my son, were in a boat! In a tornado! I immediately dialed Levi's cellphone.

"Are you okay?" I cried as soon as he answered, relief washing over me at the sound of his precious voice.

"Yeah," he said, sounding puzzled. "We're good. Why?"

"I was worried that your boat might have capsized in all the wind."

"What wind?"

"What wind?" I shrieked. "I was just in a tornado."

"A tornado? Where are you, Mom?" I could hear the worry in his voice.

"Between the cornfields."

"Mom, the wind hasn't been blowing at all. The water is as still as glass. Are you all right?"

What did he mean the wind hadn't been blowing at all? He was less than a half mile away. Surely he had to have encountered a slight breeze. Still, I couldn't allow him to believe that I had taken to hallucinations now, along with my other countless issues. "I guess."

"A little breeze sounds like a lot of wind when those cornstalks get to rustling." He should know. He had ridden his bike through these cornfields hundreds of time over the years. "Do you want me to come and get you?"

"Of course not." I laughed, even though I saw no humor in the situation." "I'm fine."

"Are you sure?" He sounded worried. "I can be there in thirty minutes."

"I just got a little spooked in the cornstalks, that's all."

"Call me the minute you get home," he insisted. "Don't forget. I won't rest until I hear from you."

"I will."

I glanced nervously around at the towering rows of corn and got back on my bike, shaking worse than the cornstalks in the punishing wind. I was mentally calculating the distance to the main road. At least five more minutes in the cornfields, then I would be back on paved road and a few miles from home. I could make it. The wind had died down and thankfully the little boy had returned to… wherever.

I pedaled furiously, not looking in any direction other than straight ahead. After a few minutes, I could see the gate to the main road looming in the distance and breathed a deep sigh of relief. I had almost made it out of the cornfields.

Increasing my speed, I absently slapped at a mosquito that was painfully trying to suck his evening meal from my neck. Hearing a steadily increasing humming sound behind me, I glanced over my shoulder hoping to see a vehicle approaching, but nothing was in sight. I screeched when one of the blood sucking insects landed on my ear and the humming sound increased to a tremendous buzzing that filled me with terror. I felt what I assumed was a wasp or a bee sting me on the back of my neck and shrieked, slapping furiously at the stinging pest.

While I devoted every ounce of energy to pedaling the bike, the relentless fog of insects was faster. Within seconds they had settled over me in a swarming cloud. I watched, horrified, as thousands quickly joined the others to cover my arms, legs, feet, head, and face to bite or sting every inch of exposed skin. Almost immediately I felt sharp stingers piercing my body through my clothes.

When I tried to breathe my throat clogged with bugs and I gagged. I was frantically slapping at them as they sank their needle sharp points into my skin. The buzzing increased in volume until I thought my head would split and my body was on fire with pain.

I was in a swarm so thick I couldn't see my hand in front of me, let alone the road. The buzzing noise the insects made sounded like a couple thousand of them had settled on my eardrums. I tried to open my eyes, but they covered my eyeballs. I felt a growing hysteria creep over me as I slapped at the insects, trying to keep the bike upright and pedal all at the same time.

Keep it together, Eve.

The gate can't be much further.

For some strange reason, I felt certain that if

I could just make it out of the cornfields I would survive this nightmare and live to tell my grandchildren about it.

I opened my eyes in time to see the gate looming directly in front of me or I would have plowed right into it at a high rate of speed. If I stopped to unlock the gate I might not be able to get back on the bike. If they got me on the ground the bugs would kill me. I was certain they would suck every last ounce of blood from my body. That settled it.

There was no way I was stopping the bike. I slowed down, jumped off and slid across the dirt road losing several layers of skin from my outer right thigh in the process, but at least I was still alive. On trembling hands and knees I crawled under the gate feeling sharp, jagged rocks slicing into my knees and palms at every move. Miraculously, when I crossed under the gate the insects were gone, just as I had expected. I looked back and didn't see a single insect.

Hallelujah.

Thank God.

I was alive.

I glanced cautiously around to see if anything else was coming my way. A raging elephant? A roaring lion? A stampeding herd of buffalo perhaps? Who the hell knows? I took a quick peek in the corn. Nothing. Good. I was covered in red itching welts, bug bites, and stings from head to toe. My knees, palms and right leg were raw and bleeding. Needless to say, I am now a firm believer in the presence of poltergeists.

I sat down on the side of the road and had a

good long cry, all the while wondering how I was going to get the bike to my side of the gate. It was full dark now and there was no way I would risk crawling back through the gates of hell to retrieve a bicycle. The kid could have it for all I cared.

As I picked my bloody, bruised, and aching carcass off the ground and began the long walk home, I heard a child's playful laughter coming from the edge of the cornfield.

Devious little shit!

Chapter Thirteen

I was soaking in a hot tub of water and baking soda that soothed the intense itching for the time being, and using tweezers to pull out the numerous stingers that had pierced my skin, when Teri called.

"Are you sure you didn't imagine it, Eve?" After hearing of my brush with death, she completely dumbfounded me by asking, "Did you fall asleep at the river and dream it perhaps? It sounds pretty farfetched even to me, and I'm a firm believer in the supernatural."

"You don't imagine a tornado and being attacked by a killer swarm of insects when you have a zillion stings to prove it, Teri."

"Good thing they weren't those killer bees that are supposed to be headed this way from South America," she giggled.

No she was not laughing at the ordeal that I had just barely survived.

"If you could see the bug bites and stings covering my entire body, you wouldn't think it was my imagination and you damn sure wouldn't think it was funny!" I was finding it hard to control my rising anger.

I mean, honestly, I could have easily lost my

life in the cornfield and she found that humorous?

"Oh, chill out." She had the nerve to laugh. "It was just a ghost sighting. That's practically an everyday occurrence. Why did you make him so mad anyway?"

"Have you been sniffing too many perm fumes?" I screeched incredulously. "What did you expect me to do? Follow him?"

"Number one, I don't do perms as you well know. And number two, I certainly would have."

Teri is a strong believer in the occult. She consults her *Ouija* board regularly and, years ago, was a member of a Wiccan Witch Coven.

She seemed intent upon making a point. "It's glaringly obvious, even to a novice like yourself, that the child wanted to show you something."

"I didn't want to see it." I knew he wanted to show me something. I wasn't that dense. I mean he *had* kept motioning with his chubby little finger for me to follow him.

I heard Teri's sharp gasp. "Oh, I just had an epiphany! I'll come down this weekend and we can spend the night at the cabin and see what the child wants. I thought you knew you were supposed to follow a ghost if one appeared. Oh boy! This will be the most fun I've had in ages."

"Forgive me, Teri. Unfortunately, I neglected to read *What To Do When A Ghost Child Tries To Kill You.*"

"He didn't try to kill you, Eve." Her giggle morphed into hearty laughter. "For crying out loud, he just roughed you up a little to get your attention. He wants to show you something and we need to find out what."

"You can cease and desist with the *we* nonsense since you will be going by yourself. I can you assure that I won't be entering those haunted cornfields ever again. I probably already have a raging case of West Nile Virus from all the mosquitoes bites or whatever bugs they were."

"You don't have anything of the sort." I could imagine tears rolling down her implanted cheeks. "There you go again, *Miss Dramatic.* Besides, you have to go. It's you he's after. He probably won't even appear if you aren't there."

"Then he just won't be appearing."

"Come on, we'll get Tamara and Mallory and have a girl's night at the river. It'll be fun. Don't be such a killjoy."

Fun? Exactly what part of my tornado and kamikaze insect attack story had sounded like fun? I had her and I knew it. Mallory scares easier than anybody I have ever known and the girl isn't about to go on a wild ghost chase. No way. No how. "If you get Mallory to go, I'll go."

"Do you swear?" she asked, taking no chance of my backing out.

"I swear."

"Okay, I'll call you right back."

That was a troublesome response. She had sounded awfully sure of herself for some disturbing reason. Why had I agreed to go if Mallory went? Knowing Teri as I do, her shrewd little mind had probably already concocted a scheme to make Mallory tag along, probably bribing her with extra highlights.

I was rubbing cortisone cream into my

bumpy, intensely inching skin when she called back. "It's all set for Friday night."

I knew it! "How did you convince Mallory to go?"

"I told her Levi was going to be there. You know she has the hots for your son."

Although Levi was a white boy, Mallory had often commented that she would love to make, yet another, exception to her *black men only* rule and teach him a few of the finer points of life.

I couldn't believe Teri had used my son as bait to lure Mallory in. "Why on earth did you tell her that? He won't be back home until Thanksgiving and that's three months away," I shrieked. "There is no way I would allow my son to get involved with a man eater like Mallory and you damn well know it."

"What difference does it make if I was off by a few months. You know Levi wouldn't give her old ass a second glance. Just let the girl dream."

"It's precisely her ass that I'm worried about," I snapped. " You know how men salivate over it."

"Oh yeah, I forgot about that."

"How about remembering it the next time you try to throw my son at her."

"I will. Anyway, I'll see you Friday night. Gotta go."

I was trying to reach my back with cortisone cream when Tamara called. "Did you really see the same little boy your dad saw?"

"I don't know for sure if it was the same little boy, but whether you believe me or not I saw him, and he tried to kill me."

Like Teri, she showed no concern whatsoever for the agony I had endured. What was wrong with these so called friends of mine? Where was the love? How could they show more interest in my alleged ghost sighting than in the pain and absolute terror that I had suffered? Couldn't they see that the evil little poltergeist had attempted to, if not kill me, at the very least send me into anaphylactic shock? You would think they could be a tad more sympathetic about my numerous injuries. I was thinking unkind thoughts about the lot of them as I clawed at my intensely itching skin.

"Do you really think he wanted to kill you?" Tamara whispered as though the child might be listening in the other room.

"At first he wanted me to follow him. When I refused, he got really pissed."

"Are you going to follow him next time?"

"Who knows? I haven't a clue what I will do if it happens again. Run like hell I suppose. At least the next time I venture into those cornfields I won't be alone. You can bet your bottom dollar on that."

Tamara was rethinking her decision to join us on the camping trip. "I can't believe I agreed to go camping down there with y'all. I have no desire to see him at all. We must all be crazy."

"Nope," I assured her. "Just Teri."

Mallory beeped in and we had a three way conversation. "Traitor." I accused her, after we had discussed the child's apparent fascination with wind and bugs.

"What?" she queried, trying to sound innocent.

"Don't what me, Mallory. I agreed to go

camping only if Teri could talk you into it, knowing full well that hell would freeze over before you agreed to spend a night in those haunted woods. Why did you agree to go?"

"I'm just curious," she lied, and we both knew it.

"About what?"

"About the little boy."

"About whose little boy, Mallory?"

"Well, I am anxious to see Levi again." With the truth out in the open she didn't even bother to hide her excitement. "Has he changed much? Does he still look as good as he did the last time I saw him?"

"Better." I wouldn't spoil the surprise. I decided to let Teri inform her that she had been duped. I would just sit back and watch the fireworks.

She sighed a dreamy sigh. "Who knows, perhaps the rest of us will get a chance to see the little boy in the corn."

I knew by the way she said it that she didn't believe a word of my story. The day Mallory saw the little boy would be the day she drew her last breath. The only reason she was trailing along was in hopes of spending some quality time, alone, with my son, in a dark cabin.

Over my dead body!

I could only pray that the child in the corn had already made other plans for the weekend and wouldn't make an appearance, even if it was my only hope of proving I hadn't imagined the entire episode. "We'll see what happens."

Hopefully, nothing.

I tried not to spend every waking moment dreading the weekend but, unfortunately, Friday arrived all too quickly. Right around dusk the girls arrived and we loaded our supplies into the back of Dad's old river truck.

"I brought the fixings for Dirty Martini's," Teri quipped. "At the river I can get drunk off my ass and not have to worry about making a fool of myself or getting pissed off by one of Lawrence's stern lectures on the dangers of alcohol. That man expects me to be as stodgy as he is and never have any fun."

Teri rarely complained about Lawrence. "Do I detect a hint of trouble in paradise."

She shook her head meaningfully. "He has way too much money for me to even consider hinting."

"Good point." The girl was no dummy. "I brought the ingredients for bloody marys. I thought I might need some liquid backbone tonight. We all might."

"I brought Corona and limes," Mallory added. "If what you said is true, and I see that kid, I'll need to be intoxicated."

We looked expectantly at Tamara.

"Y'all will just have to share."

I stopped at the gate and Mallory hopped out to open it, her eyes darting back and forth through the rustling cornstalks. "Where did you see him, Eve?"

"Hop in and I'll show you." I drove about a half mile down the road and stopped the truck. "The bugs started right about here." As I was talking a mosquito landed on my arm and I jumped so hard I almost vaulted out the window. "Ouch!" I screeched, slapping it and watching blood smear across my arm.

I jerked the truck door open and jumped, listening for the humming sound of an impending swarm. Thankfully the only noise was crickets chirping.

"Take it easy, Eve." Teri had a perturbed frown wrinkling her arched brow. "It was just one bug. Don't go into hysterics."

I drove a little further and stopped. "The wind started right about here." I pointed into the cornfield. "The little boy was right there."

I remembered the child's blood red eyes vividly. I stared into the corn, almost expecting him to materialize and motion for me to follow him. All the while I was fighting the powerful urge to slam the truck into reverse and go home.

Could someone please explain to me why I am here, again?

"Okay, keep going," Mallory mumbled nervously. "We're surrounded by corn on all sides and I don't like it. I feel trapped." Her face was turning an unsightly shade of blue and she seemed to be struggling to get air into her lungs. "In fact... I'm having... difficulty... breathing."

"Mallory, take a deep breath and chill out," Teri snapped. "Why must you get so worked up about every little thing? Eve, start driving so she can feel a breeze before she blacks out."

"Just wait." I laughed, a sound that lacked even a trace of humor when I saw that Mallory's breathing had returned to normal. "You think you're having difficulty breathing now? You ain't seen nothing yet." All three of them cut their eyes at me as I parked beside the cabin.

"I had forgotten what a lush, tropical paradise this is." Grabbing a baby wipe from her bag after climbing out of Dad's dirty old river truck, Teri daintily scrubbed her hands.

I still didn't know how the diva was going to survive a night at the river without a single luxury, although the cabin was comfortable. It had two sets of bunk beds with regular size mattresses and a tiny kitchen. The one room house on stilts had all the amenities, except a bathroom. You still had to go to the outhouse for that. I couldn't wait to see Teri's face after her first trip to the latrine.

"Let's walk to the Almond House and the graveyard before dark," she said after we unloaded the supplies. "He is, or was, a little black boy so I assume his parents were slaves on the Almond Plantation. Right? Wouldn't you think that's probably where he hangs out?" She clapped her hands together. "I can't wait to see him. I've only seen one ghost."

"You did?" Tamara asked, looking like she was already regretting the question. "When?"

"It was during my drug days and I was high on coke. Anyway, the fellow members of the witch coven and I were having a séance and a dark figure was looming, well, actually floating, in the corner. I don't remember him carrying a sickle though. That was the night I overdosed, so it was probably the Grim Reaper just waiting to swoop me to the fiery pits."

"Oh, shit." Tamara cringed.

"That's exactly what I said." Teri shuddered. "I haven't touched an illegal substance since that night."

I could tell Mallory and Tamara were fast rethinking their hasty decision to tag along. I was having serious second thoughts myself.

"Why do you want to go to a graveyard?" Mallory's voice was taking on that whining note that none of us particularly cared for. "What's so special about the Almond House anyway?"

I can't exactly say why, but everyone in the area would agree that there was something sinister about the old plantation house. It just *felt* haunted. "You'll see."

The Almond House was once a thriving cotton plantation. During research at the library I had discovered that in its heyday the plantation had produced more cotton than any other plantation in the area and the Almond's owned practically the entire town.

The family graveyard was in the woods across from the plantation house and the slave graveyard was behind it. Since the house was about a half mile from the river, I wondered if we could walk there and back before sundown, or if I should drive the truck.

"Come on, Eve." Teri joked, sensing my hesitation. "I'll protect you from the wicked witch and her winged monkeys, I mean the little boy and his evil bugs."

Teri made my decision with that comment. I could have chosen to drive the truck or walk up the road but, nope, let's take Miss Fashion Icon through the woods and a couple of redbug infested blackberry patches. Trust me, you won't understand the true meaning of the word itch until an entire community of chiggers has relocated under your skin. I was definitely going to take her on a walk to remember. "Who is going to protect you?" I asked, falling in step beside her.

Tamara and Mallory hesitantly walked behind us as we parted dense vegetation and headed through the forest. Teri quickly lost her holier than thou attitude and complained every step of the way.

"My shoes will be ruined."

"Probably," I agreed, perhaps a bit to cheerfully.

"I'll have permanent scars from all these briar scratches."

"Most likely."

"Ouch! Oh, shit!" she cried, slapping at a mosquito. "Did you bring any insect repellent?"

"Yes, I sprayed." I replied innocently. "Did I forget to offer you the can of bug spray before we left the cabin?"

"Yes, you did, twit. As a matter of fact, you failed to even mention that you brought any."

"Watch out. That's poison ivy." I warned, pointing to several vines snaking through the forest.

"Oh, dear Lord!" Teri squawked. "How do I know which green thing is poison ivy?"

"Be wary of anything with three leaves."

"Everything has three leaves," Tamara fretted, eyeing the dense vegetation.

I actually saw sweat glistening on Teri's brow. She was nervous. Good. At one point we had to crawl on our hands and knees through a tangle of thorny briar bushes. You can just imagine how thrilled the diva was at that insult to her dignity. Teri? On her knees? Without a single man in sight? Please.

"Oh, now this is simply absurd," she muttered angrily. "You didn't tell me we were going to walk through a briar patch like Brier Fucking Rabbit."

"You didn't ask...."

My anger dissolved immediately when I witnessed the breathtaking panorama before me.

We all stopped dead in our tracks and gaped at the magnificent spectacle.

"I have never seen anything like it," Teri cried. "This has to be a mass hallucination."

"Have you ever seen anything so beautiful in all your life?" Tamara cried.

"This has to be some supernatural bullshit, Eve," Mallory whispered nervously. "I want to go home now."

It was unbelievable, resembling a landscape painting more than real life.

The decaying remains of the Almond House stood in the midst of a fluffy sea of creamy yellow on all sides. A magnificent array of buttercups in full bloom as far as the eye could see. It was like the poppy field in the *Wizard of Oz*, only with buttercups.

Most people call them daffodils. I, however, grew up hearing them called buttercups by my mom and grandma, and they look like cups of butter, so I still refer to the flowers as buttercups. Sure, over the years, teachers, friends, neighbors, boyfriends and even my son has insisted that I call them daffodils, but to me, for some reason, they will always be buttercups.

They jutted up against the edge of the cornfield, all the way to the porch of the deteriorating house. The flowers spilled from stumps, over fallen trees, and obliterated the driveway that had once been on the property. The lawn was about two acres and there wasn't one square inch of earth without a gorgeous, yellow buttercup sprouting from it. It was a plethora of color the likes of which none of us had ever witnessed.

"Breathtaking!" Teri marveled as we waded through the knee deep flora.

I had been coming here with dad to pick blackberries for almost fifty years and had never seen more than a few flowers scattered randomly among the waist high pasture grass, wild blackberry bushes, and cow patties.

Tamara bent to smell a flower and pluck the stem. She would forever attribute that simple act as being the single worst mistake of her life.

Suffice it to say all hell broke loose.

As soon as she snapped the stem on the exquisite flower an unnatural clanging seemed to fall from the sky. It was loud, rattling, and deafening and I can only compare it to the sound of thousands of tin cans falling to the ground around us and beating against each other as they fell. The sound was horrifying beyond belief.

Why, why, why did I come back here?

Even the air around us seemed to buzz with a static current of electricity. Mallory was on her knees with her hands over her ears screaming hysterically. Tamara stood, paralyzed with fear, as every ounce of blood drained from her pale face. She threw the flower from her hand like it was a venomous snake as she backed toward the road with a look of terrified disbelief.

The instant she dropped the flower the noise stopped and all was quiet. Still. Calm. Deadly quiet. Not even a butterfly fluttered or a bee buzzed over the fragrant flowers.

"What in the hell was that?" Teri whispered.

"I told you." While I was shaking violently, I was also feeling somewhat vindicated. "Maybe you will believe me next time. That kid's got a mean streak a mile wide."

"Why did he do it?"

Teri wanted answers that I couldn't give. "You tell me."

Mallory jumped and screamed louder. Then, realizing the unearthly noise had stopped, she glared up at me. "He's going to kill us, isn't he? That was a warning, wasn't it? He intends to kill us."

"Of course not." I forced myself to smile, trying to calm her down. "Come on, let's get out of the flowers. I don't think he wants us bothering his buttercups."

"They're daffodils, Eve."

I looked at Tamara. Her eyes were wide as saucers and she looked like she was having difficulty breathing. "Tamara, are you okay?"

"No," she said with a tremulous voice. "Hell no, I'm not okay. What in the flying fuck just happened?"

Even Teri appeared to be slightly rattled, but she fought hard not to show it. "Maybe it was an airplane breaking the sound barrier or something."

"That was no frigging airplane!" Mallory jumped up, flailing her arms and screaming. "You know good and well it wasn't an airplane!"

"She's right, Teri," I agreed. "That was definitely not an airplane."

"I know it wasn't. Damn, Eve, I was trying to calm those two down before they go into cardiac arrest."

"Oh, sorry."

We walked carefully out of the field of flowers, placing our feet strategically among the clusters and trying desperately not to crush one, but it was impossible since they were everywhere. I glanced over my shoulder at Teri.

She was deep in thought, trying to wrap her mind around what had just happened. Like a dog with a bone she couldn't let it go. She squatted to her knees and all you could see were her shoulders and head surrounded by an ocean of velvety yellow.

"Don't!" Tamara and Mallory cried simultaneously when they saw her reach for a flower.

The supreme dumb ass picked one anyway.

Chapter Fourteen

Immediately the sky behind the house began to darken. We watched, speechless, as the blackest clouds I had ever seen began to roll toward us from behind the house, obliterating the sun. Within seconds, the angry cauldron was boiling directly overhead and it was almost as dark as night. A gentle breeze whipped our hair around our faces and caused the flowers to dip and sway in an undulating pattern.

"It will get worse!" I shouted just as a fierce howling wind descended upon us, causing the rotting shutters to bang loudly against the house. "Much worse!"

The wind sent dead tree limbs crashing down around us, and a chunk of roofing sailed from the top of the house just barely missing Tamara. A flash of lightening lit the darkness and I saw an airborne limb slap Mallory in the face.

"Oh, my God!" she shrieked, going down on her knees to cover her head and wail.

I was about to say we needed to seek shelter when a bolt of lightening forked through the dark sky and struck the ground. We felt the electricity from it singeing our skin as the current passed through our bodies and a loud boom of thunder shook the earth under our feet. Teri, Tamara and I looked at each other. Mallory was howling and beseeching the heavens.

For several seconds we were caught in an intense electrical storm with snapping currents of electricity that seemed to form an invisible barrier around us.

"He's going to kill us!" Mallory howled in between great claps of thunder as she bowed her head and clasped her hands beneath her chin. She glanced up and shouted, "Y'all better ask for forgiveness of your sins before it's too late!" She recited the first verse of The Lord's Prayer, stopping short when the first fat drops of rain slapped her in the face. Ignoring the rain she bowed her head and hastily finished her recitation.

I looked to the sky, lowering my head quickly when I saw what looked like golf balls zooming toward me at a high rate of speed. They felt like golf balls bouncing off my head.

"Eve, do something!" I heard Tamara squeal above the noise of the wind and thunder. "Make him stop!"

I didn't pick the damn flower anyway, Teri did.

All other sound was drowned out by the noise the hail made slamming down on the tin roof of the house. It produced a horrible racket, like several sledgehammers going at full throttle on the roof. I tried to shield my head as pieces of ice dug into my face and arms and legs, and especially my head. The ice was hitting hard enough to cause skull fractures.

I kept one hand over my face, covering it so

the hail wouldn't strike me in the eye and blind me. I turned to check on the others and saw a stream of blood trailing down Mallory's injured cheek. She was squalling with her hands over her ears. I couldn't be sure if her injury had been caused by the tree limb or hail.

"Get in the house!" I yelled, but they couldn't hear me. Large chunks of hail steadily pounded the tin roof drowning out all other sound. I motioned for them to follow me, then grabbed Mallory's arm and jerked her to her feet, praying that she could get herself together long enough to follow me. She did, squealing every step of the way.

Inside the safety of the house we stood huddled in a tight knot as the fury intensified outside. Jagged forks of lightening constantly lit up the room and thunder shook the old house down to its foundation, causing bricks to crumble around the fireplace. The house creaked, groaned, and swayed, but didn't collapse around our heads. Nor did the hail break through the roof as it threatened to do.

When the wind finally calmed Mallory was cowering in the corner, covering her head and chanting Bible verses. Teri gazed solemnly out a broken window at the flattened flowers, trying desperately to make some sense of what had just happened. Tamara was furiously pacing and glaring at Teri with extreme loathing.

"We told you not to pick another damn flower!" Tamara spat, glaring accusingly at Teri. "You knew he would get mad!"

"How could you be so stupid?" Mallory left her corner to stand in solidarity with Tamara. I thought for a second they might physically attack

Teri.

All of us were holding our heads and feeling like we had been hit repeatedly with a combination of iron pipes and baseball bats, and bleeding from head to toe.

"Are you hurt, Mallory? Did you get this cut on your face from hail or a tree limb?" I wiped the blood from her bruised and swollen face with the hem of my shirt.

"I honestly don't remember."

Each of us had several nasty cuts and numerous scrapes and abrasions. The hail had demanded a quota of skin from each of us.

"I have a splitting headache and I really, really want to go home, take some Tylenol, and crawl in bed and cover my head," Mallory whimpered.

"Me too." Tamara was quick to agree. "If I get out of here alive you better believe I won't ever step foot in these haunted woods again!"

What was the diva doing? Why pondering this latest turn of events, of course. She was convinced that she could solve any problem if she deliberated on it long enough, which was unusual for her. Not the thinking part, the fact that while she spent precious time pondering she was also allowing an unsightly flaw to go unattended on her porcelain skin. I would bet good money that under any other circumstance she would be on her way to her cosmetic surgeon to see if any of her abrasions should require stitches and his skilled hands.

"Why would the child get so angry because we picked a flower?" she asked. "He obsesses over his flowers worse than Lawrence obsesses over his sod."

"Who cares?" Mallory stormed. "The little demon tried to kill us! Why don't you present yourself to him as a human sacrifice, Teri, so he might let the rest of us live?"

"Oh, aren't we the humorous one now? When your caterwauling was the only sound I could heard above the deafening noise of the storm."

"You caused the storm, you stupid bitch!" Mallory screeched. "Don't you dare pick another flower. If you do, so help me, I will personally tell Lawrence about the FedEx man. And the landscaper. And the pool boy!"

All three. Mallory meant business. Her shoulders shook as she dropped her head in her hands. "Who knows what he will do to us next."

Suddenly, I noticed it was quiet outside. I didn't hear the rapid fire hail pounding the tin roof. "Listen y'all. It's stopped." All was quiet as we ventured to the door. "Be careful," I warned, as we stepped onto the porch. "These boards are rotten and you could fall through. We have incurred more than enough injuries for one day."

"Amen to that," Mallory groaned.

We carefully placed one foot in front of the other until we stepped off the porch and back into the amazing array of buttercups.

"Look at that." Tamara whispered, in awe. "Baseball sized hail and not a single flower is broken. How is that even possible?"

Tamara was right. The buttercups stood ramrod straight and tall. I couldn't even find one that had been slightly bent. Where was all the hail that had fallen? The flowers should be under at least a foot or two of ice, but they weren't. They looked exactly as they had when we first saw them. Not one flower was damaged.

"I looked out the window during the storm and the flowers were lying flat on the ground. One thing is for sure," Teri said. "The child is fond of his flowers and doesn't want us picking them. I suggest we abide by his wishes."

"No shit!" Tamara screeched.

"The rest of us were smart enough to figure that out the first time," Mallory was quick to note.

"I had to be sure." Teri dismissed the matter as she waded through the flowers and headed for a narrow path that snaked its way through the cornfield.

"Where does she think she's going now?" Mallory snapped.

"She thinks she's going to the graveyard, of course," Teri called over her shoulder like it was the only logical solution to the problem at hand.

"I am in dire need of medical attention and that demented reject from a witch coven wants to visit a graveyard." Mallory was on the verge of requiring mind numbing medication. "Did you happen to see the gash on my face? The one with the blood gushing from it."

"Please, Mallory." As usual Teri jumped in feet first to make matters worse. "Must you ever embellish? The wound has stopped bleeding and is actually dried and crusty now, most unbecoming by the way."

Mallory stood in the ocean of yellow with her arms akimbo, her eyes blaring, and her bloody upper lip in a pout. "Granted, the flow of blood seems to have subsided for the moment, but there is no way in hell I am going to a graveyard."

"I'm sure you're exaggerating the fact, as you tend to do, that your surface abrasions require medical attention. We all took the same beating from the hail as you did, and we don't require an emergency room visit. Soap and water and a few band-aids would do us all a world of good." Teri rubbed her head gingerly. "Nevertheless, if you insist on walking back to the cabin, we'll meet you back there later."

Mallory ran up to Teri, spun her around, and gritted between clenched teeth, "You know I'm not going back there alone."

Ignoring her fit of temper, Teri smiled. "Then perhaps you should stifle your incessant love of whining and follow us, or find yourself a stump among the flowers to sit on and wait for us to return. Just remember to keep an alert eye to the sky."

"I hope the little boy takes you with him the next time he appears," Mallory gritted through clenched teeth.

"No. You don't." Teri lips curved into a devious grin. "Trust me, I would haunt your ass and absolutely terrify you every day for the remainder of your natural life."

We were about half way through the cornfield when Tamara asked, "Are Mallory and I the only ones concerned that something really strange is going on and we could have died back there? That was some real Stephen King shit. Shouldn't we be concentrating on getting out of here instead of touring a graveyard?"

"I think you're being a tad over dramatic." Teri giggled. "For heavens sake, he's just a child."

"Quite frankly, my dear," Tamara said, stealing a line from my favorite movie, "I don't give a damn. It doesn't matter how old he is, he still could have killed us. That hail wasn't a joke! He may look like a two year old, but in reality he's probably more like two hundred years old."

"Well, he didn't kill us, did he?" Teri replied. "None us doubt that he could if he wanted to, so that was never his intention. He's trying to show us something. Can't you see that? Not kill us. We've just got to figure out what it is. So come on, we're almost there. Don't any of you people read Sylvia Browne?"

Some of the tombstones dated back to the 1700's. Delbert Almond had a large ornate tombstone. There was a smaller tombstone beside his with a sad little angel with outstretched arms perched on top.

"Children died young back then, didn't they? Sarah Louise, aged 11 and Eliza Jane, aged 12," Tamara read, having recovered enough to show some interest in the old cemetery. "Look how sad the little angel is on Louise and Sarah's tombstone."

Mallory was still sulking and sitting in the shade, nervously watching the sky. She wouldn't even glance at a tombstone, but occasionally shot daggers at Teri with her eyes.

"Children died very young back then, Tamara." I was eager to impart some of the knowledge I had learned at the library. "Yellow Fever came through this area in the 1800's and almost wiped out the children."

We walked past the family cemetery with large, elaborate tombstones and then to the slave graveyard with only slate rocks marking their final resting places. We heard, "Whippoorwill, whippoorwill, whippoorwill", and clutched our chests at the unexpected sound.

Whippoorwills sing at night.

"What was that?" Tamara whispered.

I looked into the trees, but didn't see anything. "It was a whippoorwill."

"You've heard about the birds, haven't you, Mallory?" Teri turned to smile at her. "One legend says that a whippoorwill can sense when a soul is departing earth and capture it. Another belief is that if you hear a whippoorwill singing it is a death omen."

"Screw you, Teri."

We were deep in the woods now and it would soon be dusk. "We really should head back," I said. "It will be dark soon and I'm hungry."

We walked back through the family cemetery and I heard Tamara gasp. "Would you look at that?"

I followed her gaze and was completely astonished. On the gravesite beside Delbert Almond lay a single magnificent buttercup.

Tamara hurried to the grave. "Seth Andrew Almond," she read. "Beloved son of Delbert Almond."

"That flower wasn't there a few minutes ago when we stood at his grave, was it?" I remembered Tamara bringing our attention to the sad little angel perched on the headstone and there definitely hadn't been a flower adorning his grave then.

"No, it wasn't," Tamara agreed as every ounce of color drained from her face.

"Why would he put a flower on Delbert Almond's son's grave?" Teri asked, puzzled. Then the candidate for the Dorothea Dix Psychiatric Hospital in Raleigh actually reached out her hand to pick up the flower.

Fortunately, a loud chorus of *Stop!* from the three of us caused her hand to halt less than an inch from the flower, most likely preventing another disaster. Teri looked around and whispered, "He must be here now."

"Here? With us! Not back at the house!" Mallory shrieked, looking like she might leave this world at any minute. Honestly, the girl looked pitiful. Her bruised and swollen face was ghastly pale under the bright red scrapes and her hair stood straight up on her head.

"Looks that way, doesn't it?" Teri smiled, seemingly unconcerned.

"Can we just leave? You can see it's getting dark," Mallory beseeched. "Who knows what he's going to do next. Can we walk on the road this time and not go through the woods?"

"Anything to make you happy, precious." Teri giggled, running over to pinch Mallory's cheeks. "It makes my day to see a smile on your little cherub face with those chubby cheeks."

Mallory slapped her hands away and began walking. "You are a bitch from the bowels of hell, Teri."

Back at the cabin everyone was ravenous, so I poured charcoal on the grill and lit it, my mind drifting in a thousand different directions. Twice I had been caught in violent storms and once had been attacked by a swarm of near fatal bugs. It was entirely possible that I now had a concussion to add to my growing list of injuries.

This latest storm had definitely been the most severe. It seemed the child had tired of playing games and was rather insistent on making a point. What that point was, I didn't have a clue.

Teri was slathering barbecue sauce on chicken when she turned to me. "You know the child is not going to rest until he shows you what he is so determined for you to see."

"Shows me what? Could someone please tell me what it is we are looking for? If not, could we at least change the subject for all of five minutes?"

"I've been thinking," she continued, ignoring my outburst.

"Just what we need. For you to brainstorm."

"Excuse me?"

"Just tell me."

"The child knew we would go inside the house when the storm came. I think whatever he wants us to find is inside the Buttercup House."

"Almond House," I corrected her. "I think he was just pissed about the flowers and that's why he sent the storm."

Mallory and Tamara were slicing potato wedges to fry. Mallory's hands were trembling so badly that I prayed she wouldn't add a chunk of meaty finger to the dish.

"This is not happening." Mallory fretted. "I mean I saw it with my own eyes, but things like this happen in movies not in real life. My head is throbbing. I'm bruised, swollen, and scratched all over and look at you, Eve. You have so many bug bites and stings you look like you have a case of the chicken pox. If we tell anybody the truth they'll have us committed."

"No doubt." Tamara agreed wholeheartedly with her assessment. "I just want to go home and forget this night ever happened. Will you take me home tonight, Eve?"

"Sure."

"Me too." Mallory added.

As was most often the case, Teri was unable to keep her pie hole shut. "You two are totally pathetic."

"I would rather be pathetic and alive than a crazy ass bitch and dead," Mallory was only too happy to inform her.

After the meal Mallory and Tamara piled their belongings back in the truck. Teri had convinced me to spend the night and discover what the child was so determined to show me.

Good Lord, I was tired of hearing that. I turned the switch on Dad's truck, tempted to go home and crawl into my own bed.

Nothing happened.

Oh shit.

I tried again.

"It's dead," I said, anticipating Mallory's screams and covering my ears in advance.

"He's not going to let us leave, is he?" she bellowed, reaching in her bag for her cell phone. "He won't rest until we're dead!" Her shrieks morphed into full-fledged wailing and gnashing of teeth. "Oh my God, there is no signal! How are we going to get home? I am not spending the night in these woods with that evil little monster!"

Checking our phones we found that none of us had a signal. "I guess you will have to walk home." Teri grinned, ignoring Mallory's keening as she calmly opened the door and got out of the truck.

"You know, Teri. You are really starting to get on my fucking nerves!" Mallory snapped, jumping out of the truck. "If we get out of this alive, I hope I never have to see your fake ass again."

"Oh, you'll see me." Teri paused long enough to raise an elegantly arched eyebrow. "Next time your cheap ass wants a free haircut."

Mallory turned several shades of red and raced toward Teri, calling her a few choice words in the process. When she got close enough Teri sidestepped, gave Mallory a little shove, and sent her plunging headfirst into the river.

Tamara and I jumped into the river with her. It was the only to wash the dried blood from our skin and it felt heavenly in the summer heat. I asked the diva to throw us a bar of soap knowing full well she wasn't about to step one pedicured toe in river water. I glanced up once and saw her using bottled water and paper towels to daintily wipe her porcelain skin.

We swam upriver allowing the current to carry us back down and cool Mallory off. "I wonder if we'll make it through this night alive?" she whispered.

"Don't think about it," Tamara advised. "With four of us, hopefully there is safety in numbers."

Mallory was quiet for once as we crawled up the bank and dried off. She might have been bruised, swollen, and terrified as all hell but it didn't stop her from scarfing down two pieces of barbecued chicken and a half dozen potato wedges. "Swimming always makes me hungry," she informed us, noisily licking barbecue sauce from her fingers.

The rest of us nibbled at the remaining food as we listened to the night critters beginning to stir. Minks and muskrats scurried down the riverbank searching for their evening meal of delectable muscles. Fish jumped playfully and plopped back in the river. An owl hooted from the tree above us as something made an awful commotion as it raced through the nearby woods. Hopefully, it was a raccoon. At any rate, we decided it was late and time to turn in.

It was evident that Mallory and Tamara were either really scared or really pissed off as they both presented us with their backs and pretended to sleep.

Teri and I climbed into the bottom bunks. I looked over to find her eyeing me curiously. "You know, Eve, I have noticed a remarkable change in you recently."

"What do you mean?" I snuggled down under the cover to get comfortable.

"I don't know. I can't really put my finger on it, but you seem more relaxed and calmer than you normally are. Actually, you seem nothing like the nervous bundle of energy that I've known for the last fifteen years. You know how stressed you always were. How you bounced from one drama to the next, falling in love with every man who looked sideways at you. It appears that the imbecile falling in love with another woman was the best thing that ever happened to you."

"It probably was the best thing that ever happened to me." I decided to come clean with them. "Visiting a hypnotist didn't hurt either."

"A hypnotist?" Tamara gasped. She and Mallory were wide awake now, sitting up in bed and stunned by the fact that I had kept such a revelation from them. "When did you go to a hypnotist?"

I told them about my visit to Marilyn.

"I noticed the change in you too," Mallory said. "I just assumed it was because you weren't having to deal with Adam's bullshit anymore."

"How much does she charge?" Mallory wanted details. "What is her phone number?"

"$60.00 an hour and worth every penny. She gave me a coupon for a free visit at a Chamber of Commerce meeting. I think you should all go see her, if for nothing more than help dealing with your intense hatred of innocent vegetables. Remind me to give you each one of her cards when we get home."

"*If* we make it home," Mallory worried. "And the Amazing Kreskin couldn't convince me to eat a cucumber."

Teri sat quietly watching me. "Did she hypnotize you to help you get over Adam?"

"She planted a suggestion in my mind. I'm guessing it was about Adam." I had no desire to travel down that road again. "Thankfully, that's all behind me now and I feel like a new woman. A tremendous load has been lifted from my shoulders, thanks to Marilyn. Well, it had until all this weird stuff started happening. If the man of my dreams comes along, fine. If not, that's fine too. Being alone doesn't terrify me anymore."

"Well, right now I am terrified enough for both of us." Mallory flipped over, showing us her ample backside again.

"Well girls, it's almost midnight and my fake ass needs some beauty sleep," Teri said pointedly to Mallory's back. Mallory refused to acknowledge the comment. "Do you want me to turn off the lanterns?"

"Do you want to lose a finger?" Mallory snapped, raising up on one elbow to glare at her.

Surprisingly, Teri only chuckled and left the lanterns on. I had to giggle as I envisioned Mallory tackling Teri to the floor if she tried to extinguish one of the two blazing lanterns that bathed the room in a soft glow.

"What's so funny?" Tamara mumbled sleepily.

"Oh, nothing." I yawned loudly. "Good night."

The next morning I was jerked roughly from a pleasant dream by the most bloodcurdling screams I had ever heard. Immediately, I felt all the breath forced from my lungs in a painful *whoosh* as Mallory landed square on my back and scurried under the cover to lay whimpering and trembling beside me. She proceeded to jerk the cover off me as she pulled it over her head. What now?

I was struggling to force air back into my lungs when I heard Tamara cry, "Sweet Jesus!"

I sat up and gasped, placing a hand over my heart in hopes that it that might still the fluttering in my chest.

Sweet Jesus was right.

Every glass, cup, bowl, pot, and pan in the cabin was filled to overflowing with exquisite buttercups, and scattered on the floor. The makeshift vases sat on the table, on the wood stove, on top of the refrigerator and stove, and on every chair.

I had brought a pack of twenty red plastic disposable cups. They were now filled with stunning arrangements of buttercups and lined in perfect little rows on the windowsills, even the windowsills behind our beds. I shivered, realizing he had to climb over our beds to get to the windowsills.

"He was here last night! With us! Wasn't he?" Mallory's muffled wail rose from under the covers.

"I believe that would be an accurate assessment."

"Why are you so scared?" Teri spun gaily around the room. "I think it was a sweet gesture. Aren't these the most beautiful flowers you ever did see?"

"I thought you didn't care for flowers?" I reminded her.

"Just roses. I love daffodils."

"Honest to God, Teri," Tamara shrieked, barely poking her head out from under the cover. "You are a certifiable nut case. You should be locked up and administered weekly doses of shock therapy."

Teri cut her eyes at Tamara, then turned to face her with her arms crossed over her chest. "Or you could grow a spine."

"So Teri," I asked scared out of my wits, but hoping to diffuse the argument before Tamara and Mallory double teamed her. "In your lofty opinion, what does this mean?"

"Well, that's obvious to anyone with half a brain."

"What about those of us with a whole brain?"

"He likes us," she marveled, waving her arms and spinning around the floral room. "This can only be taken as a grand gesture of affection."

"Affection my ass! He likes us all right!" Mallory yelped. "A near death experience from a head injury was tangible proof of that!"

"And," Teri continued, choosing to ignore Mallory's tirade entirely, "he is also confirming that my observation last night was correct. Whatever he wants to show us has something to do with the Buttercup House, hence the buttercups."

Almond House, but I didn't bother to correct her anymore. "Dare I ask what you think he wants us to do next?"

"Go to the Buttercup House, of course."

"Of course." I slapped a palm to my forehead. "Please forgive my obvious brain fart."

"Well, I'm going home," Mallory finally removed the cover from her head, although she kept her eyes squeezed shut so she wouldn't have to look at the flowers. "You can follow that little fiend straight back to hell if you want to. I am going home. Are you coming with me Tamara?"

"You better believe I am."

"Are you coming, Eve?"

"I guess I'll go back to the Buttercup House, but let me warn you. It's a long walk out and it gets spooky in the cornfields."

"I don't care how long the walk is or how spooky it gets." Mallory leapt from the bed to the door in a single bound. "I'm going home before he turns me into a buttercup. Do you want me to send your dad back for you?" She looked at Teri and snapped, "You can stay here and rot for all I care."

"Ha." Teri chortled. "If anything rots it will be the area between your legs with the vast array of semen it soaks in."

"You're a fine one to talk." Mallory sneered. "At least I'm not married."

Even Teri didn't have a comeback for that.

"Yes," I quickly said, "ask him to ride down later and check on us."

Tamara almost reached out to touch one of the beautiful flowers, thought better of it, and joined Mallory on the stairs.

"If you see the child ask him what he wants," Teri called cheerfully as we followed them outside. "Sylvia Browne says if you see a spirit just ask what it wants and it will show you."

Mallory gave Teri a murderous glare and stormed down the stairs with Tamara close on her heels.

"Do you think they'll be okay?" I worried as they trudged up the long, dusty road.

"Oh yeah, it's you he's after. He knows those two are useless."

"Gee, thanks. I feel much better now."

We fried bacon and eggs and made coffee. Afterward, we sat beside the river sipping the last of the coffee.

An hour later, with great trepidation, we stood before the glorious array of buttercups. I was terrified beyond words that if I stepped a foot into the flowers some horrible act of nature would befall us. Yet, Teri plowed right through the stunning landscape without a care for how many flowers she trampled and went into the house. I had to admire the girl's warped determination.

The house had been magnificent in its day. To the right was, or had once been, a mahogany staircase judging from the decaying remains. I imagined the plantation house as it must have looked in all its glory in the early 1800's, when Teri quickly jerked me out of my reverie.

"Quit woolgathering and get in here and help me look, would you."

Mallory was right about one thing. The girl could be a certifiable bitch at times.

We searched the house for two hours and had gotten filthy in the process. Amazingly, the diva didn't seem to notice, even though she had long strands of cobwebs trailing from her hair and was covered with soot from the fireplaces. We were still searching when I heard a truck pull up outside. It was Dad, finally.

"Did y'all find anything?" he asked, tromping through the flowers. He put his hand on his forehead to shield his eyes from the blazing sun as he gazed across the stunning sea of yellow. "I've lived him 74 years and I ain't never seen nothing like this in all my born days. Buttercups bloom in the spring of the year, not in late July."

Neither had I. "What do you make of all this weirdness, Dad?"

"I would say the child loves his buttercups. I'm sure there's a message here that you girls will have to figure out. Good luck. I would stay and help but I'm headed to the garden to pick cucumbers so Evelyn can put up some dill pickles."

"Did Mallory and Tamara tell you what happened?"

"Yep." Dad shook his head. "Them girls looked about as beat up as the two of you. They both swear they heard something running along beside them and giggling in the cornfield." He motioned toward the buttercups. "I wonder if it's the same little boy I seen almost sixty years ago?"

"I'm sure it is." Teri looked toward the flowers. "We can't find a single clue as to why he's still roaming these woods though."

"You gals gonna snoop around some more or do you want to ride home with me?"

"I'm ready to go home and take a bath. What about you, Teri?"

For the first time, she glanced down at her filthy clothes and cringed. "I guess I do need a bath, and I promised the husband I would be home tonight."

We rode with Dad to the cabin and, amazingly, when he turned the switch on his old truck it roared to life. He helped us load our supplies and I, for one, was eternally grateful to finally be heading home.

Chapter Fifteen

Two weeks later, just as I turned off the lamp and was about to get comfortable, Teri called. "How are you holding up, Eve?"

"Tired. The county contract is whipping my butt."

Don't mention the little boy!
Don't mention the little boy!

"I've been thinking about the little boy," she just *had* to say.

"And?" I knew she wouldn't allow the subject to die a natural death. "You wouldn't bring it up if you didn't have some insane notion swirling around in that salad spinner you call a brain."

"I told the husband I was coming to spend the weekend with you. I thought you might need a break from all the madness."

For Teri, that was a thoughtful gesture. "Great, we'll go shopping and out to eat, and to the movies," I tried, unsuccessfully, to change the subject.

"And to the Buttercup House."

"I'll go if you can convince Tamara and Mallory to go."

It was a joke and we both knew it. Just imagining their reaction if we even suggested they go near the house again sent Teri into a fit of giggles. "I should call Mallory and ask her to go just to piss her off, but I simply cannot tolerate the girl's perpetual whining. It's just you and me, kid."

"I was afraid of that."

"We need to finish this, Eve. I can't stop thinking about why that child hasn't crossed over."

Against my better judgment, Teri arrived at my house Friday night for another trip to the cabin. We went to Sagebrush for a great steak supper and then came home and popped popcorn for an all night movie/gossip fest.

After a delicious breakfast at Mom's the following morning, we hopped into Dad's old beat up river truck. We rode in silence, peering into the cornstalks, until I parked the truck in front of what I now referred to as the Buttercup House.

We waded through the buttercups and took another tour of the house. We searched room to room, upstairs and downstairs and inside every cupboard and cabinet.

Nothing.

Until Teri lifted a loose board on the floor in an upstairs bedroom in hopes of finding a secret hiding place and, much to her surprise, she did. She lifted out an antique porcelain doll. "Look at this, Eve."

The doll was covered with an inch of dust and her clothes were threadbare from years under the floorboards, but she was an exquisite doll. She wore a brown and green calico dress make from silk and lace and a matching hat with feathers. Her long brown hair hung down her back in corkscrew curls. Her painted eyes were blue, and her reds lips were drawn into a smile. I was amazed that mice hadn't chewed her to pieces years ago.

Teri turned the doll over and looked under her dress for any markings. "I'll bet this doll is worth a fortune."

"Probably."

"We'll split the profits." She grinned. "*If* we decide to sell it."

She dropped the doll in her bag and we continued looking for whatever it was the little apparition wanted us to find.

Again, we came up empty handed. I was sure he could speak. He could control the weather and that couldn't be an easy task, so speaking shouldn't be much of a challenge.

Why didn't he just tell us what he wanted?

"So we didn't find anything in the house, when I was sure he wanted us to," Teri begrudgingly admitted. "Maybe we missed something at the graveyard."

Once more we struck out through the dazzling field of buttercups. We had only taken a few steps when we were stopped dead in our tracks by childish laughter floating from the uppermost part of a thirty feet tall pine tree.

"He's here," I whispered.

"Yes," she squealed with delight. "He sounds like he's in a much better mood today."

The girl was touched in the head.

"Lord, please watch over us and keep us safe through whatever happens," I prayed fervently. "Forgive Teri, for she knows not what she does."

"Amen," she mumbled, glaring sideways at me.

We nervously glanced toward the tree, seeing nothing out of the ordinary. I took a few steps to the right and shifted my gaze upward to take another apprehensive look. Only clear blue sky filled with white fluffy clouds floated above us. I knew how rapidly that could change with the child being present and accounted for.

"Teri, do not say or do anything to piss him off," I warned. "You know how temperamental he is."

"I am well aware of his violent mood swings, Eve."

"Ouch!" We were carefully placing our feet between bunches of flowers when the little shit threw something and hit me on my head. "Why does it always have to be me that gets abused? Why can't he terrorize you for a change?"

Again the child giggled, seemingly from the top of the tallest tree.

"He's in a playful mood, Eve," Teri hissed. "Don't ruin it."

"For now. We'll see how long it lasts." Lord knows I was eager to humor the child and not bring his wrath down upon us. I remembered all too well his penchant for wind, lightening, hail, and biting and stinging insects.

"I think he drew our attention to keep us from leaving the house. I just *knew* that whatever he wants us to find is here. Do you think he will he come down and let us see him?"

"I hope not."

"There's only one way to find out." Moving

carefully through the flowers she leaned her hand against the tree. "Can you come down here for a second, hon?" He chose to ignore her, so she turned to me. "What did he throw at you? A pinecone?"

"I'm not sure what it was. Come help me look through the flowers and find it." On our hands and knees we rooted around the ground under the magnificent buttercups until my fingers closed over something. "I found it."

"What is it?"

It was a very old and raggedy handmade book, the pages held together with yarn. "It looks like a journal of some sort." She glanced into the tree. "Is this what you wanted us to find?"

The entire top of the tree shook.

"Apparently he got tired of waiting for us to figure this riddle out and decided to give us a little assistance."

"It's about time." Teri opened the book as gently as possible but the cover fell off and landed at her feet. "These pages are so old and fragile the book's going to crumble if we try to turn them." She held the book a few inches from her nose but couldn't read a word without her reading glasses. "Damn, I wish I could read it. Why does a person have to start going blind the instant they turn forty?"

"Ain't that the gospel?" She handed me the little book and all I could see was a blur as well. "Not being able to see what's in front of you is a royal pain in the ass. I need to have the cataract surgery my eye doctor keeps harping about, but who has the time? Anyway, let's go home and get our glasses."

"We'll be back," she shouted to the top of the tree as we climbed in the truck.

Thankfully, there was no response.

At home, side by side on the couch with my ugly reading glasses situated on my nose, I took a deep breath and read the first page:

Property of Mary Beth Almond, May 12, 1854.

"It's Mary Beth Almond's diary. She was buried in the plot with Delbert Almond, so she must be his wife? What does it say?"

Taking a deep breath, I read from the journal.

As I sit here writing this, I feel obliged to question whether I ever knew my dear husband at all. The man for whom I left my devoted family in Charleston and came to live in these Godforsaken back woods of North Carolina. The man for whom I labored and bore four children. He should thank the Good Lord above for his daughters and be eternally grateful that I chose to spend the remainder of my days here, even after I found out about her."

"Her?" Teri gasped. "Who is her? Keep reading."

May 17, 1854
Today I met her for the first time, the darkie who bore my husbands illegitimate offspring. As much as it pains me to admit, my dear husband has confessed feelings of love for the whore of a slave

woman and her bastard child.

"The little boy is the son of Delbert Almond, Eve. His name is Seth, remember?"

"We should have realized that when the child placed the buttercup on his own grave." I berated myself for having failed to come to such a logical conclusion. "When I saw the little boy my first thought was that one of his parents was white."

The next section of Mary Beth's journal concerned the general running of the plantation. I gently flipped through the pages looking for more about Delbert's son.

June 3, 1854
Unfortunately, yellow fever is sweeping the land. The darkies are dropping like flies. I fear my Almighty God will strike me dead for even thinking such a thought, however, my most fervent prayer is for my husband's whore, Buttercup, to be the very next to drop.

Teri leapt from the couch and did a little dance around the room, clapping and laughing gaily. "Mystery solved. The child's mother was named Buttercup. That explains the daffodils. They probably called them buttercups back in the day, like you do, and it was the only way the child knew to tell us who his mother was. It's probably also the reason you have insisted on calling the flowers buttercups all these years when we kept telling you they were daffodils."

"Do you think it was a sign?"

"Most definitely. You were destined to help

the child. Now, keep reading."

June 8, 1854

 The Good Lord works in mysterious ways. I prayed for the death of my husband's whore and instead he took the life of my husband's precious bastard son, Seth. My poor husband is deranged with grief and his mourning has affected his ability to think rationally. He is insisting that his son be buried in the family cemetery instead of in the slave graveyard, as would be most fitting considering the fact that his mother is a negress. Wherever did he get such a foolhardy notion? Must the entire town be made aware of his sinful ways?

 "Seth died from yellow fever," I murmured sadly.

 "Keep reading."

June 10, 1854

 My husband refused to hear the pleas of myself, or his children. His bastard child was buried in the family plot. Seth was, as he repeatedly informed us, his only son and had he lived would have one day assumed his rightful position as master of Almond House. A slave? Master, indeed!

 The child's mother caused quite a scandal outside the gate, as she wasn't allowed to step foot inside the hallowed grounds of the family cemetery. The reverend's voice could barely be heard above the woman's incessant wailing. Even she insisted that the child be buried in the slave graveyard, as would have been most proper, but my crazed husband would not hear of it.

Teri's microbladed brows were furrowed. "Mary Beth seems like quite the bitch."

June 13, 1854

Buttercup was caught today by my daughter Sarah crying over her son's grave. She had been warned repeatedly not to enter the family cemetery. I instructed the overseer that she was to receive twenty lashes for blatantly ignoring my order. Unfortunately, before the order could be carried out I was informed by my dear grief stricken husband that his whore is again swollen with his child and could not be punished.

"How could they keep the poor woman from her own son's grave?" I felt the pain Buttercup must have endured, knowing she would never be allowed to kneel at her son's grave, in my very soul. How horribly she must have suffered at the hands of her cruel mistress. I remembered the sad green eyes of the little boy as he peeked from behind the towering stalks of corn. "How could anyone be so cold and heartless?"

"Read on and see if the next child was a son or daughter."

June 18, 1854

It would seem my husband's whore has fallen at the hands of folly. She hasn't been able to warm his bed these past three nights, as she has gone missing. Delbert is beside himself with worry and grief. Even having the field hands ignore the cotton fields, which are in a sorry state and in dire need of his attention, to waste time searching for her? Such a simpering, mindless fool my dearly beloved has proven to be.

"What happened to Buttercup?"

I turned to the last page in the journal hoping to find out.

June 25, 1854

My demented husband took his life tonight. I must admit it was for the best. All his foolish ravings concerning his missing whore and the death of his child were proving to be a great embarrassment to his family. He left a note stating that he had neither the will, nor desire to continue living without Buttercup and Seth. A pity. What about his wife and four daughters? Did he care so little for us that we were not worthy of living for? My husband, who must have gone stark raving mad in his final days, had a last request of me. To search until Buttercup's body was found and bury her remains in the family plot along with him and their son.

That will never happen, for his whore's body will never be found.

"Oh, my God!" Teri shrieked. "Mary Beth killed Buttercup."

"And then hid the body where it would never be found."

Teri couldn't be still, pacing the floor in front of the fireplace. "The journal explains it all. Seth wants us to find his mother's body and bury her in the family cemetery. He needs us to grant his father's dying wish."

"There are hundreds of acres of forest around the plantation. How will we find where Buttercup was buried? You know Mary Beth didn't suddenly develop a conscious and place an elaborate tombstone to mark the other woman's final resting place. We could dig every day for the remainder of our lives and never find her gravesite."

"Seth can show us where his mother is. Just like he showed us the journal."

"I guess we should pack some food and go to the cabin, then wait for him to make an appearance." Not that I had suddenly been granted courage, I simply wanted to reunite the child with his mother.

"That's the spirit." Teri couldn't hide a devilish grin. "Pardon the pun."

We put sandwich ham, cheese, mayo, and Diet Pepsi in the cooler. Then we stuffed potato chips, a jar of dill pickles and a box of Little Debbie Raisin Cakes in a bag and hopped in the truck.

"Aren't we just becoming regular sleuths?" Teri giggled as we bounced over the rough river road.

"When either Stephen King, M. Knight Shamalan or Stephen Spielberg make a movie about our adventure it should be called *The Buttercup Girls*."

"Angelina Jolie should play me." Teri suggested her favorite actress."

"Only Julia Roberts could do me justice, but then I do have Lisa Rinna's haircut. Who should play Mallory and Tamara?"

"Definitely Rosie for Tamara."

"And Mallory?"

"Mallory would have to play herself. No one else could do the girl justice."

Chapter Sixteen

We unloaded our bags and cooler and sat down in lawn chairs to gaze across the calm river. It was so quiet and peaceful here, it was hard to believe we were waiting for a ghost to appear and show us where his mother's bones were buried.

Two hours later we were still waiting, and eating. "Why doesn't he show himself?" I was munching on a ham sandwich, chips, and a pickle and peering cautiously into the increasingly dark night filled with flickering lightening bugs. The full moon and thousands of stars reflected and shimmered on the water, casting an eerie glow over us. Crickets chirped and bullfrogs croaked like there was no tomorrow.

Teri forked out the last pickle. "I don't imagine ghosts follow a time schedule, like we do."

I was about to ask for half her pickle when I heard thrashing about in the nearby trees and almost jumped out of my carcass. Teri almost swallowed the four inch pickle whole. "I do wish you would stop using that word."

"What word? Ghost?" While she was busy peeling the wrapper from a raisin cake, her hands were suddenly trembling so badly I imagined she would have to pour the crumbs into her mouth.

"Face it, Eve. Seth is a ghost. So, poltergeist, spook, spirit, haint, specter, apparition, hobgoblin or whatever you want to call him, he needs our help."

"Must you call him Seth?"

"Why not?" Teri threw her hands into the air, sending crumbs flying. "For crying out loud that's his name."

We hadn't heard giggling or been the target of any well aimed projectiles since our arrival, so hopefully the child was otherwise occupied. "It's getting late. Maybe he's asleep."

"More likely out gallivanting with the other spooks, Eve. I don't think they sleep."

"I hope there aren't others. I don't want to be one of those people who *sees dead people*."

"Not to burst your bubble, sweetie, but you already are. Little Seth is about as dead as dead can get and you have definitely seen him."

The thrashing sound was getting closer.

Too close.

Even Teri was looking a little green around the gills. "It's probably just an animal."

"That's what I thought in the cornfields."

"Oh. Right." She took a quick glance toward the woods and pulled the last raisin cake out of the box. "It gets really dark in these woods at night, doesn't it?"

The noises around us seemed amplified. The jumping fish sounded like whales splashing in the river. The minks and beavers climbing up the riverbank sounded like Brahma Bull's pawing the earth. The chorus of insects blended to produce a high pitched steady drone. Then, suddenly, the thrashing stopped, only a few feet from our campsite. All was quiet for the longest time.

It was 2:00am and we were still sitting and trembling. We would have been eating if there was so much as a crumb left. "I can't sit here all night waiting for that little hellion to make an appearance." Teri stood, brushing the crumbs from her shirt and shorts with jittery hands.

Could it be? Was the imperturbable Teri unnerved? I knew the answer was yes when she said, "Let's go home. Apparently, Seth had other plans tonight. He's probably romping through the cornfield with the other sprites."

She was scared shitless. So was I. It took us less than a minute to jump in the truck and head up the river road. Neither of us spoke until we were past the cornfields.

Trust me, it's quite challenging to drive with your eyes closed.

Teri's waning courage returned when we were past the gate. "What's up with Seth? He showed us where the journal was, so why has he decided to be disagreeable now. Why wouldn't he show us where his mother is buried if he expects us to help him? I have a life you know."

"He doesn't, so it's probably not a big deal to him," I reminded her. "What if he doesn't know where her body is?"

"I hadn't thought of that. You're absolute right. Duh!" Teri slapped her hand against her forehead. "If he knew where she was, he would be with her. That's why he needs you. To find where his mother is buried. We're back to square one again."

Then I had an epiphany. "I wonder if Marilyn could tell us where she's buried?"

"That's a great idea. When can you go see her?"

On Monday morning, after leaving instructions with my crew, I set out for an appointment with Marilyn. I was happily munching a Twix and sipping Diet Pepsi when Kelly Clarkson's song *Because Of You* came on the radio. That song reminded me of Adam. *"Because of you I stay on the safe side so I don't get hurt"*. So true. Tell it like it is, girlfriend. It would be a long, long time before I put my heart back on the chopping block to be callously shredded into bite sized pieces again, if ever.

"I desperately need your help," I said to Marilyn as I sank down into the plush rocking chair. "I'm in a bit of a quandary."

"I see." She perched on the edge of her chair with a far away look in her eyes. "Tell me about this quandary and how I can help."

"Well, there was this lady, a slave lady, who lived on a cotton plantation called the Almond House."

"Buttercup," she said looking at something or someone over my shoulder.

"That's right." Sylvia Browne definitely had some competition with this woman. "Her name was Buttercup. I pulled the little threadbare doll out of a bag and handed it to her."

Her eyes immediately rolled back in her head. "Buttercup was Seth's mother. The child has been searching for his mother for well over a century. He refuses to cross over without her."

"Can you tell me how Buttercup died?"

Her eyes took on a distressed gaze before she closed them and leaned back in her chair. Her pinched lips turned white as a low moan escaped. "She was poisoned. It was a horrible, painful death and she suffered tremendously. She was spitting up blood. Her body was on fire and the searing pain in her stomach was excruciating. The pain seared through her stomach. She was terrified that it would reach her unborn child."

Marilyn clutched the doll to her breast as tears coursed down her cheeks. "Buttercup sees the woman who poisoned her sitting in the dark corner, smiling. She pleads for help. She pleads for the life of her child. She pleads for mercy. She pleads for Delbert. The woman only laughs and says, *"Delbert cannot help you now. Rot in hell with your bastard children."*

It took a few minutes for Marilyn's eyes to focus and her expression to return to normal. "The woman in the corner was evil."

"Very much so."

"She knew nothing about running a plantation that size. Within three years after her husband's death she was penniless. She died a lonely, miserable old woman filled with hatred. Even her own children turned against her in the end."

"Where did she bury Buttercup?"

She glanced over my shoulder, presumably at her spirit guide. "She lies beneath a buckeye tree."

"A buckeye tree?" I had never heard of such a tree. *Of course, it would be a tree I had never heard of.* I wouldn't have expected anything less.

"A nut from the buckeye tree is thought to be a good luck charm. In those days, if you carried a buckeye in your pocket it was considered to bring you good luck. Some older people still search for buckeye trees and carry the nuts in their pockets. The same way you would carry a rabbit's foot today."

"The tree didn't bring Buttercup much luck, did it?"

"The tree wasn't there when Buttercup was buried. She carried a buckeye in her pocket for luck, as did most all slaves of her time. She was buried at the top of a hill in bright sunlight and the buckeye sprouted in the moist earth, took root, and grew into a tall tree shading her final resting place.

"You mean to tell me the tree that will lead us to where she is buried grew from a nut that she carried in her pocket when she was murdered?"

"Yes," she answered solemnly.

"Where is the tree?"

"I see a tall tree on top of a high hill in bright sunlight. There is moving water in the background. That's all I can tell you."

"A river?"

"Yes."

"We think Seth wants us to dig up his mother's remains and bury her in the family cemetery with him and his father."

"That would be impossible to accomplish." She shook her head sadly.

"Why?" I cried. "We have to bury him with

his mother or he will haunt me forever."

"The roots of the tree are wrapped around her bones, or what is left of them. They would most likely be turned to dust by now."

"I hadn't thought of that."

Leaning back in her seat, Marilyn eyed me closely. "You have to dig up the child's remains and bury him beneath the buckeye tree. He can't find his mother. That's why he searches night after night, year after year. That is why he came to you for help. Seth sees you as a kindred spirit."

"Because at the ripe old age of fifty five I have begun seeing dead people."

She nodded and took my hands in hers. "If you bury Seth under the tree with his mother, they will both rest in peace."

"We just have to find the tree."

She nodded. "You just have to find the tree."

I got up to leave, but decided that I couldn't without asking one more question. "I know this is quite a departure from the subject, but how are Adam and Chia doing?"

She picked up her deck of cards and shuffled them. "Not good I'm afraid. The love he felt for her is almost completely gone. He realizes that she never really loved him, only what he was capable of giving her, and give to her he did. He is on the verge of filing bankruptcy. Their marriage is over."

"Maybe he will meet someone else and be happy again."

"He will never be happy again. In the next few months he will be diagnosed with a serious health issue." She shook her head sadly. "I told you once before that he would suffer as you were suffering, only worse. That is now coming to pass."

She *had* told me that. I actually felt sorry for Adam if he was destined to suffer worse than I had.

When I was settled in the car, I called Teri. "Buttercup is buried under a buckeye tree."

"A what tree?"

"A buckeye tree. Buttercup had a buckeye in her pocket, for luck. It sprouted and grew into a tall tree that now shades her grave. Have you ever heard anything so unbelievable?" She was speechless, so I guessed she hadn't. "We just have to find the tree. I'll go online when I get home and find a picture of one to send to you."

"Did she tell you anything about how Buttercup died?"

"Buttercup was poisoned and suffered a horribly painful death at the hands of Mary Beth Almond. The demented hag actually sat in the corner smiling, and had the nerve to tell Buttercup and her bastard children to rot in hell. Can you believe what a monster she was?"

"The evil, conniving bitch."

"Marilyn agreed that Mary Beth was evil, but the old crone got hers in the end. She couldn't run the plantation and within three years of Delbert's death she was penniless and died alone and miserable."

"Serves her right. What else?"

"Adam is miserable, and Chia has left him."

Teri laughed. "That made your day, didn't it?"

"Not really. Surprisingly, I only feel pity for Adam now. It was sort of ominous the way she said it, like his ship was headed for some stormy seas."

"Serves the buffoon right."

"Can you believe that I don't care what happens to him now, one way or the other? It's like he was a part of my life ten years ago, instead of a few months ago. It used to take me *years* to get over a man."

"Marilyn is a miracle worker." Teri stated the obvious. "She certainly turned your life around for the better. I have a head to shampoo. I'll call you tonight."

"Bye."

At home, I went online in search of information about buckeye trees. My first several finds were about trees grown in Ohio. That wasn't what I was looking for. I scrolled down to the bottom of the page and found a map. Yellow buckeyes were found in zones 4 and 8. So, I was looking for a Yellow Buckeye Tree.

The search engine produced results for the National Forestry Service that had listings for everything from how to grow a tree, to Magic Mojo websites that showed you how to cast a love spell. Good thing I hadn't found *that* website months earlier.

One website claimed the buckeye had beneficial purposes for arthritis, rheumatism, and male vigor. The wood had a variety of uses as well. Coffins and artificial limbs had once been made from the wood and, it was true, they were considered to be a good luck charm. I printed out a picture of the tree and called Teri with the information.

"I'll be over Friday when I get off work." I could barely hear her above the hair dryer blasting in the background. "Seth will be elated when we lead him to his mother."

I can hardly wait."

Teri arrived at my house the following Friday night around midnight. "The husband thinks you and I are having a lesbian affair."

"Oh, good grief. What on earth makes the decrepit soul think that?"

"Because I've been spending so much time with you lately. You know how jealous he is of our friendship. Why the man has taken to whining on a daily basis of how upsetting it is that I would rather be with you than him. I swear him and Mallory are like two peas in a pod with their incessant whining.

"Why didn't you just tell him the truth about Seth?"

"Are you crazy?" She was changing into her pajamas but paused long enough to glare at me. "He could divorce me on grounds of insanity and sometimes I think he's just looking for a reason."

I couldn't help but laugh. "Even if he didn't love you madly, which he does, he would never divorce you. I get the feeling he is slightly intimidated by you."

Adjusting the top over her triple D's, she ginned. "If he isn't, he damn well should be."

"It's late and I'm totally exhausted. Are you ready for bed?" I stood provocatively at the foot of the bed and simpered, "Perhaps you should sleep in Levi's bed since you evidently have the hots for me and might not be able to control your fevered lust."

"Honey, if I was interested in you, or any other female, I wouldn't have paid the doctor a small fortune to take a scalpel to my pecker."

I couldn't help but send her a sexy, teasing wink. "Here I thought I might get a little action tonight after such a long dry spell."

Chapter Seventeen

The following morning, we went in search of my Dad, and breakfast. "Do you know what a buckeye is?" I took a mouth watering bite of a country ham biscuit, washing it down with a cup of coffee that was strong enough to hop out of the cup and do a jig across the floor.

Mom and her sister had gone on their annual bus tour to Branson, so Dad and the rest of us were left to fend for ourselves. Fortunately, she had made a couple pans of biscuits and froze them before she left.

"Sure I do. It's a nut from the buckeye tree. As a matter of fact, I have some in a box in the bedroom closet. My daddy used to always carry one in his pocket when I was little. He said they brought him good luck."

"Do you know where a buckeye tree is?" Teri was devouring her second biscuit.

"There's one close to Rocky River. That's the only one in the area that I know of. It's on top of a hill beside the river. I ain't been to it in probably ten years. The older I get the harder it is for me to climb that hill. I guess the tree is still standing though."

It has to be. "Where is it, Dad?"

"You know that field where I plant my watermelons and cantaloupes every year?"

"Yes." The thought triggered a memory of watermelon juice running down my chin onto my shirt, and me spitting the seeds at my sister.

"The tree is on top of that hill behind the watermelon patch. Why? You girls need some luck?"

"We need to bury someone." I proceeded to fill him in on everything that had happened.

"After you bury the child with his mother, pick us a ripe watermelon." Dad didn't seem at all disturbed by my startling revelations. "Bring me a couple of buckeyes for luck, if you find any."

We hopped in the old river truck and rode down to the watermelon patch bursting with ripe watermelons and cantaloupes. "Don't point at the watermelons. Dad says they will fall off the vine if you point at them."

"Now that is just superstitious nonsense and you know it. You know how much I love your dad, but where in the world does he get his weird sayings?"

I smiled to myself as I walked ahead of her, knowing she was pointing at every watermelon she passed. "He also says that if you fish on Sunday you will catch the devil."

We made the long trek up the steep hill sweating profusely. It was almost straight uphill and my thighs were on fire. I sat down and leaned against a tree, guzzling tepid water from a bottle. "How much farther is it?"

"I think we're almost there," our team cheerleader answered. "Come on, you can do it."

I spotted a tree that looked identical to the one in the picture. It was about sixty feet tall with rough patches of flaking bark. The tree was heavy with nuts that hadn't fallen yet. "This is it." I stretched out on the sandy dirt under the tree. "Let's take a nap under the shade of Buttercup's tree."

"You go to sleep if you want to. I'm just going to rest." Teri was peering anxiously into the tree. "You know how helpful Seth tries to be. He might decide we need a shovel and toss one down."

"Good point," I agreed, coming fully awake.

"I guess now we dig up Seth's remains and bring them here."

Okay, I was almost certain that digging up someone's grave wasn't exactly a legal thing to do. Apparently grave robbing was about to be added to my growing list of law breaking activities. "You know we could get in serious trouble for disturbing someone's final resting place."

"Like I keep reminding you, Eve. Since when has getting in trouble concerned either of us?"

An hour later we were standing over Seth's grave. I was sweating in rivulets, as was the diva, but we continued to dig. With each shovel of dirt I tossed out the hole became deeper and the burning ache in my arms intensified. "How deep did they bury people back then?" We had dug at least four feet and my arms were screaming with pain. I would be in bed for a week after this. "Aren't your arms hurting, Teri?"

"I have no idea, I can't feel them anymore. What I do know is that I have never been this tired in my life. It can't be much deeper."

Teri had sweated until her mascara ran in ugly black streaks down her cheeks and her hair, that she had taken such pains with that morning, was plastered to her head. Even her high perky boobs looked limp and defeated.

I was so exhausted from digging I could have collapsed on the spot and slept in the hole in the cold, damp earth until morning. I had to rest. I sat on the ground and leaned my head against the hard dirt wall.

"Maybe we should come back tomorrow and finish," Teri said just as her shovel struck what sounded like wood.

With a sudden burst of energy I helped her uncover a tiny mahogany, elaborately carved coffin. It was at that moment I realized I was standing on a coffin and, becoming surprising agile for a fifty five year old woman, I shinnied out of the hole.

"Can you lift the coffin out?" I peered into the hole and asked from a safe distance away.

"Hell no!" the diva shrieked. "Get your ass down here and help me!"

I swallowed several sharp comments concerning her bitchiness and climbed back into the grave, helping her lift the tiny wooden coffin out. Once it was safely on the ground we went to the truck to get a Diet Pepsi from the cooler. I took a sip and glanced over at Teri. Never once in fifteen years had I seen the girl so disheveled.

Our hands were a mass of ugly red blisters and our drenched clothes were glued to our bodies and caked with mud. Teri was missing four of her French manicured acrylic nails. While we were as filthy as either of us had ever been, we had finished phase one.

"Okay, the hard part is over." Teri tilted her soda for the last swallow.

"How did you come to that conclusion when we still have another hole to dig?"

"Oh, yeah." Lying back in the truck bed, she laid a limp hand across her forehead. "I forgot about that."

After a five-minute break we lifted the coffin into the back of the truck.

"Don't you want to see what's inside?" Teri caressed the top of the coffin just itching to lift the lid. "Haven't you always wanted to know if bones really turn to dust?"

"Nope. I most certainly have not. Don't even start with that nonsense or I'm dumping your ass out right here and heading home."

"You big pussy."

I had no desire whatsoever to view the contents of the coffin. What person of mediocre intelligence would? "My best guess would be that the coffin is filled with buttercups. I'm warning you, Teri. If you lift the lid on that coffin you will walk home."

Thankfully, for once, she let it rest and climbed in the truck.

"I'm starving, Eve. My hands have blisters on top of blisters and I'm exhausted. Let's go to lunch at a nice restaurant, go to a movie, and then go shopping for a little retail therapy. We can come back tomorrow and finish this."

My sentiments exactly. "Sounds good to me."

We looked out the back truck window at the

tiny coffin, then Teri cut her eyes at me. "Do we carry the coffin with us?"

"I hadn't thought of that." For some reason I didn't think Seth would be overjoyed if we carried his coffin through the cornfields and past the gate. Still, we couldn't leave it sitting out in the open for a hunter or fisherman to find. "Come on, we can hide it in the trees, I doubt anyone will come to the graveyard today."

After hiding the little coffin I remembered that Dad asked me to bring him a watermelon. "Let's go eat a watermelon. That should satisfy the hunger pangs for a while."

"It will be hot," the diva whined, doing her best Mallory impression. "I like my watermelon already sliced, seeded, and ice cold."

"Good luck finding that down here."

At the watermelon patch I split a large Moonstar on the ground and dug out a juicy chunk. She was right it was hot, but delicious. When her head was turned I spit a mouthful of seeds at her.

"You truly are one nasty old cow," she cried. "Now that you have finally remembered your childhood, it doesn't take much to make you revert back to it."

"Here, have half." I laughed.

"I am not eating that," she insisted, crossing her arms over her chest with her full lips in a pout.

"Suit yourself." Watermelon juice dribbled down my chin and onto my shirt as I devoured half of the sweet melon. "I wish I had a salt shaker. Watermelon is so much better with salt on it."

Teri nodded toward my shirt with disgust. "Would you just look at what you are doing to your shirt?"

"Teri, honey," I replied, motioning toward her bulging chest, "take a gander at your own shirt."

She glanced down at her filthy clothes for the first time and appeared quite faint. "If anyone saw me looking like this I would be run out of Charlotte on the light rail. Here, hand me the watermelon so I can eat the damn thing and we can go home."

She dug into the watermelon like it was a slice of prime rib, daintily wiping her mouth with the hem of her grimy shirt.

After a fun evening of shopping, although it was as hot as forty hells outside and we had both sweated like vegetable pickers, we arrived home around 9:00, eager to put on some thin pajamas and get comfortable.

We went into the bedroom to lay out our night clothes when Teri noticed the porcelain doll from the Almond House perched on the dresser.

She picked up the doll as I headed for the shower.

As I stepped out of the shower a few minutes later the overhead bathroom light flickered and made a strange buzzing, staticky sound. The sound grew louder and louder, freaking me out to the point that I moved to the side so I wouldn't be standing under it if it took a notion to explode. A wet body and electricity is never a winning combination. What the heck was up with the lights anyway? There must be a storm in the area.

"Hey," Teri called from the living room. "Why are your lights flickering?"

"I have no idea." I grabbed a plush towel from the shelf, suddenly chilled to the bone. Icy cold air, much colder than what normally came from the vents, swirled around my feet and rushed under the towel. Goosebumps popped up all over my body as I clutched the terrycloth to my breasts.

Drying off, I slipped into my pajamas and reached for the doorknob, intending to make an adjustment in the thermostat setting. *Odd.* The temperature felt completely normal in the hallway. "Your turn for the..." I stopped in mid sentence and commenced to screaming like a banshee when the light bulb in the bathroom burst, shattering glass everywhere.

"What was that noise?" Teri called. "Are you okay, Eve?"

"I'm fine." Pulling the door open I stood still for a few minutes, trying to persuade my heart to return to its normal rhythm when it insisted on taking its own sweet time. "The light bulb in the bathroom exploded."

She joined me and glanced from my ashen face to the glass strewn across the floor. "There must have been a short and that's why the lights flickered."

"I suppose."

Before I could bat an eye she was back with a broom and dustpan. "Put some shoes on while I sweep this glass up before one of us gets cut."

Instead of putting shoes on I went to the sofa and curled under a blanket, channel surfing from one paranormal episode to the next before I discovered that Teri had left it on the SyFy channel. I quickly powered the TV off. "Teri, do you want a sandwich or pizza?"

"Let's call Pizza Hut and order a Super Supreme and hot wings. I'll be out in a minute."

"Okay." Dialing the number with trembling fingers I tried to relax. Needless to say, this weekend had been one for the books, so far.

The pizza arrived before Teri finished her nightly beauty routine of lotions and facial peels and such. Both ravenous, we killed a large pizza, hot wings, and breadsticks in very short order. We totally convinced ourselves that we had made it a healthy dinner choice by drinking water with lemon instead of sweet tea or sugary soda.

With our bellies full, and exhausted from a very trying day, we crawled into bed around midnight. Teri had texted Lawrence to see if he was still awake and he called just as she was settling in.

Rolling to her side, I heard her whispering sweet nothings to him as I snuggled down in my comfortable bed. Just as I was about to shut my eyes, I glanced at the bureau and noticed the doll was now sitting on top of my jewelry box. Why would Teri move it? I would ask her when she got off the phone.

I must have dozed off because the sound of the TV woke me some time later. Teri was snoring softly beside me. Why in the world did she go to bed and leave the TV in the family room on? She must have gotten thirsty after I went to sleep.
The poor girl had suffered with insomnia for as long as I could remember.

As I listened, I realized the TV was on MTV and blasting a rap song. How was Teri sleeping when the volume was set to the highest level?

"Teri." I shook her shoulder until she stopped snoring. "Why did you leave the TV on?"

"Go back to sleep. I didn't turn the TV on."

"Well somebody did." She was snoring before I even finished the sentence. Tossing back the covers I trudged down the hallway into the living room. As I did I was greeted by the distinct smell of apple pie baking.

Huh?

Grabbing the remote I pushed the power button and rushed into the kitchen to see if Teri had left the oven on during her Betty Crocker moment. Nope. There was no sign of a freshly baked pie in the oven, on the counter, or in the fridge, but both doors on my side by side refrigerator were standing wide open and a bottles of ketchup, mustard, soy sauce, and honey were dripping to the floor.

What in the world was wrong with Teri?

Was the girl crazy as hell and had somehow kept it a secret all these years?

This was really weird.

To this day, I will swear that when I turned to go back to bed I saw a black, shadowy figure past by the door. Now I am not prone to hallucinations, never have been, but I know what I saw. The gruesome sight chilled me to the marrow of my bones. "Teri!" I screamed. When she didn't immediately answer I took to wailing, "Teri! Teri! Teri! Teri!" until I finally heard her feet hit the floor running.

Sliding to a halt in the kitchen doorway she looked me up and down to make sure I wasn't bleeding or injured. When she saw that I suffered no visible wounds, she shrieked, "What's wrong with you, Eve! You almost gave me a heart attack. You know I'm too old for this shit."

"Something strange is going on in this house."

Pulling a chair out from the table she dropped down on it, looking as pale as a ghost. "Such as?"

"When I woke up the TV was on, full blast. When I came to turn it off I smelled apple pie baking and came in here to find the refrigerator doors standing open, and then I saw… something."

"What?"

Raking trembling hands through my hair, I wrapped my arms around my waist, chilled to the bone. "A black shadowy figure floated past the door."

"Are you sure you didn't have a bad dream?" She glanced toward the door. "I don't smell apple pie."

"It wasn't a dream, Teri." How could she not smell the pie? The delicious aroma of cinnamon and apples filled the house with a divine smell.

She took my hand. "Let's go back to bed. I think we both need a good night's sleep."

For someone who swears to only sleep a few hours at night, Teri was out like a light.

I lay awake for the longest time and had just gotten to the drowsy stage when I heard… crying, a woman softly crying, in the basement.

The sound of her crying was as plain as day, as though she was in the room with me. She might as well have been since only a few boards and some insulation separated us. She was in the part of the basement directly under me.

When she stopped crying she sang a sad lament about someone who had loved and lost, until she choked up again. When her crying ceased, she gathered herself and sang the same lyrics over and over. *Sweet Jesus.* I was going crazy.

I closed my eyes, determined to drown out the ominous sound. With the house finally quiet I relaxed into the mattress and was about to doze off.

When I heard footsteps.

Heavy footsteps.

Running… down… the… hall.

Toward my room.

Holy shit!

The sound of the crying woman's footfalls ended right beside my bed. She was towering over me. I could feel her presence.

Pulling the covers over my head, I squeezed my eyes shut, praying harder than I have ever prayed in my entire life.

I smelled her. She had the pervasive odor of old, damp dirt.

Graveyard dirt.

I scooted back against Teri as far as I could and held my breath, trembling until my teeth chattered as I waited for her to grab me.

I lay there for what seemed like hours, until I heard the steady creaking of the rocking chair in the corner.

Creak. Creak. Creak.

Nothing happened, just the endless sound of her rocking in the corner.

I must have dozed off to the sound of rocking, for when I opened my eyes and peeked out from under the covers the sky was just beginning to lighten. I found the courage to remove the cover from my head, crying out and covering my mouth with both hands when I glanced around the room.

My house was definitely haunted.

Every bra, pair of panties, nightgown, and pajamas I owned had been flung from the drawers and strewn randomly around the room. The closet door was open and my clothes and shoes were piled on top of us and all across the floor. My necklaces from the jewelry box hung on the corners of furniture, on the doorknobs, on the lamp, from curtain rods, and on the light fixture.

Last night when I went to bed the doll was sitting on my jewelry box. Now the top was open and a strand of pearls hung over the edge. Where was the doll?

Did I really want to know?

I found the courage to look around the room. The doll was sitting in the rocking chair, smiling at me.

Not only smiling, but showing teeth.

On a painted smile.

I opened my mouth for a scream to end all screams when my attention was drawn to the mirror. A mirror that suddenly had a smoky dark haze to it. I buried deeper under the covers as an eerie white fog began to seep out of the mirror, curling in wispy strands that reached toward me. Just as I put a hand on Teri's shoulder to wake her so she could see this, the haze began taking shape until a figure appeared.

It was a woman.

A woman wearing a black, long sleeved, high necked, very old fashioned dress. The type of dress women wore in the 1800's.

Widow's weeds.

Her hair was drawn back in a severe knot. My first impression was that she radiated pure evil. I saw it clearly in her hate filled eyes. I instinctively knew the woman in the mirror was Mary Beth Almond.

She opened her mouth and her voice was tinny, like she was speaking from inside a closed barrel. Pointing her finger at me, her eyes cut through me as she snarled, "If you help the little bastard, you will live to regret it."

I heard the mirror crack, then, she was gone.

I lay there, quiet as a mouse and trembling uncontrollably. I should go to the medicine cabinet and grab a bottle of Bayer Aspirin and keep it close by, for I was surely on the verge of a myocardial infarction.

Chapter Eighteen

I was bawling like a baby when Teri woke up. I'm not usually such a wuss, but all this supernatural shit was scaring the bejesus out of me. The doll was smiling from the rocking chair, my bedroom looked like a tornado had spun through it, my dresser mirror had thousands of tiny spiderweb cracks, and I was convinced that I would be forced to move out of my newly haunted house to escape the madness.

"What happened?" Teri finally opened her eyes and gazed around the room.

"It's been like this for hours." She was quiet as I relayed the events of the night to her.

Teri cut her eyes at the doll and leaned toward me to whisper. "The doll is haunted, Eve. We have to get rid of it."

Wiping the tears from my cheeks, I shook my head. "I'm not touching that hideous thing."

The home phone rang on the bedside table. I looked at it curiously, surprised that the cord hadn't been cut during the ghostly shenanigans. "Hello."

"Hello, Eve?"

I knew that voice. "Yes."

"Eve, this is Marilyn. How are you?"

"Marilyn?" I couldn't believe she was

calling me.

"I didn't sleep a wink last night, Eve."

"That makes two of us."

"I kept have vivid dreams about you and what was going on in your house, you poor thing."

Thank God I had a psychic who cared.

"What can I do, Marilyn? Mary Beth warned me that if I helped Seth I would regret it, but I can't go through another night like last night."

"Of course you can't, dear," she commiserated. "You must get rid of the doll." I could tell by her tone that she meant business. "To that end, you must do *exactly* what I am about to tell you."

"Okay."

"Mary Beth's spirit is in the doll you brought from the Almond House."

"I knew it." *Oh, dear God!* "She's going to kill me."

"Not if you do as I say."

My words had been more or less a figure of speech, whereas Marilyn's sounded deadly serious.

"Mary Beth can only harm you through the doll, Eve. You must get it out of your house or she will haunt you until…"

"Until what," I whispered.

"Until something bad happens." She was silent for a few minutes, allowing her words to sink in. "You are going to put the doll where she can't harm anyone else."

"Just tell me what to do and I'll do it."

"Do you have a fireproof metal box large enough to hold the doll?"

"Yes. I keep my important papers in one in

the closet.

"Do you have a roll of duct tape?"

"In my tool drawer."

"Here is what I want you to do. Put the doll in the strong box and tape the box shut with an entire roll of duct tape, use two rolls if you have it."

"Then what?"

"Go to your Dad's house and ask him for a chain and lock, he has these in his tool shed."

She even knew my Dad and the contents of his tool shed. "Will that keep her contained?"

"For a couple hundred years."

I supposed that would have to do.

"After you loop the chain over all four sides, twice, I want you to lock the chain securely. When these instructions have been followed to the letter, take the box to the Almond House and toss it in the old well in the back yard. There is a cement slab over the top of the well and it will be heavy to lift, but both of you together can slide it over enough to toss the container inside."

I looked over at Teri who was riveted to every word. "We can do it," she mouthed.

"Consider it done. Thank you for calling, Marilyn. I was at my wits end," I whispered sincerely. "I don't know what we would do without you."

"Glad to help, sweetie. You have my number on your caller ID. Call me if you need me. Oh, and Eve?"

"Yes."

"Mary Beth will not go into the container willingly." Then she hung up.

I looked at the doll with the smiling face,

then at Teri who had a troubled frown wrinkling her brow.

She leaned over and whispered, "Let's go make a pot of coffee. We need a plan."

In the kitchen we fried bacon and scrambled eggs. We were both afraid to speak above a whisper, afraid the doll would hear. "Do you think you can get her into the box, Teri?"

"I'll try my best, but I can't make any promises. I wonder how much power she has?"

"I wonder too, because she stood over me for the longest time last night, but didn't attempt to harm me physically, while mentally she had me ready to jump out an upstairs window."

Sliding the last dish into the dishwasher, Teri turned to me with her hands on her hips. "Let's get dressed and go to your Dad's for the needed supplies, and get this over with."

When we returned to my bedroom the doll was still perched on the rocking chair. "Maybe her powers don't work in the daytime," Teri whispered, hopefully.

"Don't get your hopes up. Marilyn said she wouldn't go willingly into the box."

"Oh, yeah." Taking a deep breath Teri went to stand in front of the chair. "Here goes nothing." Reaching for the doll, she grabbed it just above the wrist on her right hand and instantly swung it across the room, screeching, "The damn thing has a pulse! I felt it beating!"

How could that be?

We turned to see where the doll had landed. Apparently her head had banged against the bureau, for a crack was now snaking from her forehead, through her left eye, and down to her chin, turning her smile into a hideous frown. "I'll get the broom, maybe we can shove it into the box."

"Good idea."

Teri hadn't moved a muscle when I returned. "You try it this time, Eve."

Those were the last words I wanted to hear. Digging deep for any last remnants of courage, I bent toward the malevolent doll and swung the broom. When I did, the room was filled with a fierce wind. Clothes from the floor swirled around our heads, I had earrings in my mouth, necklaces wrapped around my neck, high heeled shoes slammed into my stomach, a curtain rod flew past me, picture frames crashed to the floor and the bed comforter wrapped around me from head to toe like a mummy. "Help!" I screamed. "Teri, help!"

I felt her tugging on the comforter, at least I hoped it was her. She shoved me to the floor and unrolled me out of the bedcovering, shouting above the noise of the ferocious wind, "You're okay, Eve. Stop screaming."

"We can't get rid of it," I cried. "Mary Beth won't let us."

Teri was suddenly filled with renewed determination. "That bitch is going in the box." She searched through the rubble until she found the strong box, duct tape, and chain. "Where's the key to the lock?"

"In my pocket."

"Give it to me." She held out her hand. "I'm going to show this bitch who she's fucking with."

I had a sinking feeling the poor girl was

about to get schooled.

Was I ever right.

No sooner had she reached for the sinister entity than we heard a whooshing sound as all the air was sucked from the room. I clutched at my throat. I couldn't even gasp. There was no air to gasp. Teri and I glared at each other with bulging eyes and raced for the door. It was jammed. We beat, kicked, and screamed silent screams of torment. We would die in this room and be trapped with an evil spirit.

The window!

On the verge of blacking out, I rushed to the side window and raised it effortlessly, filling my lungs with the sweet, sweet air. Teri was beside me. "What are we going to do, Eve?" she wheezed.

"I wish I knew." I looked toward the ground. "It's a long way down."

Teri followed my gaze and shook her head, deciding against that option. "Think hard, I don't intend to spend the night locked in a room with that fiend."

A thought suddenly occurred to me. "I keep a loaded revolver under the mattress, in case a burglar shows up. Would that cause her any damage?"

"It can't hurt to try."

I watched the doll closely while Teri reached under the mattress and pulled out the gun. "Open the strong box and be ready, on the off chance it works."

Sliding to the floor, I held the metal box in my hands, waiting.

Teri took dead aim for the doll and pulled

the trigger. Instead of shattering the doll as we had hoped, the bullet grazed her porcelain face and sent her flipping through the air. I lunged to catch her, falling face down in the carpet. Amazingly, Teri was able to grab the box and hold it directly under the doll. By some miracle, the doll fell in the box and Teri clamped it shut. "Grab the tape, Eve!"

I wrapped the box over and over and over on all sides until I had used two rolls.

"Now get the chain." Teri was wild eyed and breathing heavily. She drew the chain around the box on all sides, twice, and snapped the lock into place. We sat back against the side of the bed trying to catch our breath as the doll pounded furiously inside the box.

Teri dusted her hands and hefted the box. "Your old malicious ass is about to take a two hundred year nap."

We wasted no time loading the metal box into Dad's truck and walking through the stunning array of buttercups to the back of the Almond House. Marilyn was right, the cement slab over the old well out back was no joke. It took several tries to slide it over far enough to toss the box in.

Hearing the satisfying splash when the metal box hit the water, we dusted our hands and high fived each other. After several more struggles, we slid the cement slab back into place and breathed heartfelt sighs of relief. Now to bury Seth with his mother.

Even though the coffin was tiny, it was a chore carrying it up the steep hill. We stopped halfway up the hill to rest and catch our breath. Teri was watching me curiously. "After all these years, you were the first person with the gumption to follow Seth. Aren't you proud of yourself, Eve?"

"I can't take all the credit. I would have never returned to these haunted woods if it hadn't been for you."

"True. We share equal amounts of credit. Life will seem rather boring when all of this is over and done. What should our next thrilling adventure be?"

Please let my life be boring.

I lived for the day this adventure was behind me. "What do you say we finish this daring escapade before we plan another one."

She winked. "It never hurts to plan ahead."

"True, but back to the problem at hand, how deep we should bury the coffin."

"I wouldn't think it needs to be too deep." She took a quick glance toward the treetops. "I'm sure Seth is hiding among the branches and has already seen where his mother is buried."

Lifting the tiny coffin, we continued up the hill. At the top, we placed the coffin carefully on the ground and picked up the dreaded shovels. With blistered palms throbbing once again, we began the arduous task of lifting out shovels of earth. It was much softer under the buckeye tree and scooped out like sand. We had the hole dug in less than fifteen minutes.

After gently lowering the little coffin into the ground, we covered it with dirt and walked on it to pack the soil. We stood back and surveyed the little grave with satisfied smiles.

"All finished." Teri gazed into the tree like she expected Seth to show up with a bouquet of buttercups and personally thank us.

"Job well done." I picked up a handful of buckeyes for Dad and we headed back down the hill.

We were almost to the bottom of the hill when Teri said, "Damn, I left my sunglasses."

"Just leave them," I pleaded, wanting nothing more than to soak in a hot bath for hours. "I'm sure you can afford another pair."

"Eve, honey, those are Dolce and Gabbana, thank you. I most definitely will not leave them."

Even though I followed her back up the steep hill, I grumbled and complained every step of the way.

"Would you look at that," Teri whispered, in awe.

The sad little angel with the outstretched arms, that had been perched on Seth's tombstone, was now standing sentinel over Seth and Buttercup's grave amid a spray of magnificent buttercups. Only now, she was smiling. "The angel knows Buttercup and Seth have crossed over and she's at peace now."

I felt my eyes sting. "Mother and son are together again after all these years."

Neither of us spoke as we walked back down the hill. We trudged to the watermelon patch for Dad's watermelon, both deep in thought over all we had witnessed. It would be a long time before my nerves settled back down, and the enormity of the situation hadn't truly sunk in for either of us. For now we left with a good feeling, having reunited Seth with his mother.

Chapter Nineteen

Later that night, in between mouthwatering bites of cornbread and milk, I was explaining the events at Buttercup's gravesite to Tamara.

"Are you serious, Eve? The little angel was smiling?"

"Yes, she was."

"I wish I could have seen that."

"I wish you could too. Seth and Buttercup are finally together again."

"When are you going back to see Marilyn?"

"I'm not sure." I hadn't really thought about going back.

"I need some advice from her."

Tamara's latest boyfriend Ocela had been acting up. He lived five hours away and she had been going to spend every other weekend with him. They talked every night on the phone and several times a day. At least they had until recently, when all contact had suddenly stopped.

"I want to go too," Mallory said, when I mentioned it to her the next day at work.

Her latest love James was a good guy, but he was selfish. His money was his and he didn't like to part with it. Mallory was of the opinion that any man she dated, and allowed the supreme luxury of crawling between her thighs at night, should be willing to cover at least three fourths of her monthly bills. Now that the new was wearing off of their lusty activities they had begun fighting frequently.

"What about you, Teri," I asked later that night. "Do you want to go?"

"Nope."

Her first visit to a psychic must have been unforgettable because she was determined to never go within spitting distance of another one.

"Oh, come on. It will be fun. We can go to that outlet mall not far from Marilyn's and most of the shops are having a 50% off clearance."

I knew that would gain her attention.

"You are pure evil, Eve, playing on someone's weaknesses like you do," she huffed. "You should be ashamed. I'll ride along with y'all to the mall, but I will not be seeing a psychic. What time are we leaving?"

Saturday morning I drove to Teri's, where we all piled into her Beemer. "I don't know what to ask." Mallory was noticeably nervous about her first psychic encounter. "I need to write my questions down or I won't remember a single one. I need to ask about James, Tyreek, Eric…"

"Why Eric?"

"I've caught him staring at my butt several times in the last week."

"For crying out loud, Mallory, every man under the age of ninety nine stares at your ass."

"True, but he's been smiling at me a lot lately, and stopping me to ask questions when he knows as much about cleaning that plant as I do. I just feel a connection with him."

"You feel a connection with every man on the planet."

"I know. Still, I want to ask her if I'll ever have a chance with Eric. You know, a real chance outside of the bedroom."

I didn't have to be psychic to answer that question. Eric would never settle down with just one woman, but I kept that newsflash to myself. "You really don't have to ask anything. She may ask you a few questions, then she goes into some sort of trace and just starts talking."

"Is she scary?" She was nervous about visiting a psychic. "Like witch scary?"

I was tempted to lie and scare Mallory silly, but the poor girl had been frightened enough for two lifetimes. "Nope, not scary at all."

When we arrived at Marilyn's, Tamara went first. When she came out Mallory went in. Tamara had a dazed look in her eyes. "She is good."

"I told you. What did she say?" I listened while Tamara whispered in my ear.

"What did she say?" Teri murmured on the other side of me.

"Miquel is going to ask her to marry him by the end of the year, but there is a girl he promised to marry waiting for him in Mexico. He has to get rid of her first." I turned back to Tamara, "What are you going to do?"

"Find out who she this girl is," she said with fierce look of determination. "If he won't tell her, I will."

Mallory came out with a dazed expression. "That woman knows everything about my life."

"Is James the man for you?" I asked.

"Nope. She sees me with a man in the military." Her eyes had a glazed expression. "She saw us on a fishing boat in the middle of Lake Tillery eating fried baloney sandwiches. She's certain that James and I won't be together much longer and when I finally dump him I will meet a new man. Get this. I'm going to have another daughter with him. Can you believe that?"

"I've always felt that you and James were not meant to be together. You're too different. He concerns himself with finances and his credit score and you... don't. Plus, you've always wanted another child, and he doesn't."

"Oh, and she saw us living by the water," Mallory added excitedly. "Which must mean he is fabulously wealthy if we're going to have a house on the lake." She smiled at the thought of a lake house, not seeming overly concerned about a future without James in it.

When my name was called I sat down in the chair across from Marilyn and took a deep breath, as a feeling similar to impending doom settled over me. What was that all about? After all I had been through, surely the worst was behind me.

"I must say you have some interesting friends." Marilyn laughed.

I had to giggle. "Ain't that the truth?"

"Seth is finally at peace, Eve. Chalk one up to the Buttercup Girls."

"Thank God."

While it had been a long time since I'd given Adam a passing thought, I needed closure. "Everything happened exactly as you said it would.

Chia cheated on Adam and from what I hear, their marriage is in trouble."

"Adam and Chia's marriage is over." She closed her eyes and went to her psychic place. "Adam and Chia have frequent arguments about money. He knew she was seeing another man, someone who works at the same factory with them, but he accepted it. He pretended he didn't know it was going on and even stopped questioning her about it. She left him for the other man."

"Love is blind." I couldn't keep the sarcasm out of my voice.

"You will soon know the meaning of true love, missy. For the first time in your life you will know how it feels to love and be loved in return. The man you are about to meet will be the man you find your happily ever after with."

She gained my full and immediate attention with those words.

Me?

Happily ever after?

Doubtful.

Yet, she sounded so serious. For once, the woman was actually smiling when she foretold my future. That had to be a first. "When will I meet him?"

"Very soon."

"What can you tell me about him?" I knew she already had a clear picture of him in her head that was as plain as the nose on her face. What was the harm in clueing me in on a few of the more pertinent details?

"All I can tell you is to look for wings."

Huh?

Wings?

"What kind of wings?"

"You will know them when you see them, Eve. Just look for wings." Suddenly, the smile was erased and her face took on a serious expression. She took my hands to cradle them gently in hers. "Can you handle more bad news?"

"How much more can there be?" Amazingly, I didn't have the desire to run. I sat perfectly still, and realized that I could handle whatever she had to say. Settling back in my seat, I waited. "Tell me."

"Adam is sick, Eve."

"Excuse me?"

"He has been diagnosed with lung cancer. The chemo is making him very sick and his body is fighting it."

I couldn't focus. I couldn't even begin to think what questions to ask. "How long has he been sick? Does he realize how sick he is?"

"The doctors have told him. He recently had a lung biopsy that confirmed he was in the final stages of the disease."

Final stages? "How long does he have?"

"Only God knows the answer to that and I will not pretend to put myself on a level with him."

"Can you give me an idea." I wanted to shake her and make her tell me everything she knew. "Will it be soon?"

"All I can tell you is that time is running out. If you want to make peace with this man, do it soon."

I can't remember anything else that was said in the reading. It's all a blur. How could this be?

Adam was dying. Chia was cheating on him. He was about to lose his job, which meant he would lose his medical insurance. How would he pay his medical bills? The man's life must be a sheer, living hell.

Time was running out.

"What did she say, Eve?" Mallory asked, as I closed the door behind me.

I couldn't talk about Adam's disease, not even with my best friends in the world. I was in shock. Could Marilyn be wrong this time? I had been with the man off and on for three years. Wouldn't I have noticed the symptoms if he was in the final stages of the disease?

"What's wrong, Eve?" Teri held my hand with a worried frown.

I was unable to hold back the tears any longer and they flowed down my cheeks in rivulets. "Adam is dying?" They were all stunned into silence. "He has lung cancer and if I want to make peace with him I had better do it soon."

"Adam has cancer?" Tamara gasped.

"Maybe she's wrong this time," Mallory said. "I mean everybody has an off day once in awhile. Adam certainly gets around, if you know what I mean, for someone who is supposed to be dying?"

"That's exactly what I was thinking, but every word Marilyn ever told me has come to pass."

Tamara had tears in her eyes. "Did she say how much time Adam has left?"

"I asked her and she said… soon."

On the drive to the mall I was in my own little world as Tamara and Mallory discussed in great detail their sessions with Marilyn. I was numb as we went from store to store in the Outlet Mall where Teri loaded up. I can't believe her debit card didn't melt from overuse.

After filling the trunk and glove box of her car, she put bags in the space left between Tamara and Mallory, and even on the floorboards between their feet. Every available space was filled to overflowing with bags. We were forced to ride home, rather uncomfortably, with our feet propped high on boxes.

"Even you have to admit this is a problem, Teri." I tried to wedge my feet between a box and several bags. "I mean for crying out loud, take a look around at how you have us stuffed in you car like sardines. Doesn't that make you feel the least bit guilty?"

"Guilty? Are you crazy? I am nothing short of elated! Did you notice the bargains I got back there? Trust me, you girls can tolerate a little discomfort for savings like that."

"I can barely breathe it's so tight back here." Mallory was doing what she does best. "And my legs…" she began.

Teri swiveled around in her seat, cocking an eyebrow. "Don't you dare say a word about the indignities of having your feet jacked up in the air, when that's practically the only position they know."

Tamara and I giggled while Mallory failed to see the slightest humor in her words.

"This is beyond ridiculous." Tamara turned every which way searching for a comfortable spot. Judging from her huffing, puffing, and mumbling she wasn't being successful.

Teri pushed play on the stereo and the soothing sounds of Billy Idol, screaming at the top of his lungs, filled the car and drowned out further complaints.

Without asking, Teri pulled into Sonny's Real Pit Barbeque and parked.

We all ordered the trio platter for dinner, feasting on barbequed chicken, pulled pork, and ribs that would melt in your mouth with sides of French fries, slaw, and garlic bread. Honestly, you could hurt yourself eating at that place.

At home, I worked out the cramps from being bent like a pretzel in Teri's car, unable to think about anything but Adam. If he was really sick I would swallow my injured pride and do whatever I could to ease his pain and suffering. I couldn't imagine Chia donning the cape of Florence Nightingale. How could I approach him? Adam had always been a very closed person and kept his troubles to himself, preferring to suffer in silence.

Chapter Twenty

Even though I didn't love him anymore, I was devastated to receive a call from Justin informing me that Adam had recently taken a medical leave for an unknown illness. It was true. Adam was very sick.

Monday morning, while sipping my second cup of coffee, I made the decision to pay him a visit.

By lunch, while sipping unsweetened tea with lemon, I had worked up the courage to ride by his house. Could I do this? Could I extend an olive branch to Adam, after the unspeakable agony he had caused me?

I spotted his car in the driveway as soon as I turned on Willow Street. He was at home. I had horrible flashbacks of the afternoon I walked up his sidewalk and caught him in bed with Chia.

Please don't be at home.

I don't want to do this after all.

My flight reflex kicked in big time when I reached his door. How would I handle seeing him? I was turning to leave when Adam opened the door.

"Hey, Eve." His smile was genuine. "Long time no see."

I had been deluding myself. I wasn't over

Adam. I wanted nothing more than to take him in my arms and care for him while he was sick.

Yet, he was a married man now, and that responsibility fell to his wife. I had to remind myself that he had chosen Chia over me and politely tossed me to the curb like yesterdays trash.

"Hey Adam. How's it going?"

"Never better." He was leaning against the door frame for support, looking as weak as water. He had lost at least fifty pounds. As sick as he was, and about to meet his Maker, he couldn't resist lying.

"I've missed you, Adam." Now I was the one spouting untruths. I hadn't given him a second thought in months, until recently.

"You can't imagine how much I've missed you, Eve." He stepped out to give me a big hug. "I'm surprised to see you. I didn't think you would ever forgive me for being such a jackass."

He breathed a heavy sigh and gazed into the woods on the other side of the street. "I treated you badly, Eve. It makes me sick when I remember the things I did to you. I would give anything to relive the last year."

"I forgive you for everything that happened in the past, Adam." Surprisingly, I meant the words. "It's all water under the bridge. Let's start fresh and just be friends again. How's Chia by the way?"

"Bitchy as ever and spending money like she's married to Bill Gates." The smile fled his lips to be replaced by a melancholy frown. "She still wants to hop in the car and take vacations like we did when we first met. She doesn't think I ever get tired."

That was the most telling statement of all. In the past, he never tired. He was always up for anything, anytime, anyplace. Now he resembled a very sick old man who desperately needed a friend.

"No need to put on a pretense," he whispered softly. "She left me, Eve."

The news didn't make me giddy with happiness and leave me singing praises to the high heavens as it once would have. "I'm so sorry, Adam. I know how much you loved her."

"Yeah, well, shit happens." He shrugged his shoulders, trying to make me believe it was no big deal. "You live and learn."

I nodded in agreement. "I know you have to get ready for work, so I'll go. I just wanted to stop by and see how you were doing. Give me a call sometime." I was at the bottom of the steps, but turned back to look at him. "I will always be a phone call away if you ever need me, Adam."

He reached out to caress my cheek and I saw unshed tears glistening in his beautiful blue eyes, the only part of his body that didn't look diseased. "I will."

I could tell he was totally blown away by the dramatic change in me.

"Thanks for stopping by, Eve."

I had to hold it together until I got in the Jeep. Adam was deathly ill, that much was obvious. I turned to look back at his house and was shocked to find him standing behind me.

"Eve?"

"Yes." I tried desperately to stop the flow of tears.

He wiped a betraying tear from my cheek.

"Don't cry. I'm moving back to Massachusetts to be with my parents. They're getting on in age and need me around. I owe them that much. I guess you heard the plant is closing. I won't have a job anyway."

He wasn't going to confide in me. As always he was keeping everything, including his pain, to himself. I had to get away before I lost it completely.

"Keep in touch, Adam."

As I was opening the car door I noticed a For Sale sign in his yard that I hadn't noticed earlier.

It's funny how life throws you curve balls. A few short months ago I was fully convinced that I would spend the rest of my days in a loving marriage with Adam. Now he was going home to either recuperate from a life threatening illness, or die.

I suppose he was making a wise decision by leaving the Tar Heel state. Southerners are notorious for being extremely hospitable, as well as extremely nosy. It's inbred in us to stick our noses in our neighbors business.

If Adam left town no one would ever know the secret he hid so zealously. Everyone would assume the carefree playboy was moving back home to conquer his childhood sweethearts all over again.

My heart had been split asunder and I knew it would never be whole again. When I got home, even though it was the middle of the day, I lay across the bed and cried myself to sleep. My last thought before drifting off was to wonder if Adam's new bride knew, or even cared, about the real reason for his sudden move back home.

I still rode by Adam's lonely, abandoned house occasionally. It was a shock to see dandelions and wild onions choking out the marigolds and petunias he had taken such immense pride in. Knee high grass had gone to seed and taken over the lawn he had been so meticulous about keeping freshly cut.

How could someone who had been such an integral part of my life for two years, be so completely out of it now? I still had his parent's number. I could call and see how he was doing, but I wouldn't. Adam had left for reasons of privacy and I was going to respect them.

I was so engrossed in my thoughts of Adam that I didn't notice the man in his yard waving and riding a lawn mower. Good, the realtor had finally hired a company to mow the lawn and weed the flowers. I rolled down my window and returned his wave.

"Hi," the landscaper shouted to be heard about the mower. Wiping sweat from his brow with a handkerchief, he killed the motor. "Were you interested in the house?"

"Oh, no," I said, slightly puzzled. It took a moment for his words to register as he pointed toward the For Sale sign. "I'm… friends with the owner."

He grinned a sly grin and winked rather flirtatiously. "I'm not calling you a liar or anything, but I'm almost certain that I would remember you."

"I don't believe we've met." I didn't have a clue what he was rambling on about. Why on earth would he remember me? Were all men weird by their very nature?

He chuckled at the obvious look of confusion on my face and spelled it out more clearly. "I own this house and you said you were friends with the owner, but I'm sure I would remember meeting you."

As his meaning finally dawned on me, I felt like that the biggest dunce ever, but I couldn't help but smile. "You bought the house?"

"Yep." He pulled out a handkerchief to wipe his sweaty brow. "Signed my life away on the dotted line this morning."

It cut like a knife deep inside to know that Adam would never be coming back to this house, that my past with him really was in the past.

"I'm sorry if that upsets you," he said, accurately reading my expression as he walked toward the Jeep.

"It doesn't upset me."

"Good, I mean I wouldn't want you to be upset by the fact that I'm your new neighbor. Nor would I have wanted to steal the house out from under you, if you were interested in purchasing it for yourself." He propped his hand on the top of the Jeep and I could smell his cologne.

Jean Paul Gautier. The smell made me want to take a bite out of his perspiration slick neck.

"I'm not your neighbor." I breathed deeply of the marvelous fragrance. "I live a couple of miles down the road. I was just driving through."

"Just my luck. I was praying for at least one neighbor who wasn't entitled to a senior citizens discount." He smiled warmly. "Just joking.

Everyone I've met so far has been super nice. The house is quirky though. I've tried all morning to get the front door opened. The key goes in, but it won't turn. I guess that's why the realtor always took me through the back door."

I remembered how Adam had fought with that key until I showed him how to lift up on the handle and turn the key at the same time. I never really knew how I had figured it out. I was simply striving to impress him, I guess.

"There's a trick to it. Let me show you." I hopped out and followed him up the familiar sidewalk to the door. He handed me the keys and I lifted the handle, turned the key and the door swung open.

I immediately smelled Adam. His deodorant. His aftershave. His toothpaste. The scents blended together to overwhelm me.

"Aren't you the clever one?" He grinned. "Been here a few times have you?"

"Yes." I couldn't hide the sadness that crept into my voice at the thought of the man I had loved so deeply and lost so publicly. I handed him the keys and started down the steps. "I've been here a few times."

"Hey, wait." He pounded down the steps after me. "I believe your expertise with a doorknob deserves a reward. How about a Pepsi?"

"No, thank you."

"Oh, come on." He smiled, showing a set of perfect, snowy white teeth.

Mercy. He smelled delicious and had good teeth to boot. Don't let the man be single and have a decent paying job.

"The realtor assured me the people in this town were exceptionally friendly. Is it your intention to singlehandedly ruin my opinion of an entire town?" Merriment danced in his eyes. "You must know how important first impressions are."

He had a valid point, and since I was a member of the Welcoming Committee for our town, I was forced to rethink my decidedly un-Southern behavior. "You wouldn't happen to have a Diet Pepsi, would you?"

He shook his head. "I have Pepsi, tap water, or Michelob Light. Before you leave how about pointing me to the nearest grocery store."

"Forget nearest. There is only one in town, but it's right up the road." As a rule, I tried to avoid sugar, but in an attempt to be neighborly, I accepted his offer. "Pepsi it is then."

An intense feeling of sadness, along with an onslaught of painful memories, swept over me the minute I entered the house. The combination threatened to suck the breath from my lungs. I felt Adam's spirit floating around me.

Was he be dead already?

I felt faint and my knees suddenly went weak. I glanced around the room, desperately searching for a place to sit down. Noticing my obvious distress he, I didn't even know his name, took my arm and let me to sit on the hearth since he didn't have chairs or a sofa yet.

"Sit down and let me get you that Pepsi," he said, before hurrying off to the kitchen.

Adam was everywhere. I felt his presence as if he were sitting on the hearth beside me. I even turned my head expecting to see his dancing blue eyes staring back at me. I leaned against the bricks and glanced around the room.

It was apparent that Adam had vacated the premises in a hurry. The furniture was gone, although his pictures were still hanging on the wall and the mantle still held candles and a ship in a bottle. These precious memories of Adam shouldn't be left for a total stranger to toss in the nearest dumpster.

"What are you going to do with the pictures and other mementos he left behind?" I asked, as he handed me a can of Pepsi.

"I hadn't really thought about it." A look of deep concern marred his handsome features. "Are you alright? You looked like you've seen a ghost."

"That's exactly how I feel." I laughed and shook the cobwebs from my head, popped the top, and took a long sip of soda. It was truly nasty, like pure sugar water after years of diet sodas. "Would you consider selling the pictures and other odds and ends that were left behind?"

He gave me a puzzled frown. "I won't sell them to you, but you are more than welcome to take anything you want. I was going to load up the truck and take them to the Good Will. Help yourself."

"Thank you," I smiled with relief. "You don't know how much I appreciate this."

Together we removed the pictures, trinkets, and knickknacks Adam had collected over the years, several of them while he was with me, and carried them to the Jeep. I could store the boxes in my basement where they would be safe if Adam, or his family, ever wanted them.

"Thank you so much for your help." When

we had loaded the last box in the jeep, he opened the door on the driver's side. "I'm Eve, by the way."

"Matthew," he said, taking my hand."

He was one dreamy man. Tall, about six feet and probably one hundred and eighty pounds of what looked to be pure muscle. He had brown hair with a light sprinkling of gray at his temples and he was blessed with wrinkle free and deeply tanned skin. I would guess his age to be around forty seven or so. I glanced toward his hand, no wedding band. A definite plus, but surely someone who looked as good as he did couldn't possibly be unattached.

"Are you married?" he asked, totally shocking me by mirroring my thoughts.

"I'm divorced. You?"

"Nope, never have been." He grinned at my stunned expression. "I know, shocking right? Fifty five years old and never married? I guess the right woman just hasn't come along yet, or if she did I had blinders on."

Marilyn had said to look for wings.

He had his shirt off. No tattoos of a bird with wings, or an airplane. A fabulously broad, muscled chest, but no tattoos. *Damn!* I had assumed the wings would come in the form of a tattoo.

I glanced at his truck and there were no Harley Davidson stickers on it. Mallory had suggested my winged fellow might be a Harley Davidson man since their logo has wings. I glanced toward the garage. No motorcycle.

Tamara seemed certain he would be a military man with a set of pin on wings, or either be a commercial pilot.

"What kind of work do you do?" I asked, determined to solve the mystery of his employment, while steadfastly praying he was a pilot. I wasn't into the whole motorcycle scene.

"I own a landscaping business, have since I was twenty five."

Well, that answered that question. He wasn't a military man or a pilot.

"What do you do for work, Eve?

"I own a commercial cleaning company." I was still thinking of the wings and as far as I could tell there wasn't a set of any kind on the premises.

Damn! Damn! Damn!

"I moved here from Charlotte, to get away from the hustle and bustle of the big city. Peace and tranquility is what I seek."

"You certainly found it. It's definitely quiet around here, except during the summer when school is out and everyone heads to the lake."

"It will probably take me a while to get used to sleeping here. It's so quiet. I lived close to the airport in Charlotte and where most people count sheep when they can't sleep, I counted airbuses."

"Not much air traffic around here."

"Country living." He breathed deeply of the smog free air. Can't beat it with a stick."

"That's true," I agreed. "There's no way I could fight Charlotte traffic everyday. Give me a two lane road and I'm happy." I glanced at the bag of golf clubs sticking out of his truck. "I see you're a golfer."

"Most relaxing game on earth."

"It strikes me as the most boring game on earth." He did have at least one flaw. "I can't see myself chasing a little ball around a course, especially in the blazing sun."

"What do you do for relaxation?" He grinned. "Knit?"

Obviously he thought Eve Bryson was entitled to a senior citizens discount.

"I'm not keen on outdoor sports as a general rule, but I wouldn't exactly classify myself as a knitter. I guess you could call me an avid reader and news junkie."

"Hey, I have been known to read." He winked, causing my heart to speed up just a tad. "I even have a subscription to Field and Stream."

Now there's a magazine that should dramatically improve his IQ. "Thanks for the Pepsi, now I really have to get to work, and thanks for letting me have the mementos."

"You're more than welcome, and since you are my first friend in Hanover Falls, could I have your number and maybe call and ask advice on shopping and such?"

"Sure, and I'll give you one of my business cards in case you're ever in desperate need of commercial cleaning."

"I'll keep that in mind." He took the card and put it in his wallet. "Don't be a stranger, Eve. Stop by anytime. It gets lonely in the assisted living village."

"Thanks for the invite." I took one last whiff of his marvelous cologne before climbing in the Jeep. "Nice to meet you, Matthew." I drove away steadily perusing his outstanding physique in the rear view mirror.

Chapter Twenty One

While Matthew was a hunk if ever there was one, wings were noticeably absent. Therefore, he couldn't possibly be *the one*. I debated on who to call first and dialed Mallory's number.

"Well, he can't be the man Marilyn was talking about if he doesn't have any wings," she warned, after I had filled her in on every detail. "You know the woman doesn't miss a beat. Just keep looking for him. Who knows, if you look hard enough you might find a set hovering around Matthew. When he calls to ask you out, ask about his hobbies, that might give us a clue."

"He's not going to call and ask me out." There she was jumping to all manner of conclusions again.

"Oh, he'll call. Why else would he want your number? It's not likely that someone who owns a landscaping business would be in need of a commercial cleaning company, now is it?"

Tamara had the same reaction. "He will call. Why else would he want your number? We have a Food Lion, a Dollar General and Bojangles, how much shopping advice could he need?"

Teri's was a little different. "Forget the

wings and go for it. You could use a good lay."

"I don't think he will call. He was just being neighborly and probably felt sorry for me since I had a total meltdown in his living room."

"He'll call, and don't write him off just because he doesn't have a set of gossamer feathers attached to his back, Eve. Give the man a chance."

No problem there. "If he calls, I will definitely give him a chance."

"Well, I gotta go. I have a very large tipper ready to come out from under the dryer."

"Okay, call me later." I heard the call waiting beep and clicked over. "Hello."

"Hi Eve, it's Matthew."

Be still my heart! "

"Hi, Matthew."

"I know this is really short notice and all," he said in his very sexy voice. "I was wondering if you were free for dinner tonight?"

He certainly didn't let grass grow under his feet, now did he? I had spent a grand total of thirty minutes in the man's presence and he was already asking me on a date? It was a known fact that I didn't have any other pressing engagements and, even if I did, I could certainly rearrange my plans for him. He might be worth getting to know, even if his lack of wings was a crushing disappointment. He would be a pleasant diversion until the winged one entered my life.

"Yes, I guess I am."

"Would you like to go out, or would you care to be my very first dinner guest?"

"I would rather go out." I couldn't possibly sit down in Adam's house, in Adam's dining room and enjoy a meal with another man. Not yet anyway. "I mean, I'm sure you're an excellent cook, but I would rather go out. If you don't mind."

"I don't blame you." He chuckled into the phone. "This place isn't exactly fit for company, yet, and Bobby Flay I ain't. How does seven sound?"

"Seven is fine."

"Tell me your address and I'll pick you up."

I gave him the address, then hurried to town to purchase a new outfit.

After considerable debate, I chose a white skirt to show off my artificially tanned legs, a pink peasant top to show just the tiniest bit of cleavage, and flip flops to frame perfectly pedicured toes.

I went home and took a bath, shaved everything, dried my hair, rubbed Sea Island Cotton moisturizer all over my body, let it dry, and then rubbed bronzer on top of it. What an ordeal. During these ministrations I had to wonder why women must go to such efforts to appear presentable, when all a man had to do was stand under the shower and shave.

I twirled in front of the mirror, pleased with the results of two hours worth of hard work and determination. It was a quarter to seven and butterflies were merrily fluttering in the pit of my stomach. Good Lord, I hadn't had butterflies since… I couldn't even remember.

Please, let him be a good kisser.

As shallow as it sounds, if he couldn't kiss I knew I wouldn't give him the time of day. How crazy is that? To judge a man solely on his ability to work his lips. I'm sorry I just can't help it. To me, kissing is as important as a steady income.

Promptly at seven the doorbell rang.

Matthew grinned from ear to ear, looking me over me from head to toe. "You look great, Eve."

The way he was smiling, I actually believed him. I opened the door and invited him in. "You don't look so bad yourself." He wore khaki shorts and yellow tee shirt.

"I don't know much about this town," he admitted. "Can you steer me toward a great restaurant?"

"Well, actually, Hanover Falls doesn't boast of a great restaurant. Bear in mind that this is a two stop light town and you won't be offered the fine dining experiences of say Olive Garden, Red Lobster, Outback Steakhouse or even Pizza Hut. We do, however, have a Bojangles."

His soft lips curved into a smile. "And you said you didn't have fine dining."

I relaxed, enjoying our easy camaraderie. "Or we could drive fifteen miles to a great steakhouse. Do you like steak?"

"Love it."

"Yadkin Valley Steak House serves the best steak around. How does that sound?"

"Yadkin Valley it is."

Hotel California was playing when he switched on the ignition in his Chevy Silverado, humming along as he backed out of my driveway. "Have you lived here long?"

"My entire life." I leaned back in the seat thinking here we go again, another thrilling roller coaster ride with a gorgeous hunk. "Why did you leave Charlotte."

"I got tired of having houses on both sides of my postage stamp lawn. I want to be somewhere that if I decide to walk out on my back porch naked I can. Does that sound crazy?"

"I personally can't imagine walking out on my back porch naked. It could possibly scar my poor father for life if he glanced up one morning while feeding his bantam roosters and observed that exhibition. I do understand your need for privacy though, and there isn't much to be found in Charlotte. My best friend lives at Piper Glen and everyone knows everything about everybody in her cul de sac."

"Really, which street? I do a lot of work in Piper Glen. It's possible that I service her lawn."

I almost burst out laughing. I thought but didn't say, "If Teri ever saw you, she would insist that you service more than just her lawn." Controlling the urge to giggle I told him Teri's address.

"Oh yeah, the stately mansion on the hill. That really... ah... shapely woman that's married to that old rich guy Lawrence? Yeah, I have that account."

Told you, the typical observer would never guess Teri was once a man. "That's my Teri." I smiled. "Curvy isn't she?"

"That would be an understatement if I ever heard one. That woman is nothing but curves and I should know. She has a habit of lounging by the pool in her bathing suit when we're mowing her lawn."

"Let me guess, she's spilling out of what

passes for her bikini in every direction, isn't she?" I couldn't help but laugh. "I imagine your men get rather preoccupied when she's around."

"Speaking of that, just last week I had to replace nearly all the Hosta's around her pool fence because one of my men, Jose, was watching her instead of what he was weed eating and shredded the majority of them. Did she tell you about it?"

"Yes." I burst out laughing. "She did."

"She didn't get mad. She just told me to replace them, quickly, and her husband need never even find out. According to her, he's somewhat obsessive over his sod. Then, she invited Jose inside for some iced tea…"

"You can stop there. I already know the rest."

"I figured you would, since she's your best friend." He blushed and it was so cute. "I know how you girls love to talk. We men don't stand a chance."

I wasn't buying it. "You just keep believing that load of malarkey. I know from experience that men do their fair share of gossiping."

He laughed. "I guess we do at that.

"Do you drive to Charlotte every day?'

"Just a couple times a week. My business is well organized and pretty much the supervisors handle everything, until someone shreds eleven Hosta plants belonging to a less than friendly millionaire."

I nodded in understanding, thinking back on my own trials and tribulations of the self-employed "It's rough getting a new business off the ground, isn't it?".

"I'll say. I worked fourteen-hour days for the first twenty five years. Now, I have earned the reward of an early retirement on a golf course. Hanover Falls Golf Course is superb, by the way." He smiled and looked me straight in the eyes. "You thought I was running from a woman, didn't you?"

Matthew, it seemed, was very perceptive. "It did cross my mind."

"I'm not one to run from my problems."

Wasn't this a genuine case of opposites attracting?

"It's been several years since I allowed myself to get close to a female. The last time I made the mistake of falling in love, my fiancé decided a few weeks shy of the wedding that she loved my best friend more than me. I know," he said, and stopped suddenly, like he had said too much. "Tell it to Jerry Springer, right?"

Sensing a kindred spirit, I smiled. "At least you can laugh about it now."

"Now I can, but it took a while." He still carried the pain in his eyes. "Have you ever been hurt so badly that you weren't sure you could face another day, or even if you wanted to?"

If he only knew.

"Actually, I have."

We were at one of the two stoplights in town and he turned to face me. "It was recent, wasn't it?"

Shocked that he could be so insightful, I saw nothing but sincerity in his eyes. "How could you tell?"

"Because you almost passed out when you first entered the house, because you wanted his mementos, and because you have yet to say his name. It was his house wasn't it?"

"Yes. It was Adam's house."

Reaching across the seat he took my hand, squeezing it gently. "Did he hurt you?"

I couldn't talk about Adam. not with a total stranger. The pain was too fresh. I removed my hand and folded in in my lap. "He's... sick."

"I'm sorry, Eve. I really am. All the realtor told me was that the owner and his wife had recently split and he moved to another state."

"Let's talk about something pleasant, like the changes you're going to make to the house."

"Considerably more changes than I had originally planned."

"Why?"

"So when you come over you won't be reminded of the previous owner." He grinned that irresistibly sexy grin.

I didn't bother to tell him that for the remainder of my life when I rode by his house I would be reminded of Adam. I wouldn't tell him that if it were left up to me there wouldn't be a single change made to the house. I kept the fact that I could never be a frequent visitor to myself as well. "You do whatever you want to the house," was all I could say. "It's yours now."

I enjoyed our romantic steak dinner by candlelight. Yadkin Valley Steak House didn't disappoint. Matthew was a perfect gentleman, opening doors and pulling out my chair at the restaurant. Our conversation flowed easily with none of the awkward lulls that so often accompany first dates. We chatted like we had known each other much longer than a few short hours.

The same CD was blasting *Take It Easy* on the way home. I couldn't remember who the band was, but he was certainly a fan.

We rode around the lake as I pointed out the multi million dollar mansions close to his house and dreamed about owning one someday. It was almost midnight when we pulled into my driveway.

"Thanks for a great evening, Matthew."

He came around to open my door. "Thank you, Eve. I had a great time. I hope we can do it again soon."

"I would like that."

He walked me to the door. As my suddenly nervous fingers fumbled with the key I felt his warm breath on my neck.

"Not so clever with your own key, are you?" he teased.

I might be, if his hot breath wasn't singeing the hairs on the back of my neck. I turned my head to ask him to give me a minute, when he touched his lips to mine in a soft butterfly kiss.

Oh!

Wow!

Nice!

I'd been so worried about his kissing ability. Trust me, all worry was for naught. I melted, absolutely puddled at his feet. Our lips met only briefly and the tip of my tongue barely touched his before the key turned and the door swung open. My stomach knotted into a dainty little bow. We gazed into each other's eyes with our mouths only inches apart, his breath hot on my lips. "I'll call you later, Eve."

Then he turned and was gone.

Famous last words.

Epilogue

Teri had picked Tamara and me up and we were on our way to Mallory's house for girl's night during a torrential downpour.

"How is that delicious Matthew?" Teri asked, squinting to see through the driving rain.

"I can't find anything to complain about. The man seems to be perfect in every way, shape and form. Should we pull over until the rain slows down?"

Teri shook her head. "I can see well enough to keep us out of a ditch."

Tamara piped up from the back seat. "Marilyn was dead on about your life, Eve."

"Yes, she was, Tamara, and please watch the road, Teri."

Ignoring me, Teri took her eyes off the road to glare over the back seat. "I don't know why you would consider her to be so dead on about Eve's life, Tamara. Sure, she met a great guy, but where are the promised wings?"

"Oh, yeah," Tamara suddenly sounded dejected. "I forgot. She did say look for wings, didn't she? Come to think of it, Matthew might not be your man after all."

"She most certainly did," Teri quipped. "Speaking of perfection, have you had sex with the man yet, Eve?"

"No." Where was my lust for sex? I mean I

desired Matthew, don't get me wrong, and that desire was growing by leaps and bounds on a daily basis. Yet, since my visit with Marilyn, I didn't feel the need to jump in bed to prove my feelings for him.

"If you ask me, that is something to complain about. You've been going out for over a month and haven't had sex? What I want to know is how in the hell do you keep your hands off the man? I would have jumped his bones the first night. It still crosses my mind every time I see him, especially when he sheds his shirt."

"You wouldn't dare!" Tamara shrieked. "You wouldn't sleep with Matthew if you had the chance, would you?"

The ran had slowed to a drizzle so Teri relaxed in her seat. "Tamara, you know I love you more than my season pass to Carowinds. However, you have got to be the most gullible person on the face of the earth. Of course I wouldn't fornicate with Eve's boyfriend, you twit."

The expression on Teri's face was priceless as she rolled her eyes.

I sighed dreamily. "Matthew and I are taking it slow. There's no rush. If it's meant to be, it will happen, but let me tell you the man's kisses can tie my stomach in knots for days. If I don't feel a kiss in the pit of my stomach, the man isn't doing it right."

Tamara giggled. "That's the first hurdle. You never would give a man the time of day if he couldn't kiss."

"True." I grinned. "Let me tell you, if Matthew's kisses are any indication of his other skills, we'll spend the majority of our time at home."

Mallory met us at the door.

"What's for supper?" Teri chirped. "Chittlins?"

Did Teri have to go there as soon as she walked in the door? I swear, the girl needs daily medication.

"Backbones and spareribs," Mallory answered, much to Teri's chagrin. "I cooked chittlins this past Sunday."

Teri leaned over when Mallory's back was turned, and whispered, "I can assure you that I am not eating anything's backbone. We will be making a pit stop at McDonald's on the way home. Would it be crass of me to ask how the girl can invite us to supper and serve us bones?"

"Yes, it would." I gave her one of my *be nice* looks. "Please don't start, Teri."

When we were seated around the table, Mallory placed several meaty bones on each of our plates.

"Lord have mercy, you would have to go through a bushel basket of these to get a cupful of meat." Teri simply found it impossible to keep her mouth shut.

"Quit your belly aching and just try it," Mallory snapped. "If you don't like the spareribs try the macaroni and cheese and creamed potatoes and gravy. There is enough food on the table to fill even your pie hole."

"These are delicious," Tamara proclaimed, trying to smooth Mallory's ruffled feathers.

"Yes, they are," I concurred. "The meat is so

tender it falls off the bone."

"Do you ever prepare a normal meal, Mallory?" Teri stuck a fork in the meat and shuddered.

It was obvious that she didn't intend to let it rest. Why couldn't the girl just keep quiet for one, just one, girl's night?

"You have served me pig's feet, souse meat, beef tripe, those foul chittlins, and now some poor animals backbone." Laying down her fork she threw her hands in the air. "What do you have against a chicken leg, Mallory?"

Mallory was standing over us with her hands on her hips and eyes blaring, positively fuming.

Tamara and I knew that wasn't a good sign. If they got into a shouting match the evening would be ruined.

"If you're going to bitch and moan about what I serve, you certainly don't have to eat it. You know we eat soul food in this house."

"Soul food? Is that what you call it? Well, it looks like I will either eat it or starve, now doesn't it? Oh, get your hands off your hips, Aunt Jemima, and sit down. I was only teasing."

She wasn't and we all knew it.

Mallory was playing Snoop Dog's *Gin and Juice*.

"Thank God, I'm not having to listen to the Eagles." I laughed. "I swear Matthew plays their CD twenty four seven. He even bought a CD of their greatest hits to keep at my house. I ask you. How is a grown man still going to have posters of a band in his room?"

"I know," Mallory said filling our glasses

with tea. "I passed him in town the other day and *Desperado* was blasting from his truck. He loves him some Eagles."

"Well," Teri took a bite of macaroni and cheese and sighed with delight. "I hate to admit it, but apparently Marilyn *was* right."

"What was she right about?" I failed to see the connection.

Teri sat back looking quite pleased with herself. "Honestly, the three of you would be lost without me. Sometimes I wonder if there is a working brain cell amongst the lot of you."

"What are you jabbering about now?" Tamara asked. "I've never done a drug in my life, so I have more brain cells in my pinkie than you have in your entire head."

"If that's the case, then how is it that I have solved the mystery of the wings, in a matter of minutes, when the rest of you have puzzled over it for a month. I shouldn't even bother to tell you, since it has been as plain as the nose on your bewildered faces all along."

"Teri, honey, none of us have a clue what you are rambling on about."

She looked at Mallory. "Did you know he was a fan of the Eagles?"

"Of course. Eve says that's all he ever plays."

She looked at Tamara and asked, "And you?"

"Why, yes. Whenever I call Eve at his house it's blasting it in the background."

"Okay," Teri said. "What is the name of this group that he loves so much?"

"The Eagles. Didn't I just say that?"

"What do Eagles do?"

"Um… sing?"

"No, you damn dummy! What do Eagles do in the wild?"

"Um… fly."

"Exactly. What do they fly with?"

"Wings?"

Oh my God!

Wings!

Marilyn had told me to look for wings.

Eagles.

Wings.

"Teri you are a genius!"

"This is true and it's about damn time you all realized it. Therefore, I will be singing either *The Wind Beneath My Wings,* or *On The Wings Of Love* at your wedding. I'll need to practice, of course, to see which one sounds the best. Can one be Matron of Honor and also sing at the wedding?"

"Of course." I had to leave my seat and give her a big hug. "One can do anything one wants to *if* there is a wedding."

Teri grinned. "You said yourself that everything Marilyn told you has come to pass. She said you would find your happily ever after with your man with wings, didn't she?"

"Yes." I smiled dreamily, imagining a future with Matthew.

Teri belted out the chorus of *The Wind Beneath My Wings.* "I rest my case."

"Why didn't I think of that," Mallory groaned, hating the fact that Teri had solved the mystery and beat her at something. "It was so simple."

"Matthew is the man for you, Eve," Tamara said. "He's your man with wings."

I felt her words deep in my soul. "Matthew is my man with wings."

THE END

If you are a fan of historical romance, check out my bestselling series *Curse of the Conjure Woman*.

The first book is my gift to you.

Lynna's Rogue

Lynna's Beau

Lynna's Promise

Lynna's Destiny

Jerica's Pirate

A Heartbeat in Time Series

Clara's Song

Clara's Heart

Clara's Desire

Clara's Temptation

Clara's Forever

Also, be sure to check out these recent books added to my historical romance collection.

BRIE'S SEASON

Beauty and the Beast

and

ARABELLA'S DESIRE

Beauty and the Beast

Book 2

If romantic suspense is more your cup of tea, be sure to check out

THE DARKNESS WITHIN SERIES

STRANDED

SEASICK

SNOWBOUND

SECRETS

Note from the Author:

I truly, truly enjoy hearing from my readers. So let me know your thoughts at kittymargo.com. Be sure to sign up for my newsletter while you're there and add your name to the mailing list to be alerted when my next book is published.

If you enjoyed this book, I would *greatly* appreciate a review on Amazon, or wherever you purchased this book, to spread the word.

Thank you again for choosing my books to read.

Kitty Margo